The Soul's Mark: FOUND

Book 1 of The Soul's Mark Series

ASHLEY STOYANOFF

Published by Ashley Stoyanoff Books
www.ashleystoyanoff.com

Edited by Kathryn Calvert

Cover design by Liudmyla Supynska

ACKNOWLEDGMENTS

I would like to thank a number of people who have encouraged me to write this book, including the following: my mother Jo-Anne, my sister Jonel, and my good friend Angelle—sounding boards—without their emotional support and feedback The Soul's Mark: FOUND would still be stuck on the drawing board. Special thanks to my brother Cody for his early help in the outlining process and to my father Nelson, for all his support. Further thanks to my editor Kathryn, without her technical support the book would not have been finished. And finally, I would like to thank my husband, Jordan, for his patience while I have spent hundreds of hours working on it!

BOOKS BY ASHLEY STOYANOFF

The Soul's Mark Series
The Soul's Mark: FOUND
Waking Dreams, A Soul's Mark Novella
The Soul's Mark: HUNTED
The Soul's Mark: BROKEN
The Soul's Mark: CHANGED

Deadly Trilogy
Deadly Crush
Deadly Mates
Deadly Pack

PROLOGUE

Salem, Massachusetts, 1692

Racing through the dense woodland, a heavy cloud of smoke billowed upwards, cresting above the herbaceous border and confirming his soundless fears. Still miles away, he could already smell the pungent curdling of her blood as it began to boil, and the vile stench of searing flesh. Undeniably, the firestorm was spreading, and he struggled to drive out the image of the flames reaching up her body.

He cursed his heightened senses, wishing he could block out the ruthless chanting, "Burn the Witch!" The unyielding voices only helped his psyche run wild, and the graphic image of her tied to a post and set ablaze etched itself in his vision.

Her fear consumed him, rupturing their bond like a sudden cloudburst, and his body threatened to surrender to the inevitable fate marked for his soul. Regardless, the chain around his heart yanked him forwards. *You need to save her,* he told himself over and over, battling his body's attempts to give up and abandon the rescue. He pushed on, raw adrenaline propelling him forward. But even with the unparalleled velocity and power of a vampire, his limbs would not move fast enough.

The smoke cloud rose mercilessly, thick and black and

punctuated by the sparks of glowing embers as he broke into the clearing at Salem Commons. A mob of several hundred onlookers cheered for her execution. He watched in horror as they tossed books, chairs, and brush onto the fire that was licking up her dress.

Their eyes met, and the look of pure hatred that contorted her face was agonizing. His knees buckled, and he plunged to the ground. He focused all of his energy on pulling her spirit to him, but it was futile: no matter what he tried, she would not let him ease her pain.

The congregation's savage chanting became deafening. The flames licked at her cheeks and her long, curly locks were set ablaze, melting and sparking, but she did not howl from the pain. Silently, her gray-blue eyes remained fixed on his and flared with accusation. At that moment, he knew without a doubt that she blamed him, solely and entirely, for her cold-blooded death sentence.

His tortured wails were scarcely heard over the fevered roars of the mob. He watched, powerless, as one of the very few things that could kill him—the blazing inferno—devoured her body and his soul, turning her into nothing more than ash.

CHAPTER 1

The Greyhound bus pulled into the Willowberg station with a sucking pneumatic hiss. Amelia Caldwell shuddered as the driver announced the arrival and wondered if she could just stay on the bus. She hated moving. And she really hated change. It seemed as if that were all she had ever done.

On the ten-hour ride, she had almost convinced herself that this time would be different. This time she would make friends. She would not be the sad girl who lost her parents or the girl that no one wanted. No one would know her story; she could just start over. A clean slate. But now that the doors clicked open and she was actually here, her resolve was fading fast.

Amelia wrapped her arms around herself and looked down at her lap, hugging tightly and trying to stop the trembles that vibrated through her. She could feel the other passengers staring at her as they retrieved their belongings and made their way off the bus. People always seemed to stare.

She never really understood why she couldn't just blend into the crowd. At five foot four, she wasn't tall. With a slim figure, curly brown hair and blue-gray eyes, she felt average. Definitely not eye-catching. But there was just something about her, something she did not understand that made people notice her. It was as if they just couldn't help but stare.

Amelia kept her head down, waiting for the other passengers to leave. *It's not fair,* a voice in her head bellowed. It was supposed to be different this time, better somehow. Her eyes burned, she was shaking, and she knew she was going to cry.

Willowberg was supposed to be her new start at life. Despite all her fears of moving, she'd been so sure that she was making the right decision. It seemed like a dream come true. A full scholarship, housing arranged and paid for, and the University of Willowberg was even providing a basic living allowance so that she wouldn't have to work.

Amelia sighed, scrubbing furiously at her puffy, pink eyes. Gulping down a few breaths, she wondered why she had accepted the scholarship. Especially after she found out she would be living off campus, in a house with roommates. If they didn't like her, just as she knew they wouldn't, she would be alone. Completely alone. There wouldn't be dorm advisors that would have to be nice to her or other nerdy girls to study with. It would just be her and the roommates who thought she was a freak.

You can do this, Amelia told herself sternly, swallowing the prickly lump in her throat and stretching her cheeks into a forced—and she hoped—realistic smile. She picked up her backpack and padded her way off the bus.

Amelia had just stepped onto the platform, into the bright sun, when a clear, musical voice called her name.

"Amelia? Amelia Caldwell?"

She looked up to see a stunningly beautiful girl walking towards her. Nearly six feet tall, with silky auburn hair and big brown eyes, highlighted with a touch of liner and mascara. She looked a bit older, maybe twenty, Amelia guessed. And she was all legs, eyes and pouty lips: the perfect supermodel body.

Completely dumbfounded, Amelia just stood and stared

at this gorgeous girl, who was smiling at her, talking to her. She looked friendly and, though Amelia could not be sure, almost appeared as if she were genuinely happy to see her.

"I was getting worried you didn't catch the bus on time," the girl said, her big, childlike brown eyes wide with concern. She rushed over, throwing her arms around Amelia, crushing her in a big bear hug. "I'm so glad you're finally here."

Amelia dropped her bag, landing with a thud on the ground, and stood stiff and rigid, not returning the embrace. Affection was foreign to her. People didn't usually touch her, not like this. It took her a moment, but once the initial shock passed, she wiggled her way out of the girl's arms and took a step back.

"My, where are my manners. You must think I'm crazy!" the musical voice sang out and the girl extended her hand to Amelia. "I'm Angelle O'Connor, your new roommate."

With a shaky, unsure hand, Amelia accepted the shake, pumping it twice in a quick, fluid motion, cleared her throat, and said, "Um... Hi. It's nice to meet you."

"Oh, honey, you look as scared as a deer caught in headlights. Are you okay?" Angelle asked, giving Amelia a concerned look.

Amelia hadn't noticed how scared she truly was until Angelle said it. She could feel her body shaking and the all too familiar prickly feeling in her eyes warned her she was about to cry again. She sucked in a deep breath, straightened her shoulders, and attempted to smile, trying to conceal how much she wanted to run away and hide, and then she lied, "I'm okay. I'm just tired. It was a really long trip."

"Well then, let's get you home," Angelle said. Her big brown eyes glanced around, settling on Amelia's backpack. Surprised, she asked, "Is this all you brought?"

Amelia bit her lip for a scared second and a nervous knot emerged deep in her gut. She remembered the last time she had moved and the reaction from the other kids. They had teased her and called her names, treating her like a bum, an outcast. And for some reason, which she just did not understand, Amelia knew she would just die if Angelle treated her the same way. She dropped her head, shuffling her feet, because she really could not stand it if the girl looked at her the way others had. Kids could be just so… mean. Hesitantly, she nodded.

Angelle let out a little squeal and Amelia snapped her eyes up. "That's wonderful," she said, clapping her hands and doing a little hop. "I need a shopping trip and I've always wanted a little sister to dress up." She scooped up Amelia's backpack and said, "Are you coming?"

Little sister? Amelia wondered. She watched Angelle for just a second before she returned the smile and nodded shyly. Angelle seemed so excited. That was a good thing, right? But even if it was good it seemed… odd… and it made her feel crazy with a whole lot of uncertainty.

Angelle put a secure arm around Amelia's shoulders and steered her towards the parking lot.

Angelle had a black Hummer. In the car, all Amelia could do was gawk at her new roommate. There was something almost hypnotic about the girl. It was as if Amelia couldn't help but be drawn into her beauty. Her skin, pale and milky, seemed to glow with perfection. Her shiny hair cascading down her shoulders looked so soft, like silk.

Entranced, Amelia wanted to reach out and touch it. She could see her hand reaching out, but somehow, with great restraint, she stopped herself. Instead, she forced her eyes away, looking out the window, and tried to listen to what Angelle was saying. *She was saying something important, something about books?*

"You don't mind, do you?" Angelle asked.

Amelia racked her brain, trying to piece together the few words that popped out to her, but she was just drawing a blank. *Something about books, that was it.* That was all she could figure out.

She realized they were stopped at a red light when Angelle snapped her fingers in front of Amelia's eyes. "Earth to Amelia! Gosh, have you been listening to anything I just said?"

Amelia flushed, frustrated and embarrassed. She really hoped that Angelle didn't know she'd missed the whole conversation because she'd been marveling at her hair. God, she really hoped not. "Sorry."

When the light turned green, Angelle made a left onto a street filled with cute little cafes and overly expensive looking boutiques. Everything looked clean, almost too clean. There was no garbage floating around, the grassy areas lining the sidewalk were manicured to perfection, even the small trees were trimmed and pruned.

"No need to be sorry. How long were you on that horrid bus anyways?"

"Ten hours," Amelia groaned.

Angelle gave her a sideways look. "Wow, that's nuts. Anyways, I was saying that I picked up your textbooks and computer so at least you won't have to worry about that. It's all part of your scholarship. I know I should have waited for you, but I kinda have a teeny, tiny shopping problem." She rambled on so fast and with such a high, cheery energy, that Amelia struggled to follow it all. "I just couldn't resist the chance to spend some money." She giggled.

Angelle made a quick right, heading away from the beautiful area. "Okay, I'm completely lost. Why did you buy my books and computer? How do you even know what I need?"

"It's my job to know," Angelle replied, waving a dismissive hand. "Didn't the school tell you anything? They should have mailed you all the information last month. Oh, and speaking of the school, there it is." She pointed off to the right, but Amelia barely noticed the large buildings.

She was just so confused. "Um, I didn't get anything in the mail," Amelia stammered. "Just a phone call telling me that I won a scholarship. All they told me was that it included tuition, housing, and a basic living allowance. Then there was an email a couple days ago with the bus details."

Amelia felt a rush of pure adrenaline and her heart rate picked up, pounding loudly in her ears. *Oh God*, she panicked. *Why am I telling her all this? And why does she already know so much?* She had so desperately wanted to keep everything quiet. No one needed to know about her past or that she was poor. All she wanted was to just move on, start a new life, be... happy.

"Seriously?" Angelle said. "That's all they told you? That's ridiculous. I'm going to have to have a little chat with the administration office about that. Oh well, it will all just be a big surprise then. That's even better."

Amelia wanted to grill her with questions, but suddenly Angelle was making another right and pulling the car up to a gate. She rolled down her window and smiled at a portly, balding guard in full uniform. "Good afternoon, Ms. O'Conner," he said with an easy smile.

"Hi, Joe," Angelle said, smiling at him, and then she gestured towards Amelia. "This is Amelia. She's moving in with us today. I'll come by tomorrow with a picture you can post until everyone gets to know her."

Amelia gave Joe an awkward wave and said, "Hi." An uneasy feeling grew in the pit of her stomach as she realized this was her street. The school had told her she would be staying on Bankdale Ridge, a gated complex, but she had assumed that meant a new housing development, like the ones that seemed to be popping up everywhere with the little stone fences that surrounded a dozen or so normal houses. She had never imagined it was a gated complex, the kind with security guards and an actual gate.

"Nice to meet you, Amelia," Joe said, nodding towards her. He had a nice voice, Amelia thought. Not quite deep but not high—a comforting kind of timbre.

"Have Eric and Luke been in yet?" Angelle asked, as the big iron gate clanked open.

Joe's smile widened. "Mr. Carter came in about twenty minutes ago," he chuckled. "He was looking unusually green today."

"Green?" Angelle questioned, as she raised a perfectly plucked eyebrow.

"Oh, you'll see. Trust me, it's hard to miss," he replied, shaking his head and laughing. "You ladies have a nice day."

"Thanks, Joe. You, too." Angelle rolled up her window and thrust the car forward through the gate, climbing up the hilly street. Trees lined either side, immaculately groomed, and Amelia could just barely see the tops of the houses past them. Obviously, people here really liked their privacy.

As soon as they were clear of the gate, Amelia said, "Sorry if I sound really stupid but…" she paused and took a deep, calming breath, "what do you mean it's your job to know? Aren't you a student?"

"Don't be silly. You don't sound stupid at all. That's actually a very good question. None of us are in school. We all work for Mr. Lang managing different parts of his businesses. I manage the Dreams Come True Scholarship that you won. Out of all the applications, you definitely deserve this more than anyone I've ever seen. I just can't even begin to imagine what it must have been like for you after your parents passed away, and to be there when it happened, to see them murdered." Angelle made a sad *tsk* sound and then a long sigh.

Tiny beads of sweat popped up on Amelia's forehead, and a sudden flash of her parents ripped through her mind. Her mouth opened, and then closed, not sure of what to say. So many thoughts swirled through her brain. *No one was supposed to know.* She didn't want the sad looks and the comfort any more. All she wanted was to move on. Amelia swallowed hard, trying to loosen the orange-sized lump that was lodged in her throat. She wiped at her sweaty forehead, turned to Angelle, and said in a small voice, "You know about my parents and the foster homes?"

"I know everything, honey," Angelle replied warily,

glancing over quickly, eyes red and glassy with unshed tears. She reached over, giving Amelia's knee a little reassuring pat.

Amelia leaned against the cool window, exhausted and unhappy, and tried to get her head together. It was all happening. Everything she had wanted to hide from. Everything she had wanted to leave behind. Was she ever going to be able to move on? A thick, tense silence fell over the car, giving an ominous feeling, as if a storm were brewing, rolling in, and surrounding her with darkened clouds.

"But things are going to change for you now," Angelle continued, breaking the silence and sending Amelia a dazzling smile. "We're so excited to have you staying with us. You really are something special. How in the world did you manage to get such good grades and stay so focused?"

Amelia didn't want to talk. She just wanted to sit there, silent and miserable. But she also didn't want to be rude. She knew that would just make it all a whole lot worse, so she took a couple of deep breaths and said, "I guess I just really love to learn. Well, that and running. They're sorta my... escape." She looked at Angelle for a prolonged second, and then asked hesitantly, "Um, how many people live at the house?"

"There's Eric and Luke. You'll meet them today. They handle all the businesses Mr. Lang owns here in town. There's also Lola and sometimes Mr. Lang. They both should be back in a few weeks. I'm sure you'll just love them. You're going to fit in wonderfully. I just know it."

"Wait a minute," Amelia said, a panicked knot wrenching tighter in her stomach. "You guys all live with your boss and he's moving me into his own house? That's crazy. Why would he do that?"

"Hmmm. I guess that does sound a bit strange." Angelle paused, bringing a pink polished fingernail to her lips and then gave Amelia a thoughtful glance before turning her eyes back to the road. "I never really thought about it before. The five of us grew up together here in Willowberg so when we started working together, it just made sense to all be in the same place and since it's where it all started, we made it the base of operations. But really, he isn't around that much anymore. He stops by every few months for a quick visit and then he's off again. For you, though, it's all part of the Dreams Come True experience. You'll understand when you see the place." Angelle turned off the street onto a hidden driveway lined on both sides by weeping willows swaying gently in the breeze. "We're here!" she announced.

When they passed through the trees Amelia's jaw actually dropped. The house was not so much a house as a mansion, but it reminded her more of a castle from one of those childhood fairy tales her mom used to read her. It was all arches, turrets, and balconies, with a brown tiled roof and gray stone walls. And it exuded a magical elegance.

Amelia blinked a few times, licked her lips, and swallowed the nerves that were jumping around like grasshoppers. "You can't be serious," she blurted out, awe-struck.

"Pretty amazing, right?" Angelle chirped with a sparkle in her eyes. She maneuvered the big SUV around the west side of the house and into a motor court with large carports on both sides and parked in between a green Corvette and a mud-caked Jeep.

"That's the understatement of the year," Amelia mumbled under her breath.

Angelle turned off the car and hopped out. When Amelia didn't move, she peeked her head back in. "Are you coming in or did you just want to stay in the garage?"

Still gaping, Amelia struggled to unbuckle her seat belt, which took a few tries and when it finally clicked open, she snagged her backpack and got out.

Amelia's legs felt like rubber as she walked back out to the motor court where Angelle was waiting, looking like a glossy magazine photo in her low-riding jeans and white empire-cut long-sleeved top. She looked completely in her element standing in the expansive court.

"What do you...?" Angelle started, but was cut off abruptly by the sound of a shrill scream coming from the house. There was a clattering of pots and pans crashing onto the floor.

Angelle stiffened, and her light bubbly smile vanished. She whirled around quickly and gracefully, which Amelia would have thought was impossible in her six inch stiletto heels, and she moved in front of Amelia, taking on a protective stance, as if blocking her from some unseen danger that was about to drop.

The shrill screaming continued, relentlessly, like a banshee, and it cut through Amelia like a knife, chilling her to the bone. There was another voice, a man's voice, hollering from inside the house. Amelia couldn't make out what he was saying, but the tone definitely wasn't good. Then another clatter pierced the air, like glass breaking into a million sharp-edged shards.

CHAPTER 2

"Crap," Angelle said, relaxing her stance slightly. "It's coming from the kitchen. This can't be good." She shot Amelia a frazzled look and then dashed up the steps of the porch. At the glass double doors, she turned back and waved, gesturing for Amelia to follow. "Come on, honey," she called, before rushing into the house.

The screaming grew louder and another clatter echoed through the doorway. Amelia rushed after Angelle, jogging over the inter-locking stone, dazed, as if she had stumbled into an alternate universe. She climbed the three steps of the stone-covered porch and peeked through the open door, trying to stay out of the way of whatever chaos had been unleashed.

A faint smell of smoke washed out, followed by a man's agonized yell. Amelia glanced around, realizing she was walking into the kitchen.

"Ouch," he groaned, sounding a bit amused. His arms were raised in an attempt to protect himself from the blows of a broom swishing furiously at him. "It was an accident!" he cried out.

On the other end of the broom was an elderly woman who looked to Amelia like she was made of circles, with a round pudgy face and plump round body. She had on a flowery apron splattered with some kind of yellowy goo, and she was screaming unintelligible utterances at the man as she continued to beat him relentlessly.

Suddenly, Amelia saw the stove light up, fire crackling and blazing. Forgetting the scene in front of her, she dropped her bag and rushed in. What had her mother said about grease fires? *Baking soda, use baking soda*, Amelia thought, *that was it*. She whipped open the fridge, frantically searching, and grabbed a box of baking soda from the door. She dumped it on the burning grease-lit frying pan. The fire extinguished in a billowing cloud of smoke, and she coughed when she sucked in a breath.

"What the hell is going on?" Angelle yelled, jumping in between them. She snatched the broom out of the woman's hands and tossed it out of reach. It flew across the room, and slammed into the wall before clattering to the marble floor. "That's enough." She grabbed the man by the shoulders and shoved him away.

"He's ruining my kitchen. Look at this mess," the elderly woman said in a tizzy, surveying the mess. Amelia followed her gaze and noticed that the yellowy goo was splattered everywhere, smeared across the large cherry island, globbed on the weathered black wall cabinets, dripping from the ceiling, as if a bomb of stickiness had gone off.

The man was rubbing his shoulders, looking at Angelle as if she had really hurt him. Amelia stood back and watched, trying to stay out of the way. He was just as tall as Angelle, and bulky with muscles like a football player, a really hot football player. "I was just trying to make pancakes for Amelia," he said, smiling bashfully at Amelia. Then he looked back over at Angelle and said, "And in case you missed it, she was hitting me. Why did you shove me like that?"

Angelle rolled her eyes in a dramatic show of annoyance. "I'm sure you deserved it, Eric. You usually do." She looked over at the woman, who was now scurrying around the kitchen trying to clean up the mess. "What did he do, Mabel?"

That's Eric, Amelia realized. She giggled. He really was looking green. That's what the guard had been talking about. His shaggy, uneven, punk style haircut was dyed in a vibrant, bright green. *Hot,* she thought. Green hair, hot? Well, on him, yes, it was really hot. He was covered in the same sticky goo—pancake batter?

"He used a blender without the lid," Mabel said. Her voice was stern and a touch motherly and she had a soft accent, maybe English, Amelia thought. And she looked absolutely fit to be tied.

He just shrugged. "Stirring was taking too long."

"You're such a dork—and what's with the hair?" Angelle laughed. "You look like a little punk."

"Don't knock the hair," Eric said, leaning back against the island, arms folded across his chest.

"You can't go to the office like that," Angelle said.

"Don't have to. I've been promoted to personal chauffeur. And I think it looks great. I thought you'd appreciate it." He batted his eyes and struck a pose. "It totally matches my eyes." He looked Amelia over and then pushed off from the counter, strolling towards her with a mischievous grin on his face.

Amelia had hoped they'd forgotten about her and she really hoped she wasn't drooling, because man, he was sexy, like head to toe sexy. He stopped about a foot away from her and she met his eyes, which indeed matched his new hair color.

Eric dropped into a gallant bow and she giggled like a little schoolgirl. He took her hand in his, and kissed it lightly. "Welcome my lady," he said playfully.

Angelle groaned. "You are such a moron."

Eric laughed and dropped Amelia's hand. Wow, what a laugh. She felt it vibrate in the air. Clear, loud, and full of raw energy. He strolled back over to the island, and leaned lazily, elbows propping him up.

Amelia couldn't take her eyes off him and he was grinning at her as if he knew why she was staring. She was sure he knew exactly how sexy he was. If Angelle hadn't spoken up, Amelia would have been happy just to stay there and stare. "This is Mabel," Angelle said with laughter in her voice. "She's our housekeeper, cook, and den mother."

"Hello, dear. How was your trip?" Mabel asked distractedly.

"It was okay," Amelia answered.

"That's good, dear. Look at this disaster." Mabel let out a long, exasperated sigh. "At least I caught him before he burnt the house down." She paused, scrubbing at the counters. "Why in the world were you making pancakes? It's almost dinner time."

Eric was still leaning against the counter, watching her. Amelia could feel his eyes scanning over her and her heart started jumping, beating erratically. "She had a long trip," he shrugged. "Thought she'd be hungry."

"We just finished rebuilding the kitchen from the last time Eric tried to cook," Angelle added.

"Um, can I help clean up?" Amelia asked and took a small step towards the sink, looking for another cloth.

"That's okay, dear," Mabel said. "You two run along now and I'll clean up this mess." Mabel made a shoo-ing gesture and shot Eric a look, not a good one.

"That's her nice way of saying get out of my space," Angelle said, ushering Amelia away from the mess. "Believe me, you don't want to stay and help. Come on, I'll give you the grand tour." Angelle pulled Amelia along through the kitchen. "Eric, bring Millie's bag to her room," she called over her shoulder.

"Make the tour quick," Mabel said. "I don't want you to be late for dinner. I'm making your favorite, Amelia, Fettuccini Alfredo with chicken."

"That sounds great," Amelia said, and Angelle towed her through an open doorway, out of the kitchen.

They entered a cozy looking room with crisp white walls

and rich wood floors. "This is one of the living rooms," Angelle said. There was a fireplace on one side and on the other, an entryway to a veranda and traditional comfy-looking couches.

Amelia snuck a peek over her shoulder, back into the kitchen, at Eric who was watching her with a curious expression. His intense green eyes met hers. They drew her in and everything around her seemed to melt away. Her body flushed and her pulse quickened. She had an overwhelming urge to run to him, throw her arms around his neck, and kiss him. She was sure he would be a good kisser. Those full lips definitely looked kissable. She licked her lips, imagining how it would feel.

Suddenly, he blinked and gave his head a little shake, breaking the spell, and Amelia realized with a sucking, gasping breath that she had stopped breathing. A lopsided grin stretched out on his face, he winked at her, and turned away leaving the kitchen, Amelia guessed, to get cleaned up.

"He's… oh my God… hot," Amelia said under her breath, and Angelle shot her a surprised and somewhat confused look. Amelia instantly clapped her hands over her mouth and a fire flared in her cheeks as she flushed. "Please tell me I didn't just say that out loud."

"I'll totally pretend I didn't hear you," Angelle replied, and she wrinkled her nose, "because, *ewwwwwww*." She continued to pull Amelia through the living room out into a brightly lit hallway. "Here is a powder room," she said, pointing to the right at a closed door. They took a few more steps. "And this is my room." She pointed to the left. The door was open and Amelia was able to sneak a quick peek before being pulled up the stairs. The walls were a bright shade of buttery yellow, and the bed was covered in a fiery orange with mounds of pillows, all the bright colors of flowers and sunlight. It somehow seemed perfect and matched Angelle's bubbly personality. There were clothes strewn on every surface and spilling out of the overstuffed closet.

They started up the steps, hidden off to the side, just past Angelle's room. "To get to the second floor you can use the staircases on the east and west wings of the house and then there's also the main stairs in the foyer," Angelle explained.

On the way up the twenty-six steps, Amelia caught the muffled sounds of splashing water and a whiff of a clean, soapy scent. At the top, Angelle paused for just a second and pointed to a closed door on the left. "That's Eric's room."

He's in the shower, Amelia's mind drifted, looking at the closed door and realizing he must have snuck upstairs while Angelle was showing her around. She could almost imagine his muscular form all covered in suds. Her heart rate quickened and Angelle shot her a look, grabbed her hand, and dragged her on a bit too roughly, and she stumbled.

"Again... *ewwww*," Angelle said. "You seriously have to stop that. He's like your brother."

"What?" Amelia asked, flushing a bright cherry red. "My brother?"

"Yeah, your brother. You're part of the family now so that makes him family, hence brother." She stopped in front of the next room beside Eric's room. "This is the media room, but good luck getting it 'cause Eric's always playing those stupid video games." The room was the same crisp white and rich wood that flowed throughout the house. There were two plush couches and a few beanbag chairs. A massive television hung on the wall, and the built-in entertainment stand was cluttered with gaming equipment.

They continued on. "And this is the games room," Angelle said, before dragging Amelia onward. She caught a glimpse of what might have been a pool table, but she wasn't completely sure.

As Amelia was dragged on, a thought dawned on her, like a flash of lightening. Mabel had said she was making her favorite dinner—but how would she *know* that? "Hey, Angelle... how did Mabel know that my favorite dish is

Fettuccini Alfredo?"

Angelle shot her a sideways glance. "I think it was on one of your application forms."

Weird, she thought. Amelia was sure she hadn't written down anything about food on her applications. But how else would they know?

Angelle ushered her along a hallway that opened up and was naturally illuminated by a wall of windows. "That's a balcony, obviously, and this is the outside lounge."

Amelia noticed a shiny pear-shaped glass dome and wiggled her way out of Angelle's grasp to take a look. "Is that a pool?"

"Sure is. We open the glass in the summer. You were on the swim team at your last school, right?"

"Um, yeah," Amelia answered. The backyard was huge, lined with more of the beautiful weeping willows. Colorful flower beds adorned every corner of the lawn.

"Come on, Amelia, there's still lots to see." Angelle took Amelia's hand again, towing her away from the view.

"Sorry, I just… I mean… It's just… wow."

"I know, right? It's crazy. This is the foyer," Angelle said, gesturing to the lofty upper floor and grand double staircase that cascaded down to the main level. The stately steps were carpeted in a lush forest green. Above, Amelia observed the sunlight sparkling through four oblong skylights in the turret ceiling.

Angelle pulled her along towards the balcony that overlooked the foyer. "This room is Luke's. The other two corners are guest rooms." She looked over at Amelia with a twinkle in her eyes. "And this," she said, while opening a solid dark wooden door, "is my favorite room."

"Oh my God," Amelia gasped as they walked into a two-story oval library. "I think I've died and gone to heaven. I've never seen so many books in my life!"

All four walls were covered with floor to ceiling bookshelves, painted in a high-gloss black. Recess lighting along the coffered ceiling lit up the room in a bright glow and there were three cozy chairs with exposed legs and velvety upholstery.

"I thought you'd like it." They went down the spiral staircase in the center of the room. The smell of ancient books mixed with new paper wafted around her. There wasn't an empty shelf in the room.

At the bottom, Angelle pulled her along. "Wait a minute," Amelia said, exasperated. "I want to explore. Slow down." She just knew she couldn't wait to check out all the books. So many wonderful books.

"There's lots of time for that later and I really want to show you the rest before dinner," Angelle replied, tugging Amelia out of the library and back into the lower level of the foyer. She stopped for a second and pointed at a door. "That's the study," she said. "Office." She waved her hand. "And that horrid room is the dining room. It's so King Edward. We never use it."

"I'm never going to find anything in this place," Amelia said, flustered.

"You'll get used to it," Angelle replied, taking Amelia's hand again and towing her beyond the grand stairs. "Over here is another family room. It's just like the first one and another powder room." She kept walking, speeding up her pace, and Amelia struggled to keep up. "The other stairs," she pointed to a staircase that looked identical to the one on the other side of the house. "And this is your room." Angelle reached out, turned the knob slowly, and gently pushed the door open.

"This is my room?" Amelia asked breathlessly, looking around the sleek, fresh room. The beige walls were offset by rich, mahogany hardwood floors. "It's big enough to be its own apartment," Amelia said in wonder, and took a few steps into the room. In one corner, a massive bed sat on a raised landing with two steps leading up, covered in a rich ivory carpet. The bed was smothered in a plethora of pillows and a down comforter in bold blues, giving the contemporary styled room a splash of color.

At the bottom of the landing, there was a seating area with two brown leather chairs by a limestone-surrounded fireplace. Above the fireplace hung a large, flat-screen television and the area was brightened by a wall of windows and French doors leading out onto the terrace, showing off a magnificent view of the vibrant gardens and pool.

"Awesome, right? And check this out," Angelle said, taking Amelia's hand and dragging her up the steps towards the bed. She swung open a set of double doors revealing a walk-in closet. "That wall is for shoes," she pointed to the left, "and that side is shelving so you don't need to clutter up the room with a dresser."

There was a light knock at the door and Amelia spun around. Eric, all clean and fresh, stood there in her room. He smiled at her, a radiant smile, and her breath caught in her throat. "Brought your bag. Where do you want me to put it?" His voice sounded strained.

Amelia tried to think of something to say, but nothing would come out. Her brain was clouded by a thick fog. *He is just so cute,* was the only thought that was surfacing.

Thankfully, Angelle came to her rescue. "Oh, just drop it anywhere, Eric," she said, waving a hand at him. "And go away. Amelia needs time to get cleaned up before dinner."

He dropped it at the door, and vanished down the hallway. With him gone, Amelia was able to focus her attention back to Angelle and the cloud in her brain cleared.

Cleaned up? Amelia wondered. She realized what Angelle had meant when she was led through her room and into the attached private bathroom. She took one look in the mirror and was disgusted by what she saw. Her eye make-up was smudged, tear lines ran through her foundation, her hair was a ratty mess, and her clothes were all wrinkly. She looked as if she had just crawled out of bed.

"I'll go find you some clothes while you freshen up." Angelle glided around the room, pulling out towels, shampoo, conditioner, and soap. She filled the over sized circular tub with hot water and added bath salts and bubbles that smelled sweet and almost like pears, all with a grace and speed that amazed Amelia.

"You don't have to. I have some clothes in my bag."

"Nonsense. I have too many anyways," Angelle replied, beaming at her. "Like I said before, I have a little shopping problem. It'll be good to clear out some of the stuff. Most of it still has the tags on. Someone might as well use them."

Amelia watched helplessly, wondering why Angelle was being so nice. She was sure at any point Angelle would just throw her out the door and laugh at her for thinking that she actually liked her. That was just the way her world worked. People didn't actually like her. They just put up with her for the government checks.

The alternative was that Angelle actually genuinely liked her, but Amelia had trouble believing it.

So here she was, in her new room with a wonderful new friend. But she felt alone and scared. Really, really scared. No one had been this nice to her in years. Well, no girl had been. Boys were nice, but boys always had some ulterior motive, didn't they? Amelia hadn't planned on saying anything but she couldn't stop herself. It just flowed out in a mess of word vomit. "Why are you being so nice to me?" she blurted out, and again she blushed, embarrassed. It wasn't like her to be so blunt. She was usually so shy and quiet.

"Well, that's a silly question. Why wouldn't I be?"

Before Amelia could say anything more, Angelle disappeared, shutting the door behind her.

With a sigh, Amelia looked over at the steaming tub filled with bubbles. Her body ached with tension and the water looked alluring. She stripped off her clothes, enjoying the sweet aroma of the bath salts and slid into the tub, immersing herself in the bubbles and warm water.

It was wonderful. The house, Angelle, Eric, Mabel. *Dreams really do come* true, she thought. She could feel her body start to relax as the warm water soothed her aching muscles. She let the sweet, fruity smells fill her lungs and she lay back dipping her head under. As the tension floated away, her jumbled mind seemed to clear.

Amelia let out a soft, contented sigh and reached for the cloth. She scrubbed the smeared make-up off her face and shampooed her hair. The shampoo smelled sweet, like a fruit punch.

Finally, after, she didn't know how long, but long enough to be all wrinkly like a prune, Amelia got out of the tub, wrapped herself in a plush yellow towel and wiped down the steamy mirror.

When she saw her reflection, Amelia smiled. She could barely believe that this was happening. She felt happy and an odd sense of belonging. A quick thought crossed her mind, what if the others aren't as welcoming? But she quickly pushed it away, not wanting to ruin the peace she felt at that very moment.

CHAPTER 3

Angelle, Amelia assumed, had left a stack of clothes on the bed and she picked out a pair of black leggings and an ivory knit turtleneck sweater dress. She put on some make-up and scrunched mousse in her long, curly hair, leaving it down to air dry.

Once she was satisfied with her appearance, she glanced at the alarm clock beside her bed and realized that it was already 4:45.

On her way out of the room, in search for the kitchen, Amelia noticed another door, slightly open beside the bathroom. Curious, she reached in and flipped the light switch. It was an office. A dark wooden desk sat in front of a large bay window with a computer. Across from the desk was a bookshelf with all her textbooks. She smiled, excited to have her own little study place and then, not wanting to be late for dinner because she was sure Mabel wouldn't be happy about that, she bolted out of the room in search for the kitchen.

Amelia found the kitchen, miraculously, on the first try. But when she came around the corner, veering through the living room, so preoccupied trying to figure out if she was going the right way, she walked right smack into another cute guy. *Jeez, is this the attack of gorgeous people?* she thought as she looked up at him and mumbled a quick apology.

He smiled down at her, a smile that reminded her of a father looking down at his little girl. She knew he could not be more than twenty-five, but there was something impossibly wise and mature in his eyes. "Hey, kiddo," he greeted, ruffling her hair. "I'm Luke."

"Hi," she replied, gawking at him.

"You're just time for dinner," he said and walked over to the rounded end of the island. He draped his jacket on the back of the chair and took a seat beside Angelle. Luke was big, bulky, and at least three inches taller than Angelle and Eric. His face was warm looking, with thoughtful hazel eyes and short, spiky brown hair. He wore a dark gray-collared shirt with the top few buttons undone, showing the top of his hard muscle-lined chest, and a light blue tie loosened at the neck.

"You can sit," he said, in a deep and booming voice, with a touch of an accent that Amelia just couldn't seem to place. It was a watery mix with a hint of Irish and something else, Italian maybe. "I promise we don't bite." He chuckled, a velvety sound, and gestured to the empty chair beside Eric.

Mabel started setting steaming plates of pasta and garlic bread in front of each of them. Once they each had a heaping plate, she returned to the sink and worked silently on the dishes. Amelia had been wondering if she would join them, but she guessed not. Maybe she eats afterwards? Not sure how this whole housekeeper thing worked, she filed the question at the back of her mind for later.

"I see you found the clothes I left. I hope everything fit okay," Angelle said.

"They're wonderful, thank you," Amelia said, feeling a blush creep up the back of her neck. She didn't usually embarrass this easily and she wondered what that was about. It surely wasn't the first time someone had given her clothes. Since she had arrived, though, she had been blushing at every little thing. Maybe it was because they were all just so kind and, well, who was she trying to kid, really, really good looking.

Eric dug in, slurping up the creamy noodles. Sitting close, she was tantalized by the scent of his musky cologne. Amelia had never spent much time noticing boys before. They had always been just an unneeded distraction from what was really important, an education. But somehow he had gotten under her skin and was quickly turning her mind to mush.

"So, Angelle tells me that you are quite a math wiz," Luke said, and then took a bite of the crunchy garlic bread.

Amelia gave her head a little shake, realizing that he was talking to her. "Um, I get by I guess," Amelia stuttered, twirling some pasta onto her fork.

"Don't be so modest, Amelia," Angelle said, shooting a dazzling smile across the table. "She designed an accounting program last year for her grade twelve credit," she said to Luke. "You two should sit down some time. She could probably teach you a few things."

Luke chuckled and gave a thoughtful look to Amelia. "Yes, I think that would be a great idea if you're willing?"

"I guess I could." Amelia took a small bite of the pasta she had finally managed to wrap around her fork. The flavor of creamy, cheesy sauce exploded in her mouth and she realized that she was starving and shoveled more in. "This is so good," Amelia said between bites.

The food was so good that Amelia managed to forget Eric and the others while she continued to stuff herself. It had been ages since she had an actual home-cooked meal and the flavors were magnificent. No doubt, Mabel had made everything from scratch. You just couldn't make something that great from a can.

Amelia was so distracted by the food that when Eric reached over and yanked the top of her turtleneck down, she didn't pull away. "Why did you bother getting a tattoo if you're just gonna cover it up?" he asked.

"It's not a tattoo," Amelia snapped, her sense coming

back to her. She pulled away, fixing her top to cover her birthmark and placed a secure hand over it. "It's a birthmark, and I cover it up because I hate talking about it." Eric snickered, trying to hold in his laughter, and Amelia shot him a dirty look. "What's so funny?" she asked, her voice coming out more annoyed than she'd meant it to sound.

"Sorry," Eric said, breaking out in laughter. "It's just that you were born with the alchemy symbol for soul and you think it's just some birthmark? Damn girl, I thought you were supposed to be like a genius or something."

"I wouldn't say I'm a genius, but I'm smart enough to know it's just a birthmark." *Soul*, Amelia thought. *It means soul?* She had never really thought about it meaning something before. She always assumed that it was just some weird birthmark, a figure eight with a solid line passing behind the bottom circle. She pushed the thought back, deciding she would have to look it up later. "Can we talk about something else?"

"Of course, sweetie," Angelle chirped, giving Eric a disapproving glare that he promptly ignored.

"You know, it's the same mark from this book I read," Eric continued. "Luke, what was that book? Something about dreams, right?"

"I think it was," Luke said thoughtfully. "And about soulmates."

The humor left Eric's face, replaced with a pensive look, the same one Luke was giving her, and Amelia thought it just looked wrong on him. "Are you having any weird dreams? Like reoccurring dreams of the same person?"

Amelia froze for just a second, feeling a cold sweat break out on her forehead. He couldn't know, could he? She took a bite to give herself time to think of what, or how, to answer that. *Well, actually, yes, I do dream of the same person almost every night. You see, after my parents were murdered, I went a bit nuts and I made up this dream guy to be my friend because dealing with real people just kinda sucked. His name is Mitchell and well, after five years of these dreams, I kinda fell hopelessly in love with him. But it has nothing to do with a book or soulmates. I'm just a crazy freak.*

Yeah, that would be taken well. They would laugh and throw her out or worse, put her in a straightjacket and lock her in a padded room somewhere. She swallowed a quick gulp of pop to stall a bit longer and then instead of telling them the crazy truth, Amelia said dryly, "No, I haven't been having any dreams." She did her best dramatic eye roll. "At least not ones that I remember and please tell me you don't believe all that crap about soulmates because, seriously, no such thing. They were just made up as a marketing scheme for Valentine's Day."

"You're a really bad liar, you know," Luke said in a light voice, but his face looked tense with a forced smile. "I don't remember much of the story, but the book really is interesting. Maybe you should give it a read."

Wow. Am I really that bad at lying? Amelia wondered, speechless.

"Seriously, Millie," Eric said. "Don't you think it's a little bit strange that your birthmark actually means something?"

"That's enough, Eric. Stop scaring the poor girl," Angelle said, her voice dripping with syrup. "And Luke, I expected this from Eric, but you should know better. We will chat about this later."

"I was just saying she should read it," Luke said. "It's all very interesting and I am surprised you've never looked up the symbol, Amelia."

Angelle's smile brightened to a blinding level and when she spoke the sugar gushed from her voice. "I said that's enough." She focused her gaze on both boys and Amelia watched in amazement as they both visibly shuddered under her stare. *Weird*, Amelia thought, watching the three with curiosity. They held the stare, unblinking, and it was obvious that some silent conversation was taking place that she was not privy to. After a moment, Eric and Luke both muttered an apology to Angelle and Eric reached for the ketchup and slathered his food in it.

"That's so gross," Luke said, disgusted. "You're ruining it."

"Ketchup makes everything good," Eric laughed. "You're missing out."

They finished up the pasta and Mabel served a home baked apple pie for dessert. The sweet crumble, warm apples, and cinnamon were like a piece of heaven melting in her mouth. Amelia swallowed it down in three large bites.

When they all finished, Mabel promptly cleared the plates and left the kitchen without a word. Amelia thought for sure she would never be able to get used to this. Having someone wait on her just seemed so wrong.

She felt pleasantly full and exhausted. The bus ride, the house, her new roommates. It overwhelmed her in a delirious whirl of contentment and uncertainty. An involuntary yawn escaped and Amelia brought her hand to her mouth, suddenly afraid that they would think she was being rude. Her eyes felt heavy and it was getting hard to keep them open.

Luke reached under the table and pulled out two shiny wrapped gifts, setting them on the table. "We're glad you're finally here, kiddo," he said with a warm smile. He pushed the glittering presents towards her. "These are for you."

Amelia opened then closed her mouth, not knowing what to say. She wanted to cry. She wanted to laugh. She wanted to run out of the room and hide. They had bought her presents? Presents just for her? It seemed like such a touching gesture and, sort of, really scary. It dawned on her that maybe they felt sorry for her. Why else would they buy her things? They probably thought she was some poor little homeless girl. She flushed with embarrassment. "You guys didn't have to do this," Amelia said in a small voice. "Really, you don't have to pretend to like me. I've had enough charity to last a lifetime. I don't need yours."

"Really, Amelia," Angelle said, sounding a bit hurt. "They're nothing special. It's just a few 'welcome home and to the family' presents."

Home? Family? That sounded so perfect and so terrifying all at once. Amelia rolled it around in her mind, trying out the words. She looked around the table; it did feel like home. She hesitated for a second and then took the glittery box in her hand, gently peeling the tape, afraid of ruining the lovely paper. "It's just paper, Millie," Eric said, rolling his eyes. "You're supposed to rip it."

Amelia giggled and ripped into the paper to find a shiny pink iPhone. "I pre-loaded it with all the best music," Eric said proudly.

"And I put your class schedule in the calendar for you," Luke added. "And programmed all our numbers on speed dial."

"Mine next," Angelle said, pushing a wrapped envelope across to Amelia, not giving her a second to check out her new toy. She looked so excited that Amelia thought she was about to jump out of her seat. Amelia opened it to find a single piece of paper that said *shopping*. She looked up at Angelle, confused. "It's a shopping spree! We're spending the day tomorrow shopping and I'm buying you a new wardrobe."

Luke and Eric groaned in unison. "I tried to stop her," Luke said with amusement in his voice. "She insisted. I'm really sorry, but I just couldn't get you out of it."

"Hey," Angelle said, shooting him a look. "It's going to be fun."

"Don't worry, Millie," Eric said. "You can use the present from Luke and me to make an escape when you can't take it anymore."

"This is just…" Amelia started, tears brimming. It was so hard to believe that this was all happening. They were actually being nice to her. They genuinely seemed to like her. It was wonderful and overwhelming and she just didn't know what to say. "It's just so wonderful. Thank you."

Another loud yawn escaped and Luke gave her his fatherly smile. "You should get some sleep, kiddo." He rose from the table. "I'll walk you back to your room."

"Of course," Angelle said, standing up as well. "But nice try, Luke. We still need to have our little chat. Eric, why don't you take Millie back?" She came around the table to Amelia and gave her a big hug. "I can't wait for tomorrow. We're going to have so much fun."

Luke followed Angelle's lead and gave her a brotherly kind of hug. "Sweet dreams, kiddo," he said and ruffled her hair.

"After you," Eric said, giving a grand gesture towards the door. Amelia laughed and padded her way out of the room, Eric following behind. At the doorway, she turned back to her new friends. "Goodnight," she said with a sleepy smile.

"Goodnight," Angelle and Luke said in unison.

Eric and Amelia walked in silence through the big house towards her room and she started to feel nervous. She was alone with Eric. And he was coming to her room. And he smelled good. So good. She had to stop this. She knew it. He was her roommate and that would be weird. Trying to get her mind off him and onto something, anything else, Amelia broke the silence. "I feel like I missed something back there. What's with Angelle and Luke? Are they a couple or something?"

Eric chuckled. "No, they're not a couple. He's with Lola. Angelle doesn't like us kids hearing the adults fight."

"Us kids?" Amelia questioned. She was the youngest for sure, but the rest of them looked about the same age. Early twenties.

"So, do you have a boyfriend back home?" he asked casually, changing the subject, which she barely noticed. The question made her heart flutter.

"Ah, nope," Amelia answered lamely, not knowing what else to say. She wished she was one of those flirty girls. Angelle would've known what to do. She would've said something cute and funny. Amelia thought of the way she'd shut the boys up over dinner. She had them wrapped around her little finger and they probably didn't even know it.

"I find that hard to believe," he said, stopping in front of her bedroom door and running his fingers through his hair. "You're really cute. You probably have guys chasing you like crazy."

He thinks I'm cute, she thought in wonder. *A real boy, a very hot real boy thinks I'm cute.* She'd spent the last five years focusing all her energy on school and her imaginary boyfriend that the thought of a real boy thinking she was cute thrilled her in a way she didn't know was possible. She felt... alive. Her whole body was... alive, vibrating, hot.

Amelia smiled at him, in a way she hoped was sweet and coy. "Thanks," she said, again lamely, and she felt the blush creep up her neck.

Eric looked at her for a moment, serious, and then a sexy lopsided grin spread across his face. "Goodnight, Millie," he said and then he gave her a peck on the cheek and walked away.

Amelia watched him go, stunned. *He called me Millie, a nickname, which was good, right?* When he was out of sight, she turned back towards her room, rushed in and closed the door, leaning up against it. She rested her hand against her cheek and with a happy sigh, wiggled out of her clothes, dropping them wherever they fell, leaving a trail to her bed. She pulled on a pair of boxer shorts and a t-shirt from the pile Angelle had left and slid under the covers. She hadn't thought she would be able to sleep with all the excitement. But as soon as her head hit the pillow, she was out.

CHAPTER 4

Mitchell paced his office waiting for word of Amelia's safe arrival. Could she have missed it? Her bus was due to arrive early in the afternoon, but now the sun was starting to set, bathing Mitchell in a fiery glow as he glanced out the window. Someone should have called by now. He checked his watch again, 7:00. It was still early, maybe they were just having a good time. Yes, that had to be it. But what if something happened to her? The idea squeezed at his heart. He couldn't lose her. Not again.

"She's fine," he told himself, stalking over to his desk. Surely, he would've heard by now if things had gone... wrong. Mitchell sighed. He needed a distraction, anything to keep his mind off her and to stop the relentless tugging around his heart that begged him to close the distance between them.

He folded his long legs under the large oak desk and surveyed the stack of files that awaited his attention. Mitchell opened a folder and tried to focus on the report, but the figures blurred before him in an incomprehensible mess. *So much for distractions,* he thought, as he rubbed his forehead, before checking his watch for the umpteenth time.

Why haven't they called yet? Mitchell wondered and the

panic came rushing back in, suffocating and thick. He fished his cell phone out of his pocket and called the house again, voicemail. He tried Angelle, no answer. Luke, busy. Eric, voicemail.

Another insistent pull yanked him to his feet. Why was she affecting him so much? After all, he hadn't bitten her yet. The pull shouldn't have been this strong. Mitchell glanced down at the open file on his desk and, in frustration, he tossed it across the room, adding to the mess of papers on the floor.

Something must have happened. That was the only explanation. *Of course something happened, you idiot,* a voice growled through his mind. *You left your human soulmate alone with three vampires.*

"What was I thinking?" he breathed and a new set of fears twisted in his gut. How could he have left a bunch of vampires in charge of keeping Amelia safe? He shook his head violently, attempting to shed the thoughts. They wouldn't cross him. Not unless they had a death wish, but...

Mitchell was just about to call home again when the intercom buzzed, and his assistant's raspy voice filled the room. "Mr. Lang, Ms. O'Connor is in the meeting room waiting for you."

Panic washed over him in a flood. Why was Angelle here? The only reason he could think of was that Amelia was... Mitchell ignored the intercom and rushed to the meeting room a few doors down from his office. He threw the door open. "What are you doing here? Is she okay? Please tell me she's okay."

"She's fine," Angelle said, her big brown eyes were hard as she looked Mitchell over. She was lounging back in a black leather chair, her red patent leather heels resting upon the table.

He let out a pent up breath. "Why didn't you call then?" he shouted. "Did you forget who you work for?"

Angelle ignored him, collecting her long auburn hair together and tying it into a knot, which just increased his anger. She kept her cold stare locked on him, unblinking. "Are you sure you're doing the right thing, staying away?"

Mitchell thought about that for a moment while he tried to regain his composure. No, he wasn't sure. He wasn't sure about anything when it came to Amelia. He'd spent eight hundred odd years searching for her, and each time he was too late. He'd seen her buried too many times to count. And ever since the last time, he hadn't been able to get through to her in the dreams. Yes, the dreams were magical, he couldn't deny that, but they had physically remained thousands of miles apart from each other for way too long. It was as if she had put up a wall, a barrier of some sort to stop him from finding her again. Now that he had, he didn't know what to do.

"She's been through so much, Angelle," Mitchell finally answered, dropping into a chair. "She needs time to adjust."

Angelle's eyes washed red and her fangs popped down. "You're wrong. She loves you," she hissed with contempt dripping from her voice. She threw her legs off the table, sitting up straight in her chair.

He was almost tempted to laugh at her. Angelle was always so passionate, and she rarely thought before she lashed out, especially with him. They'd been together for so long that at times, she forgot her place. And most of the time he just looked the other way. But something inside him growled at the blatant disrespect she was showing him and his instincts kicked in before he could pull them back. "If you give me that look again, I will take that as a challenge, Angelle. This is my jurisdiction and you'd be wise to remember who you are speaking to before you flash those fangs again."

What was wrong with him? Why all the anger? He didn't get it. It was almost as if he was just turned. No control over his emotions and the blinding anger... He knew damn well Angelle wasn't challenging him. There were only two other known vampires that would even come close to his age and strength and she, by far, wasn't one of them.

Angelle shot up from her chair and slapped him across the face. His vision hazed over with crimson and his teeth sharpened at the threat. "Dammit, Mitch!" she screamed in his face, and it took everything he had not to rip her head off. It had been a long time since any of them talked back to him like this, and it boiled his blood. "I've been with you since I turned. I'm not your enemy. You aren't thinking clearly. The bond is taking control of you and you're acting like a jerk."

Angelle was right. He'd never imagined the pull would be this strong. It was as if someone were grabbing hold of him and trying to drag him towards her. A constant yanking that at times, threw him off balance. If it was this strong now, this confusing, what would happen after he bit her and solidified the bond? Would he have any control left? *No,* he told himself firmly. He wouldn't do it. No matter what, he wouldn't do that to her. He couldn't take away her choices. He wouldn't cause the pain.

He shook himself and took a deep breath. If Luke could do it, he knew he could. He was older, stronger, more experienced. He had to keep it together for her sake, if not for his own sanity. But it was taking everything in him to stay away from her.

Angelle sat back down, crossing her legs. She could sense his inner-conflict and her eyes relaxed. "Mitch, there's something else," she said softly. "She different. I don't know what it is, but there's something about her. We all feel it. It's as if some sort of power is pulsating from her. And when she gets mad..."

"Why the hell was she mad?" Mitchell snapped, cutting her off and trying to ignore the wistful look settling in her eyes. "She's only been there a few hours." The rage built up inside him, burning hot. Couldn't they just take one simple order? All he'd asked was to make Amelia comfortable. Let her get to know them.

"Eric talked about the mark." She held up her hands, gesturing for him to stay put, and he clenched his jaw.

"Before you freak, he only mentioned soulmates and dreams. She doesn't know what we are yet and she thinks it's just a birthmark." Angelle palled and averted her eyes to the floor. "There's some kind of connection between her and Eric," she murmured. "I thought it was just her, but at dinner I saw it in him, too. He's attracted to her. Maybe it's the power that's pouring off her. It's almost like a drug."

"I'm sure it's nothing," Mitchell said, glad his voice didn't waver. It was better if they didn't know, at least not until he was sure. She'd be safer that way.

Angelle huffed and shook her head. "I'm telling you, you can't wait. You need to come home. Let her know that you're real."

"Not yet," he said firmly. "She's not ready."

"What happened last time? What are you so scared of?"

Mitchell opened his mouth to tell her. Maybe it would be better to get it out, tell someone, anyone. The memory was etched in his brain. The flames, the chanting, and the hatred that blazed in her eyes. But if he said it out loud, confirmed what she was, then...

"Stay out of it," he growled as fiercely as he could.

Angelle popped up from her chair and tossed her arms up. "I'm just trying to help you."

"She's not stable enough to handle it all at once, Angelle." Mitchell met her eyes square on, pleading. "Too much has happened and if she remembers..."

"Remembers what?" she pushed, and he cursed under his breath, knowing Angelle wouldn't rest until she figured it out.

"Just please, trust me on this one."

Angelle rolled her eyes. "Fine, but when it all blows up in your face just remember I told you so." And in a flash, she was gone.

Mitchell sat down resting his head in his hands. *She has power,* he thought, the confirmation making him feel sick. He'd hoped for her sake that he'd been wrong. The bond had always only been between vampires and humans. But

God only knows what a bond between a vampire and someone...someone like Amelia could unleash. An overwhelming rush of doubt suddenly passed through him. What if it was a mistake to bring her here? Ever since the curse, his race had never seen eye to eye with hers. What if being soulmates wasn't enough?

A soft sneeze floated through the air, and a familiar scent, the sweet floral fragrance of her blood filled his nose. *Amelia.* She was here, but how? He hadn't called her soul to him.

Mitchell followed the mouth-watering scent. It was intoxicating, filling his mind and body. As he moved along the hallway, the pull become more insistent and his heart hammered in his chest with anticipation.

When his eyes found her, perching on a chair, his heart stopped beating for just a moment. She was perfection. Everything from her small frame, to her unruly curls was flawless and she was his.

CHAPTER 5

When she opened her eyes, Amelia found herself in an office. The sun glittered in through the windows and gently warmed her face. She brought her hand up to her eyes to block the glare. As her eyes adjusted, she noticed what a mess the room was. Papers and files scattered everywhere, on the floor, on the table, across the desk.

Even though it was a new location, she'd still expected to see Mitchell sitting at the big oak desk. But she was alone.

The smell of leather, mixed with Mitchell's sweet, tangy scent, tickled her nose and she sneezed.

Off to one corner were two big leather chairs and a small oval table. Amelia padded her way over, deciding to sit while she waited. There was a newspaper beside the chair on the table and she was just about to pick it up when she noticed a slight movement out of the corner of her eye.

She looked up to find Mitchell standing in the doorway. Little butterflies flew happily around her stomach as she took him in. His sweet smile sent sparks and chills racing through her body.

"Hello, love," he said, in a deep, sexy English accent. "I didn't expect to see you so early."

Amelia could feel herself getting lost in his soft, dreamy,

sky blue eyes. Her face felt hot and her heart fluttered erratically in her chest.

His soft chuckle snapped her back to reality. "Hey, Mitch," she said, hoping she sounded cool and calm. "What's with the suit and the office?"

Mitchell strolled across the room, loosening his gray and pink striped tie on the way and taking off his jacket. An involuntary sigh slipped from her lips as she admired his strong jaw and cheekbones.

He smirked. "This is where I work."

"Huh…" she breathed. Work? She didn't remember that ever coming up in the dreams before. But she decided it made sense. He was supposed to be a creation of her imagination and this was definitely the kind of office she would want her dream guy to have. Top floor, corner office. It showed he was important.

Mitchell scooped her up in his arms and sat down with her on his lap. She snuggled in closer, resting her head against his lithe chest, loving the feeling of his strong, chiseled arms around her. Mitchell tilted her chin up and their eyes met.

And then, suddenly, he kissed her.

His lips were soft at first, warm and moist and tasted sweet. He kissed her chastely for a second. But in no time, the kiss became urgent, demanding, and a surge of passion ripped through her. He buried his hands in the thick of her hair, pulling her closer to him and she found herself doing the same. Her body ignited as if fireworks were exploding within her and she tried to pull him closer. She opened her mouth under his and felt his tongue brush against hers. He groaned a throaty sound that vibrated through her, shooting sparks from head to toe.

Amelia didn't know who pulled away first, but the kiss ended just as quickly as it started. She was trembling and her breath was coming in ragged bursts. When she looked at him, she thought the expression he wore looked almost… pained. And his eyes, they seemed brighter, and were there streaks of red? She blinked, sure it was just a glare, and when she opened her eyes again, the glare was gone and he looked just as stunning as ever.

"I've missed you, love," he whispered and kissed her lightly on the forehead.

Amelia was about to tell him that she had missed him too, but an image of Eric flashed in front of her eyes and her nagging conscious screamed, *He's not even real!*

Guilt poured over her, like hot lava, but she couldn't help but remember Eric's soft lips on her hand and then on her cheek. It had been real. She could be with someone who was real. And that would be normal. She wanted to be normal, and this, this was far from normal.

Her chest hurt. It felt as if her heart had dropped to her toes, chipping and breaking into millions of pieces on its way. Was she ready to let Mitchell go? Could she let him go? Was Eric worth it? Amelia reluctantly slipped off his lap. She was shaking and cold.

Part of her had expected Mitchell to stop her. But he didn't. He let Amelia leave his embrace and she could feel his eyes burning on her back as she took a few steps and sat in the chair across from him. When she was seated, he didn't say anything. He just sat there, watching her and waiting.

Amelia took a deep shaky breath. "Mitch…" she said, glad that her voice sounded strong. "We need to talk."

Little creases indented his forehead and the corners of his mouth tilted downwards. "What's wrong, love? Did something happen today? Were your new roommates unkind to you?"

She shook her head and looked away. "They were wonderful," she said dreamily, and then huffed a gusty sound. "Absolutely perfect."

Mitchell laughed. "You say that like it's a bad thing."

"Well, it kinda is," she admitted and stood up. Her knees felt like Jell-O and she realized that maybe standing wasn't such a great idea and plopped back down on the chair before she continued. "It made me realize something."

"And what did you realize?" he questioned, leaning forward, resting his elbows on his knees, hands dangling.

"Um…" she fumbled, realizing that she really didn't know what to say. How do you tell someone that you don't want to dream of them anymore? "That it's time to let you go."

Amelia could see the wheels turning as he processed what she'd said. It was a bit intimidating, not that he actually meant it to be, but he was the kind of person you could actually see thinking. Even so, Amelia was relieved when she saw his face light up, as if he had discovered what he was looking for. "You still think this is just a dream," he murmured, bemused.

His statement left her confused. "Of course it's just a dream, Mitch," she muttered, fiddling with the hem of her shirt, twisting it around her finger. "And I met someone today. And I, um… I like him."

Mitchell laughed, and she stiffened. When she looked up, he was lounging back in his chair with a playful smile on his face. Just yesterday, that smile would have turned her into a lovesick puppy. She would have run to him, throwing herself into his arms.

But now, it infuriated her. Amelia straightened her shoulders and clenched her teeth. She could feel her fingernails digging into her palms as she balled her hands into tight fists. "This isn't funny," she bristled, and shot him a fierce glare.

"Oh, love," he chuckled. The sound made her heart skip a beat and she cursed under her breath. She hated feeling this way about him. "You met someone?" Amusement filled his eyes and he laughed, full heartedly. "Let me guess. Eric?" He got up from his chair and kneeled down on the floor in front of her so his face was at the same level as hers. "There's so much you don't know, love," he whispered, brushing her hair off her neck. He let his fingers linger, lightly tracing the outline of her birthmark.

His touch made her skin tingle, and her body lit up like a blazing fire. She knew there was something, something that he said that he shouldn't have known but with him this close she just couldn't seem to figure out what it was. He leaned in and kissed her slowly, his lips soft and teasing. This time he ended the kiss. "I love you, Amelia," he said, brushing her hair back. "You should get some sleep, love."

Mitchell bent forward and kissed her forehead. She was about to protest because she was already asleep. This was her dream and she really didn't want him to go. But when she looked at him he was flickering and fading like a television set gone to static. The room was changing, shifting, colors flashing, and then it was dark and she faded into a deep sleep.

CHAPTER 6

Morning came early, and Amelia, no matter how hard she tried, could not sleep. She glanced over at the clock next to her bed, almost 5:30. She groaned, wishing she was one of those people who could sleep in until noon because she really, really hated mornings. For a moment she thought about staying tucked into the warm, cozy blankets, but it seemed pointless. She was wide-awake and knew she was up for the day. With another agonized groan, she decided to get up and go for a run. Exercise was the only thing that made her remotely sociable in the morning and at least it would give her a chance to see the neighborhood.

Tumbling out of bed, stretching and yawning, Amelia made her way to the window. The sky was fixed in that special place at the end of night but before day, neither dark nor light. The stars were just little specks, fading into dim sparkles in the gray-blue sky.

She tossed on a T-shirt and her favorite gray yoga pants, then grabbed her water bottle and running shoes and headed out of her room. The house was completely quiet. She crept quietly down the hall, hoping not to wake anyone.

In the kitchen, she turned on the tap, letting the water run for a second. It gushed from the tap, crashing against the stainless steel sink. *There goes being quiet,* she thought and hastily shoved her bottle under the stream, not waiting for the water to turn cold.

Amelia pulled on her running shoes and went out the door into the motor court. She shivered as the brisk fall breeze touched her bare arms. There was a bite in the air and she knew she would soon have to bundle up before venturing out in the mornings. She headed down the porch steps and did a few stretches, then took off down the driveway at a slow jog, warming up her muscles.

In no time at all her blood started to pump, her muscles started to tingle and she started to feel... alive.

The street was quiet and deserted in the early morning light. The sky was turning a deep purple-blue and the sun was just starting to peek over the horizon. She picked up her pace to a sprint.

Amelia had hoped to see some of the other houses on the street and get a feel for the neighborhood, but the thick tree line blocked her view. She made out some of the houses through the breaks and from what she could see, they were all just as big and fabulous as the one she lived in.

She passed by a little opening in the trees. A small park, she assumed, with a few benches and a garden. As she passed, Amelia felt a tingle at the back of her neck. The kind of feeling she always got when someone was watching or following her. She glanced over her shoulder, not slowing the pace, but saw nothing.

Amelia pushed herself faster, adrenaline pumping, but the feeling of eyes boring into her back became more intense and prickled down her spine, rolling like needles.

A loud crack, like a branch breaking, and the rustle of leaves crunching under foot broke the silence of the morning, and she stopped abruptly. She peered into the trees where the sound came from, trying to see what was there. Nothing. She couldn't see anything but the trees. She waited, listening closely, but the crunching of leaves was gone. Maybe a squirrel? No, too loud. She knew a squirrel couldn't make that much noise. A fox?

Amelia tried to shake off the feeling, knowing it was just her imagination working on overdrive. She was in a new place after all. Reluctantly, she pulled her gaze away from the trees, turned back to the street, and screamed.

Standing in front of her was a little girl. She was so close that Amelia could feel a warm burst of air with every breath the girl took. Amelia jumped back and clasped her hands over her mouth to stifle another scream that was building up. The girl was young. Maybe eleven or twelve and she was creepy, like little kid, horror movie creepy, with unnervingly pale white-gray skin, big pale gray eyes, and straggly shoulder length thin white-blond hair. She wore an evil, devil child kind of smile.

Amelia forced her hand down from her mouth, feeling bad at her reaction. She knew the kid was probably just as scared as she was, with her screaming. "You startled me. Are you lost?" Amelia asked, her voice a little shaky.

The girl just stood there, frozen like a statue, cold dead looking eyes boring into Amelia. A chill prickled down Amelia's spine and her heart started thumping like a jackhammer in her chest. Unconsciously, she took another step back. The child still did not move, not an inch, didn't even blink. "Are you okay?" she asked, stuttering over the words.

Right at that moment, a car door slammed from behind her and Amelia jumped. She really didn't want to take her eyes off the creepy little girl, but she couldn't seem to stop herself from glancing over her shoulder quickly. She caught a glimpse of a short, chubby police officer strutting towards her. She flipped her focus back to the girl, but she was… gone. Amelia frantically scanned the street, but there was no sign of her. She'd looked away for only half a second. Gone.

Amelia turned back to the police officer, who was now only a few steps away. "Did you see that little girl? Where did she go?"

"What little girl? All I see is you. Who do you belong to?" the officer asked, not unkindly, but with a definite air of authority. He looked older, in his early fifties, Amelia guessed, with wrinkles touching his eyes and the corners of his mouth. His hair was graying, close-cropped, and his smile was friendly enough, but there was something careful and guarded and a bit unsure about it.

"You didn't see the little girl? She was standing right there," Amelia replied, flustered, and pointed to the empty space in front of her. Then his question sunk in and she replayed it in her mind. *Who do you belong to?* What kind of question was that? She shook her head, sure she'd heard him wrong and asked, "Sorry, what did you just ask me?" her voice sounding more scared than she'd hoped for.

He studied her closely, eyes scanning her over and eventually settling on her neck. She fought back the urge to cover up her birthmark. The way he was looking at it, examining it, she felt as if she were being put under a microscope. "Interesting." He folded his arms over his chest. "You must be new here. Which house are you in?" he asked, raising a questioning eyebrow.

Amelia tried not to tremble, but with the way he was looking at her it was hard not to. She was not a fan of the police. Not since the night her parents had been murdered. They brought back too many memories that she wanted to keep buried. "18 Bankdale Ridge. Did I do something wrong, Officer…" she peered at the brassy name plate on his jacket, "McLean?"

"You must be Amelia." He extended his right hand. "It's a pleasure to meet you. And no, you didn't do anything wrong. It's just that this really isn't the kind of neighborhood that a kid like you should be running around alone in at the break of dawn. It's not safe."

Amelia was sure she was looking at him as if he might be crazy. Not safe? You couldn't even get onto the street without a guard opening the gate. "I find it hard to believe this area isn't safe," she said, trying to keep the laughter out of her voice. Then a thought dawned on her, the amusement vanished, and her skin rose in goose pimples and she said, "How do you know my name?"

He gave her a long, hard stare and then shrugged, looking, Amelia thought, as if he were trying to cover up a mistake. "It's my job to know who should and shouldn't be here," he said, too quickly for her to believe. "Like I said, it's not safe, especially for those who don't belong. Why don't I take you home?"

"That's okay, it's only a few houses down." Amelia was vibrating all over. She was nervous. She knew she shouldn't be. He was a police officer. He was a good guy. But he exuded an unnamed quality that unnerved her. It was probably just her imagination, but she really didn't want to go anywhere with him. "I'm sure I'll be fine," she added when he didn't leave.

Officer McLean didn't look happy at her response and Amelia was sure she saw a flicker of fear in his eyes. Was he scared of her or scared for her? She didn't know and part of her didn't want to know. It was all just a bit too strange, the girl, Officer McLean. What kind of a town did she move to?

He sighed, a gusty sound. "Humor an old man and get in the car. It would make me feel a lot better to know that you made it home okay."

"What about the little girl?"

"Amelia, I didn't see a little girl. You're the only person I've seen all morning," he said, shaking his head. "Come on, get in the car." He waved his hand to her, a clear signal to follow, and started towards the car. She hesitated for just a moment, then, not wanting to get into trouble, Amelia followed and got into the front seat of the waiting cruiser.

It took three minutes to drive back to her house, but those three minutes felt like an eternity. Amelia wondered what her roommates were going to say when she showed up with a cop. What a way to make an impression. Not even twenty-four hours in Willowberg and she was already being escorted home.

Sweat trickled down her neck and soaked into her collar. She tried to tell herself it was from the run, but deep down she knew it wasn't. Between the scary little girl and Officer McLean, she was wound tighter than a coil of string. Of course she'd be sweating. Who wouldn't be after the morning she'd had?

Her throat was dry and scratchy, and when they turned onto the long driveway Amelia had to clear it twice before she could make her voice work. "You can just drop me off here."

Officer McLean didn't stop the car and he didn't even bother to acknowledge that she'd spoken. He drove around the side, entering the motor court and to Amelia's horror, he parked right in front of the glass doors leading to the kitchen. Without a word, he turned off the car and got out.

Amelia watched him saunter, in a way that only a police officer could, towards the porch steps. *Maybe they're still sleeping*, she hoped. With squinted eyes, she tried to see if there was anyone in the kitchen, but the frosted glass gave nothing away. She took a deep breath, reached to unbuckle her seat belt, and right at the moment that her seat belt clicked, her door flew open and before she knew it, she was yanked from the car.

"Amelia, are you okay? Are you hurt?" Luke asked anxiously. He had his hands firmly on her shoulders, shaking her like a rag doll and his face was streaked with panic. Before she could say anything, he turned to Officer McLean. "Is she hurt?" He didn't wait for the response, but he stopped shaking her, and with frantic eyes, started searching her over.

"She's fine, Luke," Officer McLean said, sounding slightly bored. He folded his arms across his chest. "I found her out running. Is Mr. Lang here?"

"No, he's out of town," Luke snapped, his eyes still scanning Amelia. What he was looking for Amelia had no clue, but his panic was rubbing off on her, and she started to shake. He finally seemed satisfied that she wasn't broken and he dropped his hands from her shoulders. "What the hell were you doing running this early in the morning?" he yelled at her.

"I couldn't sleep," Amelia answered, flinching. Anger blazed in his eyes. What had she done wrong? She didn't know, but gauging his reaction, it was serious. "What's the big deal?"

"Officer McLean!" Angelle's chipper voice came from the porch, and Amelia was thankful. Angelle—looking immaculately polished in a tailored dark gray jacket and slacks and light blue v-neck top—had captured the men's attention, effectively drawing the heat away from Amelia. "What brings you here so early in the morning?"

Luke, of course, recovered first. "He found Amelia out running." Now that he was sure she was okay, his original panic was gone and he spat the words, clearly annoyed.

"Oh," Angelle said. A flash of something that looked vaguely like terror snapped across her face so quickly that if Amelia hadn't been paying attention, she would have missed it. But in less time than it took to blink, Angelle had recovered, back to her glamorous, knock'em dead smile. "Thank you for bringing her home. That was very nice of you."

Amelia watched, stunned, as Angelle turned away from him, taking a step back towards the door, very clearly dismissing the officer. Luke followed her lead, and placed a firm hand on the small of Amelia's back, nudging her forward. Amelia had only just taken a step when the cop moved to block the stairs.

"Hold on a minute," Officer McLean said sternly. Angelle stopped and gracefully turned back to give him her attention. "Amelia claims she saw a little girl while she was out. She needs to know how serious this is. It's not safe for her to be out alone. At least not until the notice is sent."

Amelia bristled and side stepped away from Luke's hand. Did he doubt her? Did he really not believe she saw that creepy little child? "First of all, there was a little girl." *That got everyone's attention,* she thought, suddenly regretting she'd said anything. They were all glaring at her, even Angelle, and her nerve faltered. But she managed to push on. She didn't want her new friends to think she was crazy and that's exactly what the cop was trying to do. Amelia was sure of it. "I swear I saw her." She looked back and forth between Luke and Angelle, eyes pleading for them to believe her before focusing back on Officer McLean. "And I really don't know why you keep saying it's not safe. It's a gated street for goodness' sake. And there's a guard at that gate. What could be so dangerous? And what notice?"

"Millie, why don't you go inside and see what Eric's up to?" Angelle said, ignoring her questions. "I need to speak with Officer McLean for a moment."

Amelia couldn't believe what was happening. Was she being dismissed now? Were they really just going to ignore her? They were treating her like a little kid. And for a hot second that's exactly how she felt. She wanted to storm out, tell them all to kiss her butt. Luckily, she caught herself, because whether she liked it or not, she knew throwing a tantrum wasn't going to get her anywhere. It would just show them that she was in fact the child they thought she was. So instead, Amelia pushed down her boiling rage, and very calmly looked Angelle squarely in the eyes and said, "Not until someone tells me what's going on."

Angelle held her stare, but she didn't seem ruffled in the least. No, she looked... amused? Yes, Amelia thought, amused, and that just made the hot anger that was already burning her up turn blistering. After a moment, she looked away from Amelia, and smiled at Officer McLean. "Would you like to come in for a coffee?" she asked, again ignoring Amelia.

He looked at his watch. "Sure, I could spare a few minutes," he said, and as if she weren't there, the three of them turned and went inside, leaving Amelia stunned and staring after them.

Amelia watched them disappear through the doorway,

mentally chewing on a bunch of nasty comments and wanting to spit them out, but in the end, she swallowed them. She stomped up the stairs, banged the door open, and stopped just inside the door.

Luke, Angelle, and Officer McLean were already sitting at the island, busy in conversation while Mabel was serving breakfast. None of them bothered to look at her when she came in.

"You look like shit, Millie," Eric said. She hadn't noticed him, but he was lounging at the island cradling a cup of coffee in his hands, looking hot, of course, in a form fitting black T-shirt and gray and black plaid pajama pants. His hair was a mess, standing up every which way. Amelia took a moment to appreciate how great he looked all sleepy and rumpled and then she remembered she was supposed to be mad. She shot him a look, which she hoped told him to shut up.

"She went out for a run," Luke said.

"By yourself?" Eric asked. He got up, went to the coffee pot and poured another cup then handed it to her. He seemed at ease, not stressed like the other three sitting around the island sipping at their coffees. "You should have woken me up. I would've gone with you."

Amelia took the cup, gulped down a big mouthful, as the white-hot anger built up just waiting to erupt. She took another gulp, trying to calm down, and then she shouted, "Someone needs tell me what's going on!"

Eric pulled out a chair and gestured for her to sit. Amelia glared at him and shook her head, determined not to move until someone told her what was going on.

"Don't pout," Eric smirked. "It's really not a flattering look on you." He gestured again for her to sit.

Amelia looked around at the rest of them. It was clear that they were all waiting for her to sit, faces closed and guarded. She rolled her eyes and huffed loudly, then stomped her way over to the chair and banged her coffee cup onto the table.

Eric sat down beside her, taking her hand in his, gently rubbing his thumb across her palm. "Couple days ago one of the neighbors was attacked," he said. "It happened in the early morning while she was out for a walk." He paused for a moment and kept stroking her hand lightly, looking at her, Amelia thought, as if he were waiting for her to breakdown. Was she supposed to be upset about this girl? Things like that happened all the time. Anyone who watched the news or read a paper or even listened to the radio knew that. He must have read the confusion on her face because the next thing he said hit her hard and all the blood drained from her face. "It happened on our street, Millie. She was attacked behind the gates." He squeezed her hand a bit tighter, reassuring her silently. "There's been a string of break-ins, too, and we think that the attack is connected. So until whoever is behind this is caught, a curfew is in effect. That's why everyone was so worried about you."

"Break-ins? How?" Amelia breathed, their concern now feeling all too real and completely justified.

"We don't know, honey," Angelle said. "No one has been able to figure out how they're getting in. But the girl that was attacked is still in the hospital. She was really beaten up."

Officer McLean cleared his throat loudly. "When is the notice going out?"

"Today," Luke said. "Amelia, the curfew is from nine at night until seven in the morning. If you need to go somewhere, please get one of us to go with you. It's for your own safety."

"What notice is he talking about?" Amelia asked.

"It's nothing," Eric said. He let go of her hand and tapped the plate in front of her, which she guessed Mabel had brought but she hadn't noticed. When she didn't budge, he sighed and handed her a fork. "It's just to let the neighbors know you moved in. Everyone's really jumpy right now so seeing someone new raises a lot of questions."

Makes sense. "Why didn't you guys tell me all this

before?" Amelia asked, and took a bite of her eggs.

"We really didn't think you'd just wander off by yourself the first morning you got here," Luke answered, his calm and thoughtful expression back on his face. "And we didn't want to scare you."

Officer McLean must have been satisfied because he finished his breakfast in two bites, pushed back his chair, and stood up. "I'd better be going," he said, sauntering towards the door. "You take care of yourself, Amelia, and try to be careful. I would hate for something to happen to you." He nodded to the rest and then left.

Amelia quickly finished her breakfast. Now that she had calmed down, she realized how much she needed a shower. She put her fork and knife on her plate, gulped down the last bit of coffee, and stood up. "Hey guys, I'm really sorry I scared everyone."

"No worries, honey," Angelle said. "Now go get ready. We have a fun shopping day ahead of us."

Luke and Eric chuckled in unison and rolled their eyes. And Amelia couldn't help but smile, because, well, she realized with a start, as she looked at her new friends, that she was falling in love with them. All of them. It was suddenly clear to her that they were a family, not just friends, but also a real family—and she was part of it.

CHAPTER 7

Kandi slinked around the house, sticking to the shadows. She didn't dare peek in the window, but she needed to get closer. The energy was enthralling and she just needed to feel it again. *What was she?* Kandi wondered, feeling the pulse, like a heartbeat of power, coming from the house. She didn't know what it was, but the energy that radiated from Amelia was incredible, better than any blood she had ever smelled, and she knew she needed more.

She crouched behind one of the massive willows outside the kitchen, closed her eyes, and let the energy surround her. She could hear their whispers and she knew she should be listening, but it was almost as if she were high. Whatever Amelia was throwing out, it was like a mind-boggling drug.

She was sure that *He* was going to be mad. She should never have let Amelia see her. It could ruin everything, but that smell, the energy... Kandi licked her lips, imagining what Amelia's blood would taste like. *Focus,* she scolded herself and after a few shakes to clear her hazy mind, Kandi opened up her ears, stretching her senses.

"Did you guys feel that?" Eric's deep voice drifted to her ears. "It's awesome."

"Do either of you know what happened the last time

Mitch found her?" Angelle's musical voice sang and Kandi cringed. After all these years, Angelle's voice was still grating.

"All he said was that he was too late to save her," Luke answered. Kandi would never forget that booming baritone; just the sound of it sent a chill racing down her spine.

"I'm really worried about Mitchell," Angelle said. "He's a mess. The connection is screwing with him. Whatever is happening with them, something is definitely different. Honestly, I would've thought he'd already bit her by the way he's acting. He actually accused me of challenging him last night."

"Seriously?" Eric said. "But Mitch's such a push-over."

Kandi almost snickered but managed to hold it in. It sounded like there was trouble in paradise. If Mitchell was really losing it, it wouldn't be long before his trusted followers would turn against him. *He'll* want to hear this; Kandi knew it. It would be so much easier to get rid of Amelia if Mitchell wasn't thinking straight. *Score one point for the bond.*

"I'll talk to him," Eric offered.

"Not a good idea right now, Eric," Angelle said sternly. "He's not stable."

"Come on." Eric's rumbling laugh tumbled to her ears. "I'm his kid."

"Angelle, Eric's right," Luke piped in. "If he really is that unstable, Eric should go. Mitch will be less likely to feel threatened by one of his children."

Kandi heard the door swing open and she froze. *Crap!* Did they know she was listening? She waited behind the tree, staying as still as possible until she heard the purr of an engine turning over, and the tires crunching along the driveway. She snuck a quick look, making sure the coast was clear, before running as fast as she could to report back to headquarters. *He'll* be pleased. She was sure of it.

In under a minute, Kandi bolted through the door of their temporary base of operations and skidded across the linoleum floor to a halt in the living room. "She's here," she blurted, hardly able to contain her excitement.

"Finally," a grin twitched at the corners of his lips and his midnight black eyes shined. *He* was sitting on the couch, his arm draped around that useless Erin. Kandi turned up her nose slightly at the sight of those stupid overalls. And what was with the little spiky pigtails? Erin looked like a little kid and she didn't get it. Why would anyone try to look so young? Maybe she was jaded, but she'd been stuck in an eleven year old's body for seventy-four years and it sucked. Why did he keep her around? Kandi knew he had no plans to change Erin, especially if his scheme went as planned. She could only hope he'd dispose of her soon, because she just couldn't imagine spending eternity with Erin.

You've made him happy. Good work, my dear. Adam sent the message silently through their bond to her mind and winked. Kandi almost swooned at the attention from her soulmate. Adam didn't give her attention often, always paying more attention to *Him,* but when he did notice her, Kandi's heart fluttered and her body tingled all over. She had to admit, she was the luckiest girl ever.

"There's something different about her," Kandi added, hoping that this would get her more attention. "I tried to find out what it is but they don't know."

He laughed. "I'm surprised Mitchell hasn't told them."

"What do you mean?" Kandi asked, inching forwards.

He rolled his intense black eyes at her question. "She's a witch. I felt it the night I met her parents." Then he shrugged lazily. "Mitchell always suspected it."

"But if she's a witch…" Erin said with panic trembling in her voice, making Kandi cringe with annoyance. "God, what if she…"

"She won't," *he* cut her off, and Kandi giggle. At least he kept her in her place while she was around. "She probably hasn't even figured it out. She's only been eighteen for a month and without her parents, no one would have shown her how to access the power yet."

A burst of red-hot anger hit Kandi and she fixed her eyes on Adam, begging him to keep his mouth shut. She could feel the rage coursing through him, hitting her through the bond harder and harder with each moment and she knew *he* wouldn't put up with an outburst from any of them.

Adam either didn't notice her anxiety or he chose to ignore it, shouting, "Why didn't you tell us? This changes everything. If they strengthen the bond, we won't stand a chance against them."

"Enough!" *he* bellowed, eyes washing red. Kandi winced, man he could be scary. "I've waited too long for this." *He* kept his terrifying gaze on Adam for a long and painful moment, and Kandi held her breath, terrified. But then his lips twitched into a cruel, little grin and he shifted his gaze to Erin, who was still cuddled in his arms. "You're up. See what you can find out."

CHAPTER 8

Amelia's feet hurt. Her back ached and her legs and just about every muscle in her body screamed at her to sit down. She peeked out of the dressing room door and watched Angelle glide around the store grabbing more clothes for her to try on. They'd been at it all day and this had to be at least the fifteenth store they'd been to. She glanced at the storefront window, through which the golden rays of the setting sun were entering the room. It would be dark soon and with the way Angelle was going, Amelia was sure they were not going to stop anytime soon.

I should have listened to Eric and Luke, she huffed. Amelia looked longingly at her new phone, debating on whether or not she should call in a rescue mission. They'd tried to warn her. But really, she'd never thought it would be this nuts. Angelle didn't just have a little shopping problem, she was bordering on an addiction, the kind of addiction that there really should be meetings for. Her shopping was not a hobby. It was a sickness.

Amelia watched for another second, and then she shut the door to the dressing room and looked back in the mirror. She had to admit that her friend had a great sense of style. It had been a long time since she'd been shopping, and even longer since she'd had clothes that fit properly. Most of her wardrobe consisted of hand-me-downs. And even though she felt a little like a dress up doll and she was exhausted, it was kind of, just a little bit, fun.

She took off the little black dress that Angelle had said, correctly, would look fantastic, pulled on her jeans and hoodie, slung the keepers over her arm and ventured back out to the chaos that was Angelle.

Amelia had only made it a few steps from the dressing room when a girl popped up in front of her. "Excuse me. Are you Amelia Caldwell?" she asked, looking nervous. She was a touch taller than Amelia was and about the same age with short, bleach blonde hair pulled up in two spiky little pigtails, accentuating her sharp nose and cheekbones.

Amelia had just opened her mouth to reply when Angelle was suddenly there, pushing her back and placing herself right in between them. "That depends," Angelle said, sugar dripping from her voice. "Who's asking?"

Amelia's mouth opened, then closed, stunned at her friend's reaction. The girl looked sweet, wearing baggy corduroy overalls and a long-sleeved white T-shirt. Nothing about her suggested a threat. So what was with Angelle's protective demeanor? She recovered from her shock, stepped out from behind Angelle, and gave her a dirty look. "Jeez, Angelle, don't be so rude."

"It's okay," the girl said to Amelia, and then turned her attention to Angelle. "I'm Erin Truscott, ma'am."

Ma'am? Amelia wondered, thrown off by the formality. *Who even says that anymore?* And Angelle was not what Amelia thought qualified as a ma'am. She was too young, too pretty, too… well, really not ma'am material.

Angelle stuck out her arm and gently, but firmly, pushed Amelia back behind her. "Erin Truscott, hmmm, that *does* sound familiar."

Erin really didn't seem to be bothered by Angelle's attitude. She was acting as if this were normal. "I've lived in town for a few years," she said.

Angelle put her hands on her hips and raised a questioning eyebrow. "What do you want with my little sister?"

"Angelle," Amelia snapped, appalled. She snuck out from behind Angelle and managed to dodge Angelle's attempt to stop her. "I'm sorry about my friend. I'm Amelia. Can I help you with something?"

"Wow, Amelia Caldwell in the flesh," Erin said, grinning like a fool. "I can't believe I'm actually meeting you. Your favorite color is purple, you love animals, and you're majoring in mathematics and specializing in mathematical finance, right?"

"Um, yup," Amelia said. The cashier came up, took the armload of clothes from her, and went back to the counter. Amelia mouthed a *thank you* and looked back at Erin, questioningly. How in the world did she know so much? "Sorry, but have we met before?"

"Nope, you're kinda a celebrity around here and I'm in the same program at school. Hey, you're like a genius, right? Maybe we can study together. I really suck at math." Erin rolled her eyes and put up her hands, showing that she knew exactly how idiotic she sounded, and without taking a breath, kept rambling on. "I know, I know… why take it then, right?" She shrugged. "Didn't have a choice. It was either take the program or don't go at all. Then I would have to do the whole getting a job and working thing and that really didn't sound like much fun."

Amelia gaped and eyeballed Erin in disbelief. She hadn't thought it was possible, but she might have just found someone that could give Angelle a run for her money in the talking without breathing department. Was every girl in this town super excited and bubbly? She hoped not, because living with one, not that she would change it for the world, was more than enough.

"Erin," Angelle interrupted, "did you really come in here to talk about school?"

"No, ma'am," she answered and the animation on her

face was replaced by the original nervousness. "Sorry. I was shopping," Erin held up a blouse to prove she really was, "and this girl came in when you guys were in the dressing room. She was young and sorta sick looking, like really pale and grayish. She shoved this at me." Erin handed a single long stemmed rose to Amelia. "She asked me to give it to you with a message."

"What message?" Angelle asked, impatience tinting her tone.

"She said tell Amelia we've been waiting for you. I tried to tell her to do it herself, but she vanished before I could."

"What's that supposed to mean?" Amelia asked, twirling the rose between her fingers, inhaling deeply the sweet fragrance. At first glance she'd thought it was deep red, but on closer scrutiny, she realized that the large velvety bloom was black as night.

"Not sure," Erin shrugged. "Like I said, she just vanished. Never got a chance to ask."

"Thank you, Erin," Angelle said. "Was that all?"

"Yes, ma'am. Sorry to bother you guys. Maybe I'll see you at school, Amelia." Erin turned to walk away. But there was something she'd said that caught Amelia's attention. A girl with pale, grayish skin. Could it be? The kid from this morning? And if it was, why a black rose? And why was she waiting for her? Waiting for what?

"Hey, wait a minute," Amelia called after her. "You said it was a girl that looked really pale. Was she young, maybe eleven or twelve with white-blonde straggly looking hair and really creepy looking?"

"Yeah, why?" Erin asked, curiosity creeping up in her eyes. "You know her?"

"Millie," Angelle said, shoving another stack of clothes at Amelia. "You've got to try this stuff on."

Amelia sighed, loud and gusty, and looked at the heavy stack that had been dumped in her arms. She smiled at Erin apologetically. "I have to get back to the torture. Thanks for the message."

Erin nodded and darted out of the store, leaving Amelia with more questions than answers. Why couldn't she just leave it alone? Accept the rose and chalk it up to a nice welcome to town kind of thing. But who would give a black rose as a welcome? Black never meant welcome.

Amelia caught Angelle before she could add to the pile, grabbed her hand, and towed her into the dressing room. When they were in and the door was securely closed, she dumped her burden onto the floor and shoved the rose in Angelle's face. "What is this about? What did that message mean? Why did Erin say I'm like a celebrity? How does she know my favorite color? And what is your problem?" The questions just poured out in a stream of frustration. Out of the top weirdest days ever, this one was sailing right on past and kept sky rocketing upwards.

Angelle grinned. "Of course everyone's gonna know who you are. Mr. Lang owns half this town and in case you missed it, you did just move into his house. That's pretty big news around here. Now hurry up and try this stuff on. We still have a few more stores to hit." She gave Amelia one of her overly bright smiles, snagged the rose, and zipped off over to the racks and started rummaging through the clothes again.

Amelia stood there, watching Angelle flutter around and listening to the chatter of the other shoppers, and all of a sudden she wanted to cry. It seemed silly because everyone had been so nice to her.

She rubbed at her eyes, took a deep breath, and closed the dressing room door to try on more clothes.

CHAPTER 9

The clicking of the calculator was a soothing sound as Mitchell punched in some figures, and it helped to ease some of the tension that had built up in him during the last twenty-four hours.

This was what he needed. To bury himself in work. Keep his mind occupied. Stay at the office. And away from Amelia.

"Amelia," he breathed and rubbed at his face. Staying away was torture and he was sure that the pain it caused in his heart was worse than dying.

Mitchell sighed and forced himself back to work. He knew if he kept thinking about her, he would drive himself crazy and that wouldn't do either of them any good.

In no time, he was back at it, buried in the mound of work before him. The tension was slowly easing away and he was starting to feel normal, at peace.

The peace was short lived. Suddenly, his office door swung open, cracking against the wall. "Yo, Pops, you work too much," Eric said, that stupid half grin spread across his face. His green punk styled hair was sticking up every which way and he was wearing a gray tracksuit.

Mitchell groaned, annoyed at the disruption, and leaned back in his chair. "What are you doing here, Eric?" And what were they thinking sending him? He assumed they probably figured he wouldn't hurt Eric, but Mitchell wasn't so sure. If he couldn't trust himself with Amelia…

Pain flashed across Eric's face. "Do I need a reason to visit you?" he asked, unsure of himself.

Shit, Mitchell thought, annoyed, confused, and all-round pissed off at himself. "Of course you don't need a reason," he said, desperately trying to sound welcoming. He got up from his desk and gestured towards the empty chairs in the corner. "What's on your mind?"

Eric plopped down, stretching his legs out and crossed them at the ankles. He was still so young and carefree. Mitchell wondered if Eric would ever be able to take his place. Not that Eric knew yet, but that had been Mitchell's plan and Eric still had a long way to go before he was ready.

"What's going on with you? Angelle told me you lost it on her last night."

"It's about time you guys learn your place," Mitchell said sternly, and instantly regretted it.

Eric's face seemed to crumple at his harsh words and his shoulders slouched. "Dude, did you really just say that? What the hell?"

Mitchell sighed, long and loud. "You shouldn't be here, Eric. I…"

"Why are you doing this?" Eric asked. His looked so desperate, so unsure of himself that it pulled at Mitchell's heart. Eric looked up to him; Mitchell knew that and dammit, he wasn't setting the best example for his child. "She's your soulmate. Why are you hiding from her?"

"It's complicated. You wouldn't understand."

"Fine." Eric threw up his hands. "You want to sit here and hide, then fine. But she's really special and if you wait too long something might happen. Whatever it is, it pours from her and it is…" Eric licked his lips and a dreamy look clouded his face. "It's going to attract the others and if you don't claim her soon you might not get a chance to."

"Eric, I know you think that I should be there but I just can't," Mitchell said carefully. "And to be honest, it doesn't really matter if I'm there or not. They won't touch her and I won't bite her." He spoke with so much passion, that it almost seemed like he meant it. He wanted to mean it but... No, he did mean it. And until he was sure that he could trust himself, he would stay away. "She needs time. I can't push this on her. I won't."

"Dude, she's broken. What she needs is love. Not time. She needs a family. She needs friends," Eric persisted.

Mitchell opened his mouth to speak but then stopped. He couldn't explain it all. He didn't even understand it himself. The connection between them was already stronger than he'd ever imagined and he wasn't even in the same house as her. If he couldn't keep his emotions in check with his family, how the hell would he be able to do it with Amelia? He knew he would never forgive himself if he let things get out of control. It would only take a second and they would both regret it. He loved her too much to let that happen.

Eric glared at him in disbelief, got up from his chair, and headed for the door. At the doorway he turned back to face Mitchell. "By the way, there was an incident this morning."

A cold sweat broke out along Mitchell's brow and his stomach clenched. "What do you mean an incident?" he asked, barely a whisper. Something had happened to her. It all made sense. That's why they sent Eric.

Eric must have noticed his panic. "Chill out. It's not what you think," he blurted out. "Millie went for a run at like 5:00 this morning and she claimed she ran into a little girl. It sounded like Kandi."

"But she's okay?" Mitchell asked, holding his breath. It couldn't have been Kandi. They wouldn't think of coming back here. Not after the last time.

"Yep, Officer McLean found Amelia and brought her home. I had to make up some stupid story about the curfew and break-ins." Eric's expression turned serious and Mitchell held his breath. "Dad, come home. Please. If you won't do it for her, do it for me. I can't stay away from her and I need your help."

Mitchell felt like he had been slapped in the face. Eric hadn't called him "Dad" for over a hundred years now and the term of endearment pulled on every single heartstring he had. But even though he wanted to cave in, he forced himself to stay strong on this, knowing he would be no help to them by coming home. And maybe this could teach Eric some much-needed restraint. *Yes, this is a good thing*, he told himself. "I know you won't touch her, Eric," Mitchell said encouragingly. "Have a little more faith in yourself."

Mitchell thought Eric was going to argue with him, but then that goofy grin spread across his face again and he ran his fingers through his hair, making the leafy-green strands even more disheveled. "Sure, you're probably right." And then he slipped out the doorway.

CHAPTER 10

There was no sign of Eric or Luke when they got home. Mabel had left a note on the table letting the girls know that dinner was on plates in the fridge and all they had to do was heat it up, but Amelia wasn't hungry. She was too tired and, extraordinarily, too wired to eat.

Angelle helped lug all her new treasures into her room. It took nine trips between the two of them. They unpacked the fifty-eight bags, spreading all the items out on Amelia's bed.

Angelle perched on the edge of the bed and started folding a T-shirt. "Millie?" she said, looking up; the beginnings of frown lines were appearing on her forehead. "I know we just met. You've been through a lot and you probably won't believe me but..." she paused briefly, looking at Amelia with sad eyes. "I want you to know you can trust me. I mean it. I'm really sorry for the way I acted earlier. I was rude and there's really no good reason. It's just that, it's really hard to explain, but I feel connected to you somehow. It's like I've known you forever, like we're sisters. When Erin came up to you I... I don't know... I guess I just feel really protective of you."

Amelia didn't know what to say so she picked up a stack

of pants and started putting them on hangers. She knew what Angelle was talking about. It wasn't just Angelle, though; Amelia felt connected to all of them. It was like she was finally home.

Amelia finished hanging the pants and sat down beside her on the bed. "I know what you mean," she said faintly. "As soon as I met you I felt the same thing."

"So I was thinking," Angelle mused, the frown creasing deeper, "you look like you need someone to talk to and well, you can talk to me... if you want to."

They stared at each other for a long, hard moment. Amelia hadn't meant to say anything. At least nothing that really mattered, but once she started, she just couldn't stop. It poured out of her like water gushing through a broken dam. She talked about her parents, about the murder, and about how she'd been tied to a chair, bound and gagged, and forced to watch as they bled to death. Amelia cried about the guilt, about how she couldn't do anything to help them. She even confessed to the dreams, and told about how she'd fallen in love with Mitchell.

When she finished, Amelia felt faint. She'd never told the whole thing to anyone—at least not anyone who wasn't a doctor. What was Angelle going to think? Would she treat her differently now? Would she look at her with pity all the time?

"Oh, honey," Angelle said. She had tears in her voice as she pulled Amelia into a hug.

"It's okay." Amelia pushed her off and got up, picking up a top and putting it on a hanger. "Really. I don't want your sympathy. It's not going to bring them back. It won't change anything."

"It's not sympathy," Angelle said and shifted her gaze towards the bed. She picked up another top to fold before continuing. "This is going to come out wrong, but I don't feel sorry for you. Everything happens for a reason and, well, even though what happened to you sucks, it's all part of life. It's the cold hard reality. We all have loss and pain, some more than others, but it's made you the strong person you are. So I don't feel sorry for you, but I am sad for you."

Wow. No one had ever spoken to her like that. It felt cold and harsh, but it was also... nice—*honest*. The last thing Amelia wanted was more people walking on eggshells around her. She'd had more than enough of that over the last five years to last her a lifetime.

Angelle continued, "You be careful with all that guilt, though; it will eat you up if you let it." Angelle met Amelia in the eyes. "You want to hear a secret?"

Did she? Of course. She had just bared her soul, spilling her deepest secrets. The thought of hearing someone else's was just too tempting to pass up. "Do you even have to ask?"

"You've got to promise not to tell anyone," Angelle said. "Especially not the boys."

"Duh..." Amelia replied, rolling her eyes and plopping back down on the bed. "I wouldn't dream of it."

She shoved her pinky at Amelia. "Pinky swear?"

Amelia locked her finger with Angelle's and repeated, "Pinky swear."

Angelle smiled, but there was something forced and sullen about it, nothing like her usual dazzling smile. "When I was sixteen, I was fat and really awkward. No one liked me. Even my parents shunned me."

"Yeah, right," Amelia laughed. "Not even possible."

"Seriously," Angelle continued, shooting her a look that clearly said *Shut up and listen*. "I hated high school. Kids can be just so vicious. Anyways, that's not the point. I had an imaginary guy, too. Just like you and the dreams. His name was Derek and for two years, I pined over him. For awhile the dreams were more real than life and I just lived to dream."

That peaked Amelia's interest to a whole new level and a happy little voice inside her yelled out, *You're not alone and you're not as crazy as you think.* She needed to know more. She had so many questions, but she wanted to play it cool, so she asked, "So what happened?" as casually as possible.

Angelle shrugged. "I slimmed down, had a growth spurt and became popular, and the dreams just stopped. I guess I just didn't need him anymore and then life just sort of happened."

"Huh." Well that wasn't what she'd hoped for. And it really wasn't all that reassuring. Amelia was eighteen. She wasn't going to have a growth spurt and become beautiful over night. She would never be popular because, she had to face it—she was a bookworm and kind of a nerd—and nerds were never popular. And if she told herself the truth, she didn't want the dreams to stop. She might have said that she did last night, but she really didn't mean it. Life without Mitchell was not something that Amelia thought she could deal with.

Angelle must have read it on her face because she continued, looking distant, as if recalling a great loss. "It was hard for awhile. My life revolved around him and to tell you the truth, I still miss him sometimes." Then she smiled another sad and fake smile. "But hey, look at me now."

"Why are you telling me all this?"

"I don't know. I guess I just wanted you to know that you're not alone." Angelle picked up the stack of clothes she'd folded and set them on a shelf in the closet. When she came back out, her normal bubbly disposition had returned. "Enough of this serious crap, you still hot for Eric?"

Amelia blushed—a bright cherry red—and flung a pillow at Angelle. She dodged it, and snagged it out of the air just before it hit the ground and then threw it back at Amelia playfully. It hit her square in the face and they both burst out in laughter and collapsed in a giggling heap on her bed.

They talked for hours—strictly girly girl talk. They divulged their most embarrassing moments, trying to one-up each other (Amelia won by a landslide with a story involving two foster brothers, a bar of soap, and a shower curtain malfunction.). They chatted about their favorite romantic movies, and remembered their first kiss. Angelle grilled

Amelia on fashion, a subject on which she was clueless, but Angelle promised to whip her into shape.

The hours slipped by, and the yawns kept emanating from Amelia no matter how hard she tried to keep them in. She'd stopped adding anything valuable to the conversation, because her sleepy brain was no longer forming any thought that was even remotely comprehensible, and before she knew it, she had drifted off to sleep.

CHAPTER 11

On Saturday morning, Amelia slept in. She was usually up at the break of dawn, but this morning she just couldn't pull herself out of bed.

Lying on her side, curled up in her king size bed, she stared at the alarm clock, watching the glowing red digital numbers change...8:30...8:31...8:32. Maybe if she just stayed in bed and closed her eyes, she would fall back asleep and he would be there.

It was sad and it made her feel a bit sick, but some part of her had secretly hoped that Mitchell could be real. But of course, he wasn't real.

The words of her psychiatrist echoed loud and clear through her mind. "Mitchell is a figment of your imagination. It's all very normal, Amelia. You have created a fictional character, an imaginary friend if you will, to help you deal with your loss."

That was the logical explanation. And Amelia was usually all about the logic. But if Dr. Roth was right, then that meant Mitchell wouldn't be with her forever. Sooner or later, she wouldn't need him anymore. Maybe that's why she hadn't dreamt of him last night. Maybe it was because she actually had real friends now. Maybe this was her psyche trying to tell her that she no longer needed him. Maybe she would never dream of him again.

The thought of never seeing him again hurt, sticking her like a knife through the heart. She shivered as a prickling sensation enveloped her skin as if she had lain down on a pincushion. *Wow. This is just sad,* she thought. *Pull yourself together. Look around you. You have friends who actually care about you and you live in a castle. You're following your dreams and going to University. You even have a housekeeper.*

Life was finally starting to look up. She was finally starting to see the light at the end of the tunnel. So why did she still feel so empty? So alone? It was as if something were missing, something important. There was a void inside her that seemed to stretch out forever, leaving her filled with misery.

Her eyes started to sting and she squeezed them shut, willing away the tears that threatened to spill. She sucked in a gasping breath and got out of bed. She craved fresh air and yearned for exercise. Running was like her coffee. It woke her up, giving her that jolt of raw energy she needed to start the day. And it was late enough that the curfew was over so that meant it was safe. Right?

In about two minutes, Amelia had pulled her hair up into a bun and slugged her way into her yoga pants and hoodie. She snagged her water bottle off the table and frowned when she caught a glimpse of herself in the mirror. She looked like crap. And what was the dark, puffy circles under her eyes about? She poked at the saggy looking skin and sighed. It looked as if she hadn't slept in weeks and she wondered if she could sneak out of the house without her stunning roommates seeing her. *Probably not.*

A tantalizing whiff of pancakes, maple syrup, and freshly brewed coffee drifted from the kitchen. Amelia's stomach rumbled, but she didn't want to eat because if she ate, she would have to sit at the table and smile and pretend that everything was fine. Right then that seemed like way too much work.

Trying to stay as quiet as possible, she inched her way down the hall, hoping to avoid her roommates. But, of course, it was just her luck she ran into Angelle in the hallway, just outside of the kitchen. She was in pink today— a frilly, hot pink mini skirt, matching hot pink camisole and a light pink open cardigan. Her hair was tied up with an assortment of pink ribbons and her lips were painted in a soft pink shine. For most people, it was just way too much pink, but on Angelle it was somehow perfect.

Hit by a sudden twinge of jealousy, Amelia wondered if there was anything that wouldn't look good on Angelle. She instantly felt guilty for the thought and fire burned in her cheeks; she blushed, embarrassed. She wasn't one of those catty girls and she wouldn't start now. Nevertheless, seeing her drop-dead gorgeous roommate looking so spectacular did not help her sour mood.

"Good morning, sunshine," Angelle chirped in a bubbly voice and if Amelia hadn't been sour before, she definitely was now because no one should be that happy in the morning. The cheerfulness surged through her like nails running down a chalkboard.

"You're way too perky for this early in the morning," Amelia groaned.

Angelle's big brown eyes widened and her lips curved into a playful little smile. "Someone woke up on the wrong side of the bed I see." Amelia rolled her eyes and slid past her into the kitchen.

Mabel, who was busy loading the dishwasher, gave her a warm, motherly smile. "Oh, you're up. Did you want breakfast now? The rest just finished."

"No thanks. I'll grab something later," Amelia replied, dragging herself over to the sink and filling up her bottle. *Why couldn't everyone still be asleep?* she thought sourly.

"Morning, Millie," Eric greeted. She hadn't noticed him when she walked in, but he was sitting at the table looking just as chipper and awake as Angelle, in jogging pants and a faded beer logo T-shirt. He beamed at her. "You look like shit by the way." She didn't bother to answer him but shot him a look that clearly said, *Screw off,* which just made him laugh.

"Someone's not a morning person," Angelle chirped, gliding in behind her and gracefully perching herself at the island, newspaper in hand.

Eric laughed harder and Amelia felt the ice melt just a little. What a laugh, so clear, almost musical. She gave herself a little shake, clearing the fog that seemed to suck her in whenever he was around, padded towards the door, and jammed her feet into her running shoes.

"Hey, where are you going?" Eric asked, hopping up from the table.

"Run," she grunted, and opened the door.

Eric darted around, putting his hand up, stopping her just before she made it outside. "I'll go with you."

"You'll just slow me down," Amelia said, and weaved around him, ducking under his arm, and out into the cool, crisp morning.

Eric followed her out, not taking the hint that she just wanted to be alone. "I doubt that," he said with a lazy, lopsided grin.

Amelia gritted her teeth and clenched her fists into little balls. "Fine. Whatever. But I'm not slowing down for you."

She skipped her usual stretching, annoyed that he was insisting on coming, and took off down the driveway at a sprint, not bothering to warm up her muscles.

If Amelia had been worried he wouldn't be able to keep up, she was wrong. After ten minutes, she was breathing hard, in short bursts and dripping sweat, and he looked like he was just out for a leisurely stroll. *At least he wasn't talking to her,* she thought, glad for the silence.

As if he could read her mind, in that instant he said, "Millie?"

"What?" she gasped, short of breath, and pushed on, harder and faster.

"What's made you so crabby this morning?" he asked, shooting her a sideways glance.

Crap. Not what she wanted to talk about. What was she supposed to say? *I didn't see my imaginary boyfriend last night?* If she had any hope of impressing him, and she really did want to make an impression, because he was, really, oh-my-God-hot, that really wasn't the topic to do it with. "Just run," she said and hoped she didn't sound sad. The running helped cover the tremors in her voice and she picked up the pace.

"I get it," he said. "You don't want to talk to me. But you can if you want. I'm a good listener and you're not alone anymore." He sounded a little strange, tired, and a touch too serious.

Amelia didn't know what to say so she just kept running. She suppressed a wide smile. Not alone. That was good, right? It sure felt good.

****

By 11:30, Amelia was curled up studying on one of the marshmallowy chairs in her room, a soft fleece blanket wrapped around her. It hadn't been her first choice for spending the day, but Luke had some emergency business meeting, Eric was playing video games, and Angelle was busy doing God only knows what.

Amelia flipped open her Linear Algebra I textbook. *The main structures of linear algebra are vector spaces. A vector space over a field F is a set V together with two binary operations...*

She hadn't gotten very far when Angelle burst through the door in a frenzy. "There you are!" she said. "I've been looking all over for you. You have guests."

"Guests?" Amelia questioned, closing her book, "But I don't know anyone." And she really didn't want to meet anyone, at least not in yoga pants and a hoodie. She hadn't bothered getting dress up since she'd planned to study all day.

Angelle swooped over to Amelia, tugging the blanket

away, and yanking her up. The book that Amelia had on her lap fell to the floor with a thud. "It's time for you to meet the neighbors," Angelle said, looking her over with a look that clearly said she didn't approve of her attire. "I bought you so many nice things yesterday. Why are you wearing this?" Angelle picked at the hoodie like it was filthy and she didn't want to get her hands dirty. She sighed loudly. "Well I guess you'll just have to go out like this. Your guests have already been waiting too long." She grabbed Amelia by the hand and towed her out of the room.

"Wait a minute," Amelia said, trying to pull away. It was a useless effort. Angelle was a lot stronger than Amelia had guessed and she didn't waver at any of her tugs. "Let me have a shower."

Angelle ignored her and dragged her down the hallway, up the grand stairs, and straight out to the outside lounge. The second Amelia's bare feet hit the cold balcony she shivered, but Angelle pulled her on to where a crowd had gathered, lounging on some fancy chairs and chatting amicably.

One of the girls turned around and squealed, "Amelia!" and she rushed over, smothering Amelia in a hug.

Amelia stiffened. Why did everyone keep hugging her? What happened to shaking hands? Amelia thought the girl would have gotten the hint from her stiff stance, but it didn't ruffle her in the least and she was starting to think the girl wasn't going to let go.

"Jessica," a man said, chuckling softly. "Let the girl breathe."

"Oh, sorry," Jessica said, stepping back from Amelia and looking bashfully at the man who, Amelia assumed, had saved her from the hug. She was short, not more than five feet tall, and she looked like a miniature Barbie doll—busty and curvy, which really stood out in her low rise blue jeans and yellow scoop neck T-shirt that fit like a second skin. "I'm just so excited. She's finally here." She looked back at Amelia and grabbed her hands jumping up and down excitedly. "We are going to be the best of friends."

"Hello, Amelia. I'm Doug and you've already met my Jessica." He stepped forward out of the crowd and Jessica dropped Amelia's hands. He was taller than Amelia but not by much and he had a deep tan. The kind of tan you could only get by spending hours out in the sun. He had on a white button up dress shirt with a tie and black slacks, a bit formal for a Saturday, but Amelia quickly noticed that all the men were in the same sort of get-up. He gave Jessica a look that made Amelia blush. It was the kind of look that should be private, filled with raw passion, devotion, and pure love. His eyes lingered on her for a moment, before turning back to Amelia. "Aren't you a cute little thing!"

"Um, thanks I guess," Amelia said, thrown for a loop. What was wrong with this town? The idea of spending the day studying was looking better every minute.

"Look at her hair," another girl said, stepping out from the crowd. She was tall with an hourglass figure and looked like she had just stepped off the runway. Everything about her shined, from her long silky black hair right down to her patent leather bright red heels. She took one of Amelia's hands and examined it closely. "And oh my God, she's a biter. Those fingernails are hideous." She put her hands on her hips, drumming her perfectly polished fingernails against them, and looked Amelia over with a scowl. "And what in the world are you wearing? How could you possibly think that yoga pants and a baggy sweater are flattering?"

"Wow, did you really just say that?" Amelia said, looking the girl over. Who did she think she was?

"I'm Fiona by the way," the rude girl said. "And we won't be seen with you if you don't make an effort Amelia. You aren't some trailer trash anymore. You're one of us now and you need to act like it."

Amelia bristled. "You seriously need to back off."

"I could give her a manicure," Jessica offered timidly, looking back and forth between Fiona and Amelia as if she were waiting for the claws to come out.

"And I might be able to do something with this frizzy mess," another girl said from behind Fiona. She stepped out and gave an apologetic smile to Amelia. She looked like a knock-off of Fiona: same hairstyle, same clothes, and same make-up. The only difference was that while Fiona was hard looking and mean, this girl looked... friendly. "I'm Amber," she introduced herself.

"Now ladies," Eric said, strolling in and draping an arm around Amelia's shoulder. "Millie looks just fine."

"Right, and you would know," Fiona sneered, and Eric laughed, putting up his hands in surrender.

He winked at Amelia and mouthed *I tried* and then sauntered off to the gathered crowd of people, who were watching the girls, all with amused smiles.

"There's nothing wrong with the way I look," Amelia said through clenched teeth. What kind of guests came into someone's home and acted this way?

"Amelia, you're a VIP now," Fiona said, wagging a finger at her as if she were a child that needed to be reprimanded. "You can't be seen in the community looking like... like you just rolled in from the streets."

Amelia looked at Angelle for help. "Don't look at me," she said, her overly bright smile plastered on her face. "I think it's a good idea. You never know, you might actually have fun."

With Angelle's okay on the situation, the three girls grabbed Amelia and dragged her off, promising she would look like a beauty queen when they were done with her.

CHAPTER 12

There were twenty-two houses on the gated street, Amelia found out, all owned by Mr. Lang.

After the three hour makeover, which she had to admit was fun, Amelia was set in the living room like an expensive museum piece on display. For two days, the residents of the little community came to meet her. They all fawned over her, telling her how pretty she was, which was crazy. Amelia had never seen so many flawless looking people in one place and she couldn't help but wonder if they all used the same plastic surgeon, because no one could look as perfect as they did. It just wasn't natural.

While on display, Amelia also found out that all of the people in the little gated complex worked for Mr. Lang in one way or another, since he really did own most of the establishments in town. It was mind-boggling; she wondered how old he was. She'd assumed that he was the same age as her roommates, but that would make him too young to be as important as he was. Maybe it was family money? Whatever it was, she was getting more and more nervous about meeting him.

When Monday morning finally rolled around, Amelia jumped for joy because she couldn't take much more of the meet and greet that had been happening all weekend. She just couldn't understand why any of them cared about her. Was it normal for neighbors to make such a big deal about a poor scholarship kid moving in?

If she'd hoped that the buzz would die down, she was mistaken. As soon as Amelia hopped out of the car at the University, people flocked to her as if she were some kind of rock star. She soon found out that the majority of them had grown up in Willowberg or had been around long enough to know who Mr. Lang was, but their excitement was rubbing off on the other students and before long, everyone wanted a chance to meet her.

When her first lecture started, Amelia had never been so happy to listen to the monotone drone of her professor, who clearly wanted to be anywhere but teaching. Professor Patterson started right into the what-you-can-expect speech. He went through the lectures, the labs, the assignments, and the grading system he used. He told when everything would be due, and explained his no make-up policy. Basically, no make-ups unless you're dead and then you don't need to make anything up anyways.

People stared at her throughout the class. Amelia had thought she would be used to it by now. People always stared at her. But this was different. They weren't staring at her because she was new; it was because of whom she lived with.

The three-hour lecture ended too soon. Amelia didn't rush out because she really wasn't ready to smile and meet more people. She stayed put, finishing up her notes, and tried not to notice the line of people who were waiting for her.

"What are you guys staring at?" snapped a female voice. "Have you never seen someone writing notes before? Shoo. You vultures need to find somewhere else to be. Nothing to see here."

Amelia's eyes snapped up to see the girl she'd met shopping. The one who had given her the rose. She searched her brain, trying to remember her name. Erin? Yes, she was pretty sure it was Erin who was expertly dismissing the gawkers.

Once Erin had herded the last of them out the door, she plopped down next to Amelia. "It's worse than I thought," Erin said, grinning.

"Yeah, you really weren't kidding about the celebrity thing," Amelia sighed. "I just don't get it. I'm just a scholarship student. I'm not important."

Erin's grin faded and she looked Amelia over as if she were crazy. Had she said something wrong? If she had, Amelia didn't know what. After a long moment, Erin's grin returned and she shrugged. "It just goes with the territory. You live with the rich kids and well, most of us don't get to see them. They're all pretty secretive and keep to themselves so you're like the shiny toy and everyone wants to see what's behind the gate."

"Well it sucks," Amelia groaned. "I don't think I like this popularity thing very much."

Erin laughed and rolled her eyes. "You better get used to it 'cause it's only gonna get worse. Let's go grab something to eat before the next class. I can sneak you into the cafeteria without anyone seeing you."

Erin kept her word and managed to get Amelia to the cafeteria almost undetected. They went through the library and down a service hall and ended up in the back of the cafeteria before Amelia knew it. It was frustrating that she had to hide and sneak around. She really wanted to see the school, check out everything, but with the constant people or sneaking around, she'd barely had a chance to explore.

Erin sat Amelia in a far corner shielded by some fake trees and went off to order their lunch. She returned with a couple of egg salad sandwiches and bottles of water. She handed over a sandwich to Amelia and had just sat down when her eyes widened and she groaned loudly, "Here comes the Barbie Squad."

The Barbie Squad? Amelia turned around scanning the

room to see what Erin was talking about and then giggled. Fiona, flanked by Jessica and Amber, were heading straight for her, all wearing identical, and unflattering, scowls. And they did kind of look like Barbies.

"Amelia," Jessica said, rushing over. She blew delicate air kisses on either side of Amelia's cheeks and sat down beside her.

"Hi, Jess," Amelia said, forcing a smile. Couldn't she just have a quiet lunch? The three of them looked magazine perfect. For most people their outfits would have been everyday boring, but with their flawless skin and curvy figures, the low rise jeans and snug turtleneck sweaters, all a slightly different shade of purple, looked stunning. Each wore a sparkly diamond pendant around their neck.

Fiona and Amber didn't bother to greet Amelia; instead, they glared at Erin, a cold, hard glare that made Amelia's skin crawl. "Did you forget what side of the fence you're from?" Fiona said. "The trash gathers over there."

Before Amelia could say anything, Erin jumped from her chair so quickly it clattered to the floor, and she got right up in Fiona's face. "We aren't behind the fence, Fiona. You're on my turf now."

"Amelia will not have lunch with the likes of you," Fiona sneered. "Scram, Erin, no one here wants you." Annoyed, Fiona shoved her hard, causing Erin to stumble back a step.

Frozen, Amelia watched, unable to believe what she was seeing. Erin struggled to regain her footing.

A second of tense silence filled the air before Erin said, "You better be careful, Fiona. All that frowning is going to make you wrinkle." Her lips twitched up into a smile and she folded her arms across her chest. "And by the way, Millie's a big girl. She can pick who she wants to have lunch with all by herself."

Amelia didn't think it was possible, but Fiona's frown grew even deeper. "Run away, freak, before I change my mind in letting you go so easily."

"Fiona!" Amelia snapped, finally finding her voice.

"Pretty sure you're the one that needs to run away. What the hell's gotten into you?"

"She's just looking out of you, Amelia," Amber piped in, fidgeting back and forth, clearly nervous. "You don't want to be seen with that freak. It'll ruin your reputation."

Fiona ignored Amelia and took another step towards Erin, and Amelia jumped up and got in between them just as Fiona raised her hand to slap Erin. She slapped Amelia instead. Hard. Hard enough to bruise, hard enough that Amelia almost screamed out. White-hot rage bubbled up inside her; all Amelia saw was red. "I think it's time for you guys to leave," Amelia said tightly, clenching her fists into little white-knuckled balls.

"Oh my God," Fiona said, her face turning paper white. "Amelia, I'm so sorry." Her voice quivered, and she was shaking visibly. She backed up with terror in her eyes. "Please forgive me. I didn't mean to hit you."

"She didn't mean to, Amelia," Jessica added, eyes pleading. "Please don't tell him."

"You guys need to screw off," Amelia hissed through clenched teeth. She felt her cheeks flare red with anger. They must have seen it because all three whirled on their heels and scampered off like scared little mice.

"Way to take a stand, Millie!" Erin chirped, giving her a high five and doing a little happy dance. "I've never seen them back down like that before. Are you okay? You know you're probably going to get in shit for that when you get home, right? They all stick together and you just dissed them. They're not going to let that go." She was rambling again, the words tumbling out in a fast, excited stream.

"Whatever," Amelia said, and sat down hard. Her cheek was throbbing, pulsing, and tingling and she could already feel the bruise forming. She took her bottle of water and held it against her cheek, easing the sting a little.

Wow, Fiona could hit hard, Amelia thought. And who wasn't she supposed to tell? Eric and Luke? What would they care if she got into a little fight? And who the hell did they think they were? And why was Fiona so freaked out that she'd hit her and not Erin?

"So, I'm having this party on Friday," Erin said, bringing Amelia back from her thoughts. "You in?"

Amelia didn't have time to answer, because just then some guy slipped into a chair beside her. "Hey, Erin. Who's your friend?" he asked, giving Amelia a lopsided grin. He had shaggy, light brown hair which was styled perfectly messy, falling just above his deep brown eyes, and he was sporting a bit of stubble on his chin.

"You're kidding me, right?" Erin rolled her eyes. "Damn, Ty, where have you been? This is Amelia Caldwell. Like Amelia Caldwell from the Lang house."

"Shit, sorry," he apologized, blushing, just a soft hint of color. Amelia thought he may be cute, but with Eric, who was droolicious and Mitchell, who was absolutely dreamy, her cute radar was kind of off these days. He was dressed in faded blue jeans, and a form-fitting white T-shirt that showed off his abs, but they definitely were not Eric or Mitchell kind of abs.

Amelia smiled, which stung her tight cheek. "Actually, it's refreshing to find someone who doesn't know who I am."

"What happened?" he asked, nodding towards the bottle she held against her cheek.

"Run in with the Barbie Squad," Erin said. "Millie here was defending my honor and got in the way of Fiona. You should have seen it. The look on Fiona's face was priceless. I've never seen her so scared."

Tyler laughed. "Nice. Bitch had it coming, that's for sure. You want some ice?"

"Nah. I'm okay," Amelia said, the anger finally starting to fade. She set the bottle down on the table with a thump. "Who the hell does she think she is anyways?"

"Most of them are like that," Erin said, and shrugged. "They think they run this town because they live behind the gate."

"I'm Tyler Armstrong by the way," he said. "I've got class but…" he shot Amelia a big-eyed puppy dog look. "You're coming to Erin's party, right? 'Cause," he ran a hand through his messy hair, making it stand up on end, "I'll be there and it'd be cool if you were."

"Um, yeah maybe," Amelia said.

"Cool." He gave her one last grin, got up, and strolled away. Amelia watched him walk away, enjoying the view. She admired the way his jeans hung loosely on his hips and perfectly cupped his round and all-too-grabbable butt.

"He's hot, right?" Erin said, and snickered. "He's totally into you."

Amelia felt herself flush; it burned up her neck and she just knew her face was turning a bright red. She looked back at Erin and shrugged. "Yeah, he's alright I guess," she said and they both burst out laughing.

****

Erin was in all of Amelia's classes, and she knew every short cut and hiding place in the school. She escorted Amelia, showing her all the back ways and least traveled halls to get to classes. It made the day a bit easier and by the time her last class ended, Amelia was starting to feel slightly better about her new status.

She meandered towards the main parking lot to meet Eric and made it out without another run in with the Barbie Squad. Eric was waiting in the car right outside the doors to the Math Building. He was hard to miss in his flashy green Corvette. Amelia went straight to the car, jumped in, and buckled up her seat belt without a word. What would he say about Fiona? Did he already know? Should she tell him? Now that she was with him, she didn't know what to do.

Eric squealed away from the curb. She could feel him watching her from the corner of his eye. He was the first to break the silence. "Rough day?"

"You could say that," Amelia said. Her voice cracked

and tears stung her eyes. She wiped at them, furious at herself. She'd had worse days. She'd been hit before. This shouldn't bother her. Most of the people were nice. Everyone wanted to know her. She was popular. This should be a good thing, so why was she shaking?

"It'll get easier," he said, and looked at her quickly before bringing his eyes back to the road. "They'll get used to you being around."

"God, I hope so."

"I heard about Fiona. She hit you pretty good, too, I see."

Amelia hadn't bothered to look, but she knew there had to be a bruise. She could feel the tight skin and any facial movements made her feel like her face would crack. She flipped down the visor hastily and opened the mirror. There was a bruise all right. She had a clear handprint imprinted on her cheek that was turning a nice purple-blue. "That's nice," she huffed. "Just what I needed."

"It doesn't look that bad, honest." She shot him a look and he laughed. "Well, okay it does, but you can cover it up."

"How did you find out already?"

"Amber called Justin freaking out. Justin called us. Angelle and Luke are over there now with the five of them." He gave Amelia another quick look.

Crap. Amelia's temperature dropped and all of a sudden, she felt cold as ice. Why were they getting involved? She had enough problems without them making it worse. And Amelia could look after herself. She'd been doing it for five years now. It made her feel uneasy, especially with the way people were treating her. She wasn't important, so why was everyone she met treating her like a rock star?

"Why?" Amelia blurted. "Why can't you guys just stay out of it?"

Eric chuckled. "It's better that we deal with it then for Mr. Lang to find out. He wouldn't be happy and Fiona was out of line. Besides, you're part of the family now and we look out for each other." He shot her a mischievous look. "So, it's just us tonight."

Just us? Was it wrong that her heart did a little flip at the thought? Amelia quickly forgot she was supposed to be mad and the stress of the day, well, the stress of everything that had happened since she had arrived in Willowberg fluttered away. Since when had she become so boy crazy? She didn't know, but with Eric this close to her, so close she could smell his musky scent and feel the heat of his skin, all reason flew out the window.

"I was thinking I could take you out for dinner," Eric continued cautiously. "Somewhere nice."

Was he asking her out? On a date? No, he couldn't be. He wouldn't. He was just being nice, she was sure of it, but she couldn't help but hope maybe, just maybe, he was. "Okay," Amelia said, trying to keep the excitement out of her voice.

"Awesome," he said, flashing a lazy, and very sexy, grin.

****

Dinner was fantastic. Eric had taken her to a swanky little place in the downtown core. Amelia had been so nervous at first that she almost knocked her drink onto his lap. Luckily, his reflexes were extraordinarily fast and he caught the glass, not spilling a drop.

In no time, Eric had made Amelia forget all about her nerves. His laugh, his smile, his charismatic, easygoing personality, everything about him made her at ease. By the end of the night, to Amelia's surprise, she was flirting and inching closer to him. Even more shocking, he was flirting back.

When they got back home, he was a gentleman and insisted on escorting her to her door. That was when Amelia remembered her nerves. They came back, jumping and flipping like acrobats at a circus. As they got closer to her room, she was suddenly all too aware of her body and his body and the closeness between them, like an electric current, coursing through her limbs, waking up parts of her that she didn't even know existed.

They reached her room all too quickly and part of her wanted to rush in, shut the door, and hide. What if he kissed her? Did she want him to? *Yes.* But what if she didn't do it right? Would he laugh at her? In theory, she knew how to kiss. She'd kissed Mitchell hundreds of times, but that was just a dream. He wouldn't tell her if she sucked at it.

Amelia was getting herself so worked up that she felt nauseous. Her stomach was flipping so fast it was as if she were on a rollercoaster, hanging upside down, and looping around. She stood in front of her door, staring at her feet and fidgeting with her watch, turning it over and over on her wrist. She could feel him watching her and could just imagine his laughing, vibrant eyes. The silent tension was spine tingling, and the urge to flee became overwhelming, but she just couldn't make her body work.

Just when she thought she would scream in frustration, he reached out and gently tipped her chin up, so she had to meet his eyes. Then, as if it were slow motion, the world around her stopped and he leaned in and kissed her.

He tasted sweet and his lips were soft and oh so gentle. She'd thought it would be just like kissing Mitchell but it wasn't. Not one bit. Her lips tingled, and it was nice, but the passion, the need, it wasn't the same. Not bad, just... different.

When he broke away, he licked his lips and looked down at her, eyes hungry. "Shit," he breathed and backed away. "Shit, that shouldn't have happened."

"No, it's okay," Amelia said. That really wasn't the reaction she'd hoped for. What had she done wrong? She took a step towards him. Maybe if she tried again. This time she could use her tongue. Maybe that would work.

He held up his hands to stop her and his expression turned cold. "It's really not okay. Don't look at me like that."

Her heart sank, feeling like boulders were tied to it, dragging it down to her toes. The way he was looking at her, as if he couldn't stand to be near her hurt. It hurt really badly, way worse than Fiona's slap. "Like what?"

"Like I'm some chocolate sundae. You're going to be the death of me if you keep that up."

"Eric, we didn't do anything wrong," she pleaded, tears filling her eyes.

"Dammit, Amelia!" he yelled and slammed his hand against the door so hard the walls rattled. "Yes, we did. I have to go." He turned away from her and shuffled off.

"Eric," she called after him, but he didn't stop and the tears spilled over, gushing like a waterfall. She scrubbed at her face, hiccupping and gasping for breath, not understanding what she'd done so wrong. Was she really that horrible to kiss?

Amelia stared down the empty hallway for a cold, lonely minute, praying he would come back, but he didn't. Finally, she went into her room, slammed the door, fell into bed, and cried big heart-wrenching sobs.

CHAPTER 13

There was no sign of Eric the next morning, and to Amelia's relief (and dismay), he stayed away for the rest of the week. After their little kiss, he'd left abruptly, supposedly on some business trip and no one seemed to be able to tell her when he would be back. She knew sooner or later that he would come back. It would be awkward and they would have to deal with it, but she was glad she didn't have to face him, at least not yet.

As the days went on, Amelia's shiny new toy status didn't fade in the least. It only seemed to grow, especially after the Barbie Squad formally and publicly apologized to her.

With Eric gone, and no sign she would be able to just blend in, Amelia focused on school, burying herself in books. Studying was the best, and really the only, distraction she could think of and she was glad classes were tougher than she'd expected. It was nothing like high school and by the time Friday came around, she'd already taken (and aced) two quizzes, and had a report to write by the end of the weekend.

The energy at school on Friday was nuts; there was a palpable buzz in the air. Amelia could feel it like a soft vibration, radiating and pulsing. By the time 7:00 came around and her last lab class ended, the buzz had grown, and seemed more like a tidal wave of anticipation. At first, Amelia thought it was a bit strange. Erin was not Miss Popularity by any stretch of the imagination, but from what she'd heard Erin's annual party had grown a reputation of an event not to be missed. Amelia had been asked at least a hundred times if she would be going to Erin's party. And with Amelia's celebrity status, all the girls wanted to know what she'd be wearing, when she'd be getting there, if she had a date, if she would have her hair up or down. It was so flattering and all the attention, whether she wanted to admit it or not, was going to her head.

Now, at 8:30, Amelia was sitting on her bed amidst heaps of clothes, watching the clock flip away the minutes. The reality had finally hit her. This was her first real party and with all the attention she'd been getting she knew she had to look just perfect and everything seemed… wrong. Every outfit she tried on made her look fat or just didn't work.

She picked up a black skirt, held it up to the light and then tossed it across the room. "Everything is just wrong," she huffed to herself. Her nerves were on hyper-drive and the knot in her stomach twisted agonizingly tight.

With a sigh, she got off her bed, wrapped her housecoat around her, and stalked out of her room. She knew it was stupid and she was overreacting, but there was so much pressure on her to be some perfect, glamorous movie star that it made her feel sick and she just knew she couldn't go. *I'm not the party type anyways,* she thought, and watching a movie and hanging out here would be… better. And how could she look perfect when the bruise on her cheek was starting to turn a horrid greenish-yellow.

Amelia slipped up the stairs and headed straight for the media room, the thought of chilling out and watching a movie was sounding better and better to her by the minute. When she passed Eric's room, she stopped for a moment, taking in a deep breath of lingering musk. Her heart sank as she looked at his closed door and wondered if he was ever coming back. She gave herself a little shake, forced her eyes away, and padded down the hall to the media room.

The room was dark and quiet, and Amelia reached in and flicked on the lights. She was half way to the television when she saw him.

Eric.

Amelia had expected it to be awkward, and it was. Seeing him again hit her hard, like a punch in the gut, knocking out all the air from her lungs. They locked eyes for an incredibly long minute. She wanted to pull away, break the contact, but she couldn't. So many feelings rushed into her, suffocating her. Hate, anger, lust, more anger. She felt like she was drowning in the intense rush of pure emotion.

It wasn't until he grinned at her with that mischievous grin of his, the one which at one time had turned her into a giggling fool, that it hit her. A part of her, a purely animal part, wanted to pounce on him and kiss every inch of his magnificently sculpted body. That was her biggest worry. She'd been terrified that when she saw him again she would act like a lovesick puppy dog. But now, as she looked at him, it was crystal clear that her attraction to him was completely and utterly sexual. She didn't love him, not even a little. And somehow, for some reason that little bit of realization stopped her from making a complete and utter fool of herself.

"Oh, sorry," Amelia said, pleased at the strength of her voice. "I didn't know you were back."

"It's okay." Eric looked so calm and cool and she wondered if he was feeling the same mix of confusion that she felt. "Thought you were going to that party tonight."

She shrugged and continued on to the entertainment stand. "You thought wrong."

"Oh, come on," he whined, and Amelia had to work hard not to look over at him. His voice was almost captivating and it called to her. She focused with eyes unseeing on the shelves of movies. "I was looking forward to it. Go get ready."

"I'm not going so drop it," she snapped, annoyed at how much he affected her. "And even if I were, you wouldn't be coming with me."

Amelia hadn't heard him get up, but she could feel his breath, warm and tantalizing, on the back of her neck. "Why?" he asked, a soft, seductive whisper in her ear.

She was suddenly hotly aware that the only thing under her thin housecoat was a lacey black bra and thong panties and he was standing so close that she could feel the heat of his skin warming her body. "I have nothing to wear and I look fat in everything," she breathed, broken and strained.

Eric laughed, loud and hard, and Amelia spun around. "Fat?" He staggered back a few steps, laughing hysterically and holding his stomach. "Come on. What are you, a size six?"

Amelia bristled. "A size six! You think I'm a size six! You're such an ass," she yelled. She grabbed a DVD off the shelf and flung it at him; it missed and banged off the wall.

Eric sobered quickly, looking at her with confusion and that look made her blood boil. "What did I say?" he asked, and held up his hands in protection as she grabbed another DVD and whipped it at him.

"What's up with you two?" Angelle asked, appearing in the doorway as another DVD was sent airborne at Eric. "And why aren't you ready?"

"I'm not going," Amelia snapped, grabbing another case off the shelf.

Angelle glided into the room, and before Amelia knew it, she'd snatched the next case out of her hands and placed herself in between them. "What the hell did you say to her, Eric?"

"I didn't say anything," he said, exasperated. "She said she looked fat and I said she was a size six."

"You didn't," Angelle gasped and put an arm around Amelia, more to keep her from attacking Eric than anything else. "God, Eric. Didn't anyone ever tell you to just keep your mouth shut about that kind of thing? She's a size four." Angelle paused for a second and gave Eric a hard glare. "You just have so much class, Eric," she said, her voice oozing with sarcasm. "All lower, but so much class." She turned her big brown eyes on Amelia. "It's okay, Millie. I'll help you find something to wear. Don't listen to him. He's an idiot." And then she ushered Amelia off, promising to help her get ready.

"I think I should cancel," Amelia said when they got to her room, her voice a little shaky. Why had she let Eric get to her like that? She knew it was crazy and he really hadn't said anything wrong, but dammit, he could get under her skin so easily.

"Don't be stupid," Angelle laughed. "You were so excited yesterday."

"That was yesterday," she replied, letting out a long gusty huff and curled up in bed, tugging the blankets around her. "This whole party thing is overrated anyways."

Angelle bounced across the room and ripped the blankets off her. "Oh no you don't," she said, wagging a finger at her. "You're going and it's gonna be a blast. Now go jump in the shower. I'll pick out something for you to wear."

"That's the problem," Amelia said, glancing back towards the closet and around the room at all the clothes scattered. "I have nothing to wear." She ran her hand through her mess of curls. "I've been looking for the last hour and I have absolutely nothing. Everything is just wrong."

Angelle erupted in laughter. "You've got to be kidding me." She put her hands on her hips and made a great show of an exaggerated eye roll. "We shopped for like ten hours and I bought you a whole new wardrobe. You're being a bit dramatic, don't you think?"

Amelia felt the giggle bubbling up and tried to cough and cover it, but it ended up sounding like a choked laugh. She had to admit it. Angelle was right. For the first time in years she had lots to wear, but nothing seemed right.

Angelle yanked her up out of bed and ushered her into the bathroom, keeping a firm hand on the small of her back. "You better hurry," she said, giving Amelia another nudge towards the shower. "I promise I'll make you look fantastic."

With a theatrical, drawn-out sigh, Amelia reached in and turned on the water. "Fine, but I want to put it on record that I don't think I should go."

After a quick shower, Amelia emerged from the bathroom draped in a fluffy white robe. She laughed when she saw her office door open. Angelle had transformed it into a mini beauty parlor.

"Sit," Angelle ordered, pointing to the desk chair. Amelia obediently padded her way over and sat down, perching on the edge.

"I'm pretty sure I can handle getting ready myself," Amelia said, jutting out her bottom lip in a pout.

"Stop pouting, Amelia. You are going tonight and you are gonna have fun," Angelle said sternly, clipping the diffuser into place on the hair dryer. Grabbing the mousse, she squirted out a blob of tangy, sweet-smelling foam and worked it into Amelia's long curls. Then she turned the dryer on, scrunch drying the masses of hair.

It took almost thirty minutes for Amelia's thick hair to dry into soft spiral curls. Angelle parted it right down the middle into two loose pigtails and tied them with short black ribbons just below the ears.

"Pigtails?" Amelia questioned, feeling the knot return to her stomach.

"Just trust me. It's the little bit of sugar; now we will work on the touch of spice." Angelle dumped her make-up bag onto the desk and started rummaging through the contents. "Close your eyes. I don't want you to see the colors I'm picking."

Amelia huffed but closed her eyes. The brushes tickled as they were swept across her face. She'd never been one for much make-up, never really knew how to wear it.

"Okay, spice complete. Now take the clothes from the bed and get dressed," Angelle ordered like a drill sergeant. "But do not go into the bathroom. I'll turn around. You can't look yet."

Amelia hustled over to the bed and looked at the clothes that had been laid out for her. It all looked so basic. A pair of dark vintage blue boot cut jeans that had the worn-in details on the thighs and a snug looking black cashmere scoop neck sweater. "I can't wear this," Amelia said, a tinge of disappointment in her voice.

"Will you just trust me and put it on!"

Against her better judgment, Amelia pulled on the clothes as Angelle had instructed, trying not to mess up her hair. "Okay. I'm dressed. Can I look yet?"

"Nope," Angelle chimed. She went back into the closet and returned with some accessories. "This is for a touch of color and it's so hippie chic." Around Amelia's neck, she draped a colorful scarf like a woven tapestry of the rainbow. "And this will give you a little bit of edge." Then she placed a charcoal gray fedora on her head. "Just put on these boots and then I'll let you look." She handed Amelia a pair of black leather ankle boots with three-inch heels and Amelia pulled them on. "Perfect!" Angelle gushed as she looked over her masterpiece. "Okay, now go into the bathroom and look in the full length mirror."

Amelia tried to move slowly and act like she didn't care, but she was just a touch excited. She looked in the mirror and gasped. *Wow. It's amazing what the right clothes and make-up can do*, Amelia thought, as she looked herself over. She barely recognized herself. Her normal, straight body was all curves and she looked... sexy. She broke into a big glossy smile and made a mental note to ask Angelle to show her how to do the smoky eye thing later.

"I told you you'd look fantastic," Angelle said from behind her.

"Thank you." Amelia could feel the tears welling up, and

she cursed under her breath. When had she turned into a blubbering baby? She didn't know and she really didn't like it.

Angelle squeezed her shoulder and smiled, a friendly energy packed smile. "Enough of that. No tears allowed. You'll smudge."

On impulse, Amelia turned around and flung herself at Angelle, giving her a big hug. "You're the best," she whispered, trying to keep the joyful tears from falling.

In the kitchen, Eric and Luke were standing at the door, deep in conversation. Amelia took a moment to admire them. Even in their casual jeans and knit sweaters, they were a sight for sore eyes.

Eric noticed her first and she was thrilled to see his jaw actually drop and his eyes travel over her, taking in every detail. After what he'd put her through, taking off, leaving without so much as a goodbye, it was nice to see she had some kind of effect on him. She felt the beginnings of a flush rushing hotly up her neck. "Wow. You look…" he said, looking her up and down. "Wow."

Luke cleared his throat loudly, ruining Amelia's moment. "You look great," he said, smiling at her. "We all thought we would tag along if that's alright with you, since it's past curfew and all."

"Fine," she said, keeping her calm. She didn't want them to know that she was glad they were coming because truthfully, she still really didn't want to go. But with them with her, maybe it wouldn't be so bad. And she was sure Angelle would be a blast.

Eric grumbled something unintelligible, clearly not happy with her lack of enthusiasm, and stomped off, out the door.

****

If Amelia had been worried they wouldn't be able to find Erin's house, she was wrong. The glow was visible from four blocks away. When they reached the house, she saw why. Lights adorned every corner: bright white spotlights lazily circled on the roof, tiki torches lined the walkway, blue and red strobe lights flashed.

Erin's home looked like, well, it was hard to tell really what it looked like between the flashing strobe lights and all the drunks spilling out all over the lawn. It could have been anywhere from white to black in its color scheme, but Amelia just couldn't tell. It was smaller than her house, maybe an eighth of the size, but then she lived in an enormous castle so comparing it was hard, and it looked, Amelia thought, well used, not run down, just well lived in. The sight reminded her of all those frat party movies she'd seen. Red plastic beer cups littered the lawn and the line of people waiting to get in had formed their own party outside.

Luke parked the car, miraculously finding a spot right in front of the house, and the second Amelia got out, people rushed to her, greeting her, complimenting her. She felt as if she were walking down a red carpet.

Her friends were on it and faster than she could follow, they moved in front of her, blocking the drunken mob from getting too close. And Amelia was grateful. All through high school, she'd wanted to be popular. She'd prayed for it. She'd wished for it. But wow, she'd never thought it would be this much work. It was exhausting having people like her. Amelia never thought it would be possible, but now she was starting to wish she could be that girl no one liked again, because this smiling and being happy thing was not as much fun as it looked. *Why did anyone care she was here?* she wondered, and looked at her friends. They were the ones that should be noticed. She lived with them and still had a hard time not gawking. They were just so perfect it almost hurt her eyes to look at them.

Angelle noticed her hesitation and linked arms with her. "You ready?" she asked, and before Amelia could answer, Angelle was pulling her forward through the crowd and the four of them strolled up the walkway straight to the door.

It was quite a sight, the four of them. People, drunk and

sober, jumped out of the way to let them through. She guessed that was one plus of her new status. She didn't have to wait in lines.

They made it to the door just as it banged open and the low thumping of music spilled out mixed with chaotic laugher and slurred hollers of people having a good time. A couple staggered out more involved in each other than anyone else, and Amelia wasn't really sure how they were walking. They were wrapped around each other like pretzels. *Well that's new,* Amelia thought, blushed, and turned away, letting them by. They didn't make it far, landing in a heap on the lawn, and kept right on going.

"Millie, you made it!" Erin cried from the door. She reached out, snagged Amelia's hand, and pulled her in, not paying any attention to her friends. "Let's get you a drink," she suggested, looking back at Amelia's entourage. "Come in or stay out, but shut the door," she yelled over the music and pulled Amelia down the hall, through the living room, and straight into the kitchen.

By the time they pushed their way through, Amelia felt filthy. She'd been groped God only knows how many times, had a least one drink spilled on her, and she was covered in sweat, which wasn't all her own. Her boots felt sticky, like suction cups taping her to the floor.

The kitchen was a little slice of heaven compared to the crowded living room that had been transformed into a dance club. There were still too many people, talking way too loud, but the noise level was down about six decibels. She could actually make out the words people were saying in there.

Erin snagged two beers, popped the tops, and handed one to Amelia. "Thanks," she said, and hesitantly took it and looked at it, not sure if she should drink it or not. She'd never been much of a drinker, or actually had alcohol before. Amelia took a quick glance over her shoulder, noticed Eric was already flirting it up with some trampy looking thing with a huge, bulging chest and a skimpy little skirt that shouldn't even be legal, and all caution rushed away. She tipped the beer up and gulped a mouthful. It was sour and fizzy and it tickled her nose, but she took another gulp anyways, hoping the taste would get better.

After she forced down half the beer, she looked over at Erin, who was watching her as if she had never seen her before. "Better slow down, lush," she said. "I'm betting you've never drank before and you don't want the hottie to know he's getting under your skin."

The beer was hitting her hard. Amelia already felt a bit tipsy and she couldn't stop the giggles from erupting. Her ears were ringing and pleasant warmth was spreading through her. "What, Eric? You've got to be kidding me. Didn't even notice him," Amelia said with a tight smile plastered on her face.

"Sure you didn't." Erin rolled her eyes and took a dainty little sip of her beer. She looked too young and innocent to be drinking, Amelia thought. But then, she was too young to drink in the grand scheme of things. But Erin looked like a kid with her bleach blonde hair tied up in little spiky pig tails—like usual—and she was wearing overalls and a spaghetti strapped ocean green tank. She had a purely "little girl" kind of cuteness. "Bet you didn't notice that skank he's hanging onto either," Erin added.

Amelia took another swig, downing the rest and banging the empty can onto the counter. She glanced around, noticed that Angelle and Luke were chatting it up with some people she vaguely recognized and she thought one of them might have been Justin, one of the Barbie Squad's boyfriends, but she wasn't sure.

In the corner, some kind of drinking game was in progress. It didn't look that complicated. There was a ping-pong ball and six red beer cups in a triangular formation on each end of a table. "What are they playing?" she asked Erin, nodding towards the game. Amelia watched as someone tossed the ping-pong ball, bouncing it off the table and into one of the cups.

Erin laughed. "You really were a sheltered kid. It's called beer pong, Millie."

There was a bunch of hooting and hollering coming from the game and Amelia looked back to see Tyler chugging a beer. Maybe it was the beer, but he was looking pretty yummy in jeans and a buttoned up long sleeved denim shirt. He had the shirt open half way down his sun-bronzed chest and she watched as a drizzle of beer splashed onto it.

As if he knew she was watching, he finished the drink and looked over at her with a brilliant smile. "Millie," he called, waving her over. "Didn't think you were going to make it."

Erin giggled, bringing Amelia's attention back to her, and she blushed. "He's got it bad for you," Erin said, grinning like a fool.

Amelia raised her eyebrow. "Really?" She glanced over at Eric, who was now sucking face with the blonde tramp. She pulled her eyes away, grabbed Erin's hand, and with a great deal of focus, walked over to Tyler, swaying her hips with every step.

She was relieved that the kitchen wasn't too packed and she made it to the table without tripping over anyone, because that one beer was making everything a tad fuzzy. But she made it, hoping she had pulled off the sexy walk she had been aiming for. And by the look on Tyler's face, and every other guy around the table, she had.

"You look hot," Tyler blurted, and then he blushed, a deep red. "I mean... you look..." he fumbled over the words.

"Are you trying to flirt with me?" Amelia asked, giving him a look that she hoped was extra flirty.

He grinned and visibly relaxed. "Maybe, is it working?"

Erin looked back and forth between them. "Hey, Millie," she whispered into her ear. "Looks like hottie noticed you making eyes at Ty."

Amelia glanced over her shoulder just as Eric strolled up.

He wrapped a possessive arm around her waist and gave her a sloppy kiss on the cheek. "Hey, babe. Who's your new friend?" he asked, jaw clenched, and he narrowed his vibrant green eyes at Tyler.

The whole room froze, silently watching. All the buzzing stopped, the drunken laughter, even the music, stopped. It was quiet as night; everyone watched them as if it were a movie playing out for their enjoyment. Amelia tried to wiggle out of Eric's arms, but he had a firm hold on her. She caught the look on Tyler's face, confused, hurt, and worried. He took a step back, leaned against the counter, and put his hands up. "Sorry, dude. Didn't know she was with someone."

"I'm not." Amelia kept wiggling and managed to get Eric's arm off her. Erin had backed off a few paces and was nervously watching the scene. Amelia completely understood it because the vibe Eric was giving off was ice-cold.

Eric snagged Amelia's hand before she could move out of his reach and his eyes softened slightly. "You break my heart," he said dramatically, putting a hand over his heart and gave her a wounded look.

Amelia shot him a look that she hoped told him to *Screw off* and pulled her hand away from him. It must have worked because he put his hands up in surrender. "Don't you have something else to do?" she asked.

"Come on, Millie." Eric reached out to touch her again. She pulled away before he could. "Don't be like that."

"Stop it, Eric!" she snapped and rested up against the counter beside Tyler, who was clearly uncomfortable. He was about the same size as Eric and Amelia thought they would be well matched in a fight if it came to that, but there was an animalistic rage brewing in Eric's posture that was cold and frightening.

Tyler slid away from her and he looked as if he were trying to make himself smaller. He gave Amelia a sad, sorry look. "Hey, I don't want to get in the way here."

"No, it's okay. He's just my roommate and he was just leaving." Amelia glared at Eric. "Your trashy friend looks lost over there, Eric," she said icily. She wasn't sure if it would work, and for an eternal minute he didn't even acknowledge her, just kept his intense glare fixed on Tyler. Then he shrugged, grinned, and walked away.

Amelia looked after him, stunned and utterly confused. The tension had obliterated her pleasant buzz, and she snagged a couple of Jell-O shots from a passing tray, and slurped three, one right after another. That was the cue for the party to start again, and she was glad when the music picked up and the drunken banter started up again.

Amelia glanced over at Tyler. "You know what?" she said, taking another shot and pounding it back. "Let's have some fun."

"Fun sounds good," he said, smiling, and handed her a beer. Amelia glanced around for Erin and didn't see her. But she didn't blame her for sneaking out. If Amelia had been able to she would have as well, because that was really, really, uncomfortable. She joined in the beer pong game and in no time, she forgot about Eric and was having a blast.

Amelia didn't know how many shots or beers she consumed. Every time she finished one, Ty handed her another. And since she wasn't a drinker, it was hitting her pretty quickly. In no time, she found herself leaning into him. And flirting. Man, was she flirting!

At some point, he sat down and somehow she ended up on his lap but she didn't have a clue how and she didn't really care. Tonight was about normal, reckless teenage fun.

"I think I should cut you off," Tyler announced, as he handed her another shot.

"Probably, but you're not going to!" Amelia replied seductively—she hoped—but even to her own ears it sounded sluggish and slurred.

"But I really should. Eric doesn't look too happy over there."

"Forget Eric." Amelia glanced up at Tyler. She didn't

know if it was the booze or the party, but he was looking pretty cute. Suddenly, she found herself thinking of Mitch. Mitch... she missed him. Missed him horribly and Tyler was no Mitch, but... and then, before she knew what she was doing, she kissed him. She felt herself leaning into him, blending, and molding.

His lips tasted like raspberries. *The Jell-O shooters*, her brain told her.

"Amelia," Eric growled from behind her and Tyler broke away.

"Um," Tyler said, looking from her to Eric and then he untangled himself from her and stood her up.

"What do you want, Eric?" she huffed. "I'm a little busy if you didn't notice."

"It's time to go," he replied coldly.

"You can leave whenever you want to." Amelia tried to sit back down on Tyler's lap, but she missed and landed on her butt on the floor. And for some reason she thought that was funny, but she really didn't know why, and started giggling uncontrollably. She giggled so much that her stomach hurt, but she couldn't stop.

Eric reached down and yanked her up so hard that she could feel bruises forming under his fingers. "Let go, Eric!" she screamed. "You're hurting me." A hushed tension fell on the room, the party stopped and everyone froze, staring at them.

"What's going on here?" came Angelle's sugary voice, and Eric dropped his grip on Amelia. Angelle gave the room her sweet glamorous smile. "Don't stop the party on our account," she chirped and then waited. After a moment, the buzz and chatter started up again.

Amelia was cradling her hand, and blinking back tears from the burst of pain. "Eric was just leaving," she choked out.

"You're drunk, Millie, and he was all over you," Eric sneered.

Tyler shifted uncomfortably beside her, inching away

under the stare of her roommates, which was made even more intense by Luke. "Maybe you should go," Tyler said, obviously trying to look anywhere else but at her.

"What?" Amelia asked. She tried to take a step towards him, but he backed up. "Whatever, I'm going for a walk." She turned on her heels, lost her balance, and almost toppled over again but managed to catch herself and stomped off, out the patio door into the cool night air.

Behind her, she heard Angelle's voice. "Let her cool off, Eric. She'll be fine."

It was chilly and it turned out that the fresh air did not do wonders for her buzz. It only seemed to make it hit her harder and with every cold, crisp breath, her head spun. Amelia hung onto the railing, glad it was there, and focused on breathing which turned out to be a hard task. If the deck would just stop moving…

Before she heard his drawling, southern voice, Amelia smelled him coming. It was a rancid smell, like meat rotting in the summer heat. "What do we have here?"

With every ounce of concentration she could muster, Amelia managed to turn around and prop herself against the sturdy railing, again silently thanking it for supporting her.

"That's Amelia," said some girl. Amelia had to blink a few times to clear the double vision, but when it did, she almost screamed. The girl, the creepy little girl she'd seen running, was just inches away. She grabbed Amelia's chin and tilted her head, examining her neck.

"Let go of me," Amelia yelped, stumbling sideways and landing on her butt. Her head was swimming, and she suddenly wished she'd never drunk.

The girl's eyes stayed fixed on Amelia. And the guy, thin and wiry looking, moved in closer. "Her bodyguards shouldn't have left her alone," he said, a malevolent smile creeping up on his face.

Amelia tried to stand up, but she couldn't make her legs work. "Leave me alone," she said, sliding away from them.

"Why would he let you wander around all alone," the

creepy girl murmured, watching Amelia scoot across the deck and lean in against a corner. "Very careless, don't you think?"

"Very careless, indeed," he agreed. His grin spread wider, and a flash of white sharp teeth popped down.

Amelia felt cold. She was shaking and her head was still spinning. She couldn't believe what she was seeing. It was the booze. It had to be the booze, but those teeth... they looked real, sharp, and... scary. "Who are you guys?" she choked out.

They ignored her question. "And look at her mark," the man said. "He hasn't even bothered to claim her yet."

Claim her? Amelia knew that sounded important, but the ringing and buzzing in her ears wouldn't let her brain put it together. She could see the party carrying on through the glass patio doors. No one noticed her outside, probably trying to ignore her, she thought, and with all the drama she had caused, she didn't blame them. She tried again and managed to get to her feet. She started backing away towards the party. If she could just get back in the door. Eric would see her. He would help her.

"Leaving so soon?" the girl questioned. Amelia hadn't seen her move, but suddenly, she was right in Amelia's face. Amelia screamed as she got a look at the girl's eyes. Blazing red. And she clasped her hands to her mouth. *It's just the booze*, she told herself. *This isn't real. You're just drunk.*

The man chuckled unpleasantly. "Oh, Kandi. Stop scaring the poor thing."

"But, Adam," she whined, "Listen. Just listen. That beat. It's musical. And he obviously doesn't want her. He would be here if he did."

Amelia scrambled backwards and tripped over her own feet. She crashed down, smacking her head hard against the railing, the railing that just a minute ago she'd thanked for being there. A shooting pain pierced her skull and, mixed with her drunken stupor, sent her stomach into somersaults. Bright spots flickered in her vision and she closed her eyes tightly, only succeeding in making her spinning head speed up. She blinked a few times in an effort to make it stop. A hot and sticky feeling trickled down the back of her neck, and she caught the harsh red glow of eyes and white flicker of razor-sharp teeth, and she knew the stickiness was blood.

Amelia heard the piercing scream, bone chilling and terrifying, and it took her a moment to realize it was coming from her lips.

"Kandi, Adam, did you miss the mark?" Amelia heard a new voice, familiar and booming with authority and the screaming stopped. Luke. "She's taken."

"We were just having a little fun, Luke," a girl said. Amelia's mind was moving slower and it was getting hard to remember whose voice belonged to whom. They were all melting together. She forced her eyes open; trying to see what was happening. She wanted to shout for Luke to run away. She needed to warn him. But warn him of what? She wasn't even sure. A little voice was screaming *Vampires*, but her brain was telling her she was drunk.

"Kandi," Adam snapped, moving in front of her as if to shield her. *From what?* Amelia thought. They were the monsters, not Luke. "We were just chatting with her. We weren't going to hurt her," Adam continued.

Suddenly, Eric was hovering over her. "Millie… Millie, try to focus." Eric's eyes bore into hers. "Are you okay?" Amelia focused on him. There was something wrong. His face was contorted, eyes blazing… red. "Luke, she's bleeding."

Amelia tried to move. She needed to get away. Eric. Luke. She frantically looked around. Call for help. She needed to call for help. Then she saw Angelle. Looking sweet and deadly. A dynamic mix of sugar and fire; the sight made Amelia shudder.

"Get away from her, Eric," Angelle growled. She turned to Adam and Kandi, who were cowering like scared little dogs, and the sweetly syrupy voice poured out. "If I ever see you near her again, I won't hesitate to rip you apart."

One second they were cowering and the next they were gone, leaving Amelia with her roommates. "What's going on?" she cried. Her hurting head was spinning out of control and everything around her was taking on a static-like, grayish tone. "I don't understand what's happening."

Before she knew it, she was in Luke's arms, cradled like a child against his chest, and they were back in the house heading towards the front door. "Don't worry, kiddo. I'm going to take you home."

Home. Yes, home sounded good. Amelia snuggled in and closed her eyes. She thought she heard Tyler and Erin, but it seemed so far away, like a dream. Everything else was just too loud. Music was pounding, pumping out, and she buried her head deeper into Luke's chest, hiding from the noise.

The next thing she knew, she was in Luke's car, cradled on his lap. Amelia fluttered her eyes open. Eric was driving she noticed and Angelle looked worried. But why? They were vampires. Why were they worried? Nothing made sense because logically, she should be the one that was scared. She looked up at Luke, through half closed, sleepy eyes. "I think I should be scared of you guys," she murmured.

Luke chuckled and it rumbled through his chest, jiggling her, "Why's that, kiddo?"

"Because... you're a vampire." Then she giggled and rested her head back against his chest, closed her eyes, and let the darkness consume her.

CHAPTER 14

Someone was calling her name. It was frantic and relentless, calling and calling, over and over. Amelia struggled to open her eyes. They felt so heavy, and sharp stabbing pains radiated from her head, pulsing through her entire body. It was dark, black as the dead of night, and she looked around trying to find who was calling her. With every move of her head, hot pain mixed with dizzy drunkenness overwhelmed her, attempting to suck her back into a cold, dark hole.

She struggled to keep her eyes open. It was getting brighter. There was a soft, white light shining down. Amelia looked up. Sunlight; it was the sun. Was it morning? Why was she outside? She blinked a few times. It was so quiet. The calling had stopped and she was alone in the soft grass under a big oak tree. Strips of sunlight peeked through leaves and branches from above, warming her skin where it touched.

A soft hand brushed hair from her eyes. Her gazed shifted, and beside her, looking like a fallen angel, was Mitchell. "Amelia, what happened?"

"I hit my head," she slurred, feeling woozy and closed her eyes again.

"Are you drunk?"

Drunk? That sounded right. She remembered going to the party. "Yup," she said and giggled, and then a thought dawned on her. "Wait, how am I drunk? I shouldn't be drunk in a dream. And what are you doing here?"

"You're bleeding." He poked around at the back of her head which did not feel nice, and she tried to bat his hand away.

"Tyler's a really good kisser," Amelia blurted. "So is Eric, but you're better." Then she smacked her hands up to her mouth in red-hot embarrassment and giggled some more. She wasn't really sure what was funny, but well, even her voice sounded funny, a bit slow and slurred.

Mitchell took her face in his hands and pulled her attention back to his sea blue eyes. "Try to focus, Amelia. What happened to you?" He looked so scared. Someone else had been scared, too. Who? She didn't know and it didn't matter. Mitchell was back. She'd missed him and now he was back. Then Amelia saw him realize something, and his face turned cold, and he went deathly still. "Who the hell is Tyler? And what do you mean 'so is Eric'? You kissed Eric?" The words came out snarled, contorted with anger.

"He's really cute," Amelia said, and then clasped her hands back to her mouth. Why couldn't she stop talking? "He tasted like raspberries. I like raspberries."

"You were with another guy," he spat the words at her.

"My roommates are vampires," she giggled. "But they aren't scary like the other ones. I need to sleep. I wonder if Tyler will call me tomorrow."

"Forget about Tyler," he growled and dropped his hands from her face. He got up and started pacing back and forth, back and forth. Amelia tried to follow him, but the movement was too much and it made her dizzy.

She closed her eyes and yelled, "No!" She took a deep breath. "I don't want to forget about Tyler. I like him. Go away, Mitch. Leave me alone. I don't want you here anymore."

Right at that moment, Amelia moved. She didn't mean to move and she didn't think she did it on her own, but she was floating. And Mitchell was gone. No. She wasn't floating, she realized. Luke was carrying her. There was so much commotion around her. Angelle was yelling and poking at her head. Amelia wanted to tell her everything would be okay and that she was fine, but she couldn't keep her eyes open. It all seemed like too much work. Someone tucked her into bed. The world spun around her and she passed out.

****

Something was wrong. Amelia could feel it deep in her bones. Her bed was moving. No, not moving. It sagged. Someone was in her bed. She jumped awake and opened her eyes. Too fast. It was way too fast; the room moved around in circles and she clamped her eyes shut. She could hear the covers rustling and someone touched her hand. *Open your eyes*, she thought. *You need to open your eyes.* It seemed to take forever and she thought she would never be able to pry them open again. A tangy, sweet scent drifted to her nose and as if she could not control it, her eyes fluttered open. "Mitch," she groaned. "Why can't you just let me sleep?"

"How are you feeling, love?" He looked rumpled and tired. He was in a suit and it looked as if he had been hit by a truck.

Amelia closed her eyes again, relaxing back in bed. "Drunk and sore," she whined, "I don't want to be drunk anymore."

"I know." He scooted over and gently pulled her into his arms. Amelia snuggled into the hollow of his neck. Tears stung her eyes, prickling like bee stings. If the room would just stop moving everything would be okay, she was sure of it.

"I don't want to love you any more either," she choked

out through the tears. "Why won't you just stay out of my dreams?"

"You're not dreaming, love." He kissed her lightly on the forehead. His lips felt warm, and she sighed. "I'm sorry, Amelia. Please forgive me." He sounded so sad. Sad and lonely.

She peered up at him, not understanding. Why was he sad? Why was he sorry? What had he done? And did it even matter? He wasn't even real. "Forgive what?"

"You've left me no other choice, love," he murmured and brushed her hair back, trailing his fingers lightly down her neck. "Remember that I love you. Please, just remember that." He closed his eyes for a long second, and when they opened, Amelia gasped. They were no longer blue and heavenly, but tinted with streaks of red.

Amelia squeezed her eyes shut. *It's just a dream. You're drunk. It's not real. He's not real.* Suddenly, there was a sharp pain, like two little needles jabbing into her neck, breaking the skin. She gasped. The pain grew, burning, hot, like scalding water. It was her birthmark. It was on fire. She tried to reach up her hand to stop the burning, but her hands were stuck. Not stuck... restrained... He was holding her wrists.

Just as fast as it started, the fire stopped and her body tingled. A warm floating sensation engulfed her. Was she dying? Was this it? The end? There was something else. She could feel it. A connection. A link. A chain. Yes, that was it. A chain, tethering itself around her heart, gently tugging her closer, closer. Closer to what? She needed to get closer, she knew that, but to what? An uncontrollable need to get closer to him. To Mitchell. The room was still spinning too fast, and it hit her. If she could get closer, he could make it all stop. He would help her.

Amelia tried to get closer, but her body wouldn't move. She tried to speak, but the hard lump in her throat trapped the sound, pushing it down. Her hands were cold, and the spinning room was taking on a grayish tinge, getting darker... darker... darker... She tried to keep her eyes open, but her eyelids were too heavy. A soft hum filled her ears, getting louder and louder, buzzing like bees. And then it was dark.

****

Amelia woke up with a pounding headache. Every muscle in her body throbbed, and she felt weak and lightheaded. Her mouth was parched and a stubbly film covered her tongue. She smacked her mouth, opening and closing, trying to get the saliva moving. The horrid taste was as if she had licked a wet dog, and she wrinkled her nose. How much had she drunk last night? *Obviously way too much*, she thought and silently vowed never to drink again.

From somewhere in the house, she heard a door slam followed by muffled voices. She couldn't make out the conversation, but the tones were enough to let her know that an argument was underway. She pulled a pillow over her head, trying to drown out the noise, but it was no use. Another door slammed and footsteps pounded down the stairs.

Frustrated, Amelia flung the pillow across the room. The sun glittered through the window on the west side, letting her know that she'd slept most of the day. She glanced over at the clock, 3:30. With a groan, she dragged herself out of bed and staggered to the bathroom.

After guzzling three large glasses of water and popping a few Advil, she brushed her teeth to get rid of the rancid taste in her mouth. The toothpaste wasn't much better and the sharp mint caused her stomach to heave and turn.

Amelia sunk to the floor, resting her head between her knees, gulping in a few deep breaths. She racked her mind, trying to remember what she'd done last night, but everything was fuzzy. A few foggy images coursed through her head. Jell-O shooters, Tyler, Eric, but they were all jumbled and torn, nothing was making sense.

A couple minutes later, her stomach settled and she slowly got up off the floor. Hot bolts of pain shot through her head. She ran her fingers through her hair and discovered the source of the pain. A goose egg the size of a plum rested at the back of her head and her hair was matted and crusty around it. The lump was throbbing as if it had its own pulse.

How had that happen? Amelia leaned up against the counter to get closer to the mirror and with a little handheld mirror, she examined the lump. She noticed a gash as well. She stared at it, trying to think, but couldn't remember anything.

You need to remember, a small voice echoed through Amelia's mind. She needed to figure out what happened.

Amelia couldn't breathe. Her chest felt tight, as if something was squeezing around her heart and tugging, pulling her off balance, and she stumbled, righting herself on the sink ledge. She caught a glimpse of her reflection in the mirror, gasping for breath. Her eyes were veined red, and her skin had a pale, grayish pallor. She splashed some water on her face and the coolness helped a bit, but the tugging at her chest continued. Each tug was more forceful than the last. She sucked in a few ragged breaths and stumbled towards the door. She needed help. If she could just make it out of her room, someone would help her.

"Amelia, are you okay?" Mitchell's panicked voice sounded loud in her ears and she stopped abruptly looking around her, but she saw nothing—no Mitchell. It was just her, alone in her room. She gave her head a shake, convinced she was losing her mind, and staggered out the door.

Amelia could hear the hushed voices of her roommates floating down the hallway and she pushed herself forward. She felt as if her body were giving her the finger, but she kept going. Her legs felt like they were weighted down by boulders and every time her feet hit the floor a stabbing pain shot through her head, but she didn't allow herself to stop.

As Amelia approached the kitchen, a new, but somehow familiar voice, trickled into her ears and an odd warmth settled in her stomach. For a moment, she thought she was going to be sick and stopped, leaning against the wall.

An image of Mitchell flooded her mind. Mitchell kissing her. Her lips tingled at the memory and her face flushed. The sensation resurrected another memory. When he had kissed her neck, there had been a sharp pain, like needles breaking her skin and then burning. Her neck had been burning. She shook her head, trying to toss out the disturbing memory. *It was just a dream,* she told herself.

Amelia felt another tug, as if there were a chain around her waist yanking her forward, and she stumbled. Her feet were moving again, but she didn't feel like she was in control of the movement. It felt like she was being pulled. Her pulse quickened and her stomach fluttered with anticipation, almost as if her body knew what was waiting for her.

Amelia made it to the living room, following the sound, when Luke's booming voice broke her stupor. "That's enough!" followed by the sounds of a struggle and the crack of a fist connecting with solid flesh. A few more incoherent shouts and grunts blasted from the kitchen.

Suddenly, bits and pieces of the night before came flooding back. Tyler's raspberry lips and Eric's ridiculously protective outburst.

Amelia remembered storming off. She hadn't been alone. Had there been a young girl? Yes, that creepy kid… Kandi and a man named Adam. Images flashed quickly, red eyes, blazing like fire. Her blood hot and sticky trickling down her neck. Eric's contorted face with flecks of crimson filling his vision. And she'd told Luke he was a vampire! Did that really happen?

"Where are you? Are you hurt?" Mitchell's voice burst into her thoughts.

"Get out of my head," she screamed out loud. Shaky and dizzy, she needed to sit down before she passed out and she crumbled to the floor. Her breath was coming out hard and ragged.

You need to pull yourself together, Amelia told herself. She felt hot, too hot, and her eyes prickled as tears spilled over the lids. She buried her face in her hands. *It didn't happen. None of it happened. There's no such thing as vampires.* A sick feeling flooded her body.

Amelia heard someone shuffle into the room and sit down beside her. "Are you okay, love?" He attempted to keep his voice gentle, but there was an unmistakable edge to it.

She could feel him watching her, scanning her over from head to toe. He sat so close that she could smell his sweet, tangy scent. "No," she murmured, and a fresh avalanche of tears cascaded down her face. She looked up at him and her body flushed hot. Her breath caught in her throat. He was close enough that she could feel the heat of his skin. But even with this closeness, Amelia felt as if they were painfully far away from each other. She felt a tug, as if she were being pulled towards him by an invisible chain and without realizing it, she slid closer. He reached out, brushing away her tears and leaving behind a sizzling trail of sparks where his fingers had touched her skin. Her heart beat erratically, thumping like a jackhammer. Amelia drew in a shaky breath and shook her head. "No, Mitch, I'm not okay," she breathed, and then everything went dark.

CHAPTER 15

A buzzing noise filled her ears and Amelia tried to breathe, in and out, slow and steady, and after what felt like hours, the buzzing deteriorated, and the soft whispers of her friends came into focus.

"Hey man, you weren't here last night." That was Eric. Amelia recognized the voice. She kept her eyes shut, trying to listen. "You need to trust me on this. She's a scared and confused teenage girl. You gotta think of her like a time bomb and you, my man, are the bomb squad. Proceed with caution. If you push too hard or move too fast, she'll go kaboom."

Kaboom? Time bomb? What was he talking about? Amelia didn't know. She was about to open her eyes when someone tucked a warm blanket around her and said, "Shut up, Eric."

Mitchell.

Mitchell was real. He was here. He was a vampire. They were all vampires. The thoughts were coming in a rushed blur. Her pulse picked up, beating painfully fast, the thumping of her heart was drowning out the conversation around her. She felt cold like ice. Were they going to kill her? If they wanted to, wouldn't they have already done it?

What had her dad said to her when she was a kid? It was something about bears when they were camping. Play dead and they won't bother you? Does that work with vampires? She didn't know, but she thought she would give it a try.

Mitchell chuckled, a warm sound, velvety and soft. "No, love, playing dead with vampires doesn't work. We can all hear your heartbeat so you might as well open your eyes." His voice seemed to speak directly to her heart and she felt the chain tugging and tightening and as if she had no control over her body, her eyes fluttered open and landed on him.

Amelia's breath caught in her throat and warmth flooded in. Mitchell stood over her, looking down, a bright lemon yellow glow around him, shooting out in strips, like rays from the sun. Amelia blinked, trying to clear her vision, but the yellow haze stayed around him. The strips of color reminded her of the second or two after you closed your eyes and flashes of colors appear before turning black. The brain wave came to her like a smack in the forehead; she could see his aura. That's what those flashes of colors were. She remembered reading about it once. Amelia studied his face. There was so much love in his brilliant blue eyes. Not just in his eyes, she realized with a start; she could feel it, coming from him, it was as if they were linked, and his feelings were radiating from him and pulsing into her.

Amelia didn't think she could speak. The sight of him in front of her was absolutely awe-inspiring. The dreams had not done him justice. He'd always been striking, but with the yellow glow outlining his chiseled and perfectly sculpted six foot-three frame and mixing with his soft light brown hair, he was so stunningly beautiful that it nearly hurt to look at him.

Her mouth felt dry and the awful pulling around her heart urged her to get up, to go to him, to touch him. Before she could stop herself, Amelia was off the couch, the warm fleece blanket falling to the floor around her feet, and she was reaching out to brush her fingers across his cheek. "I can see your aura," she breathed, more to herself than to him. "How are you here? You're not supposed to be real."

Mitchell took her hand in his, holding it against his cheek, and leaned into it. She could vaguely feel the presence of her roommates, but it didn't matter. At that very moment, nothing mattered more than he did.

Someone cleared their throat loudly, drawing Amelia reluctantly back to the present, and Mitchell dropped her hand. "How did you know what she was thinking, Mitch?" Eric asked. He looked mad, Amelia noticed, hands balled into white fists and red tinting his face and neck. There was something staining his white shirt, which was ripped in a few places. Something brownish-red—blood? Yes, it looked like dried blood and there was some dried up under his nose and smeared on his cheek, too. He had a black eye, which to Amelia's disbelief, was getting lighter with every passing second.

"Yeah, Mitch, how did you know?" Angelle added. She was suddenly standing in front of them, glaring daggers at him. "Because I know you wouldn't do that to her." Mitchell didn't bother to answer, and Amelia thought he may have looked ashamed, which made no sense at all. What did he have to be ashamed of?

Angelle and Mitchell stared at each other for a long, tense moment. "Dammit, Mitch!" she said under her breath, looking away from him. She took Amelia's chin in her hands and gently tilted her head looking over her neck. "When?" she yelled at him and Amelia had to fight hard not to whimper, because hey, she was alone in a room full of vampires and there was an angry one holding onto her and her eyes were such a glowing red, who wouldn't want to whimper and find a rock to hide under? This wasn't the sugary sweet girl Amelia knew. This thing standing in front of her, holding onto her chin, was a monster.

"Leave it alone, Angelle," Mitchell said tightly and started pacing the room. The beautiful yellow that surrounded him was fading and quickly shifting to a muddied red. It only took Amelia a second to realize what the change meant—a rising tide of anger, so strong it was suffocating.

I should run, Amelia thought, as she watched the red deepen and black flecks, like spots of dirt, appeared. *Just run. God, why can't I run? Stupid flight reflexes. What's wrong with me?*

You don't need to run, love. No one is going to hurt you.

Amelia trembled and a shiver rushed in, straightening her spine. "You didn't talk," she said, the tremors coming out in her voice. "Your lips didn't move."

"You project very clearly, Amelia." Mitchell chuckled softly, and looked at her, some of the anger lifting away, and his soft smile returning. "It's kind of like one of those amplifiers. Your thoughts just blast in, loud and clear."

Angelle wrapped her arms around Amelia hugging her closely. For a moment, Amelia stayed ridged and held her breath. Her lungs started to burn and like a balloon popping, she let out a pent up breath in a gush and all her resistance seemed to rush out with it. There was something about Angelle that reminded her of a mother bear protecting her cub, and Amelia felt herself relax into the hug and let herself be pulled back onto the couch. "Oh, honey, it's okay," Angelle whispered in her ear, the way her mother used to when she'd had a bad dream and rocked her softly in her arms. "You're safe. You're going to be okay."

"I can't believe you're really here." Amelia glanced over at Mitchell just for a second and her heart fluttered happily in her chest. She supposed she should have known he was real, but she'd never really let herself think about it. But now that she thought about it, really thought about it, he'd given tons of hints over the years and they were not always that subtle. Come to think of it, she was sure he had even mentioned vampires before. A sudden, uncontrollable giggle erupted from her lips and she quickly covered her mouth, trying to hold it in. Was this shock? It had to be shock. That was the only logical explanation. So if she was in shock then none of this was okay. She would soon realize that.

Amelia pulled back from Angelle's arms, just enough to meet her square in the eyes. "It's not okay. None of this is okay. I'm sitting in a house full of vampires. Vampires. This is completely insane." The last words came out in a yell.

"What's done is done," Luke said matter-of-factly. Amelia hadn't noticed him sitting in the corner. But there he was, relaxed and composed in an armchair, watching everyone with those thoughtful eyes. "All of this yelling isn't going to change that. I think we all need to just calm down and deal with this. She loves him. We all know that, otherwise the dreams wouldn't have happened for five years. I think you all may be underestimating her ability to handle this. Amelia is more mature than you give her credit for."

"But she wasn't ready. She's still not ready!" Angelle raged, tightening her grip on Amelia.

"I don't care if she is ready or not," Mitchell said, jaw clenching. "I'm not going to let her run around with that boy!" He shot Eric a challenging look. "Or with you."

"You did this to her out of jealousy," Angelle choked and continued to stroke Amelia's hair.

"Dude," Eric said, giving Mitchell a look of pure disgust, but bit his tongue on anything else he might have been about to say when Mitchell flashed him another terrifying look.

Amelia couldn't imagine what was so horrible, but the grim expressions on her roommates' faces made its graveness very clear. She pushed her way out of Angelle's arms and stood up on shaky legs, wobbling like a tightrope walker. A sickening feeling engulfed her, and she suddenly felt a flash of cold and waves of hot all at once.

"I don't understand what's happening here," Amelia blurted.

"Tell her, Mitch."

"This is not the time, Angelle." Mitchell sat down on the couch and pulled Amelia onto his lap, cradling her in his arms. Every place their skin touched set her on fire, burning hot. His tangy scent filled her head, pushing away all her fears. Amelia knew she should push away, but her body just didn't want to. "Drop it."

"Mitch, buddy," Luke said, completely calm and in control. "She has a right to know. Think about it. It's better to just tell her so you can both be careful. Believe me, you don't want it to just happen."

"He bit you, Amelia." The bitterness in Angelle's voice was as black and violent as a thunderstorm. She reached out, as if she were going to touch her, and then drew back, thinking better of it.

"Angelle," Mitchell roared. Suddenly, Amelia was standing, teetering unstably, and Mitchell had Angelle off the couch, holding her against the wall by her shoulders. He looked scary. Cold, hard, and overpoweringly scary, and Amelia could feel everything. She could hear his thoughts; he wanted to hurt Angelle, and she could feel it, the cold, bitter anger. She wanted to do something. She needed to stop him but she couldn't. It was as if she were frozen in place and the only thing she could do was whimper like a little baby.

"Mitch!" Luke's voice boomed. Amelia didn't see him move, but he was now behind Mitchell, holding him tightly, arms pinned behind his back.

Amelia couldn't take it anymore and she crumbled to the floor. Her emotions were already a jumbled mess and feeling all his anger was exhausting. How could anyone have that much hatred? That much rage? She just couldn't imagine. And why could she feel everything he was feeling? "Someone really needs to tell me what's going on," Amelia said in a small voice.

She didn't think anyone would answer her. They were all tense, watching Mitchell like a hawk. Luke must have been satisfied that he was under control because he let go of Mitchell and sat back in his chair. He never dropped his eyes from him, though, watching closely for any sign he wasn't completely in control of himself.

Mitchell didn't look at her and, surprisingly, that hurt more than all his anger. How could he not look at her? Amelia just didn't understand because she couldn't seem to look away. Like a moth to a flame, she was hopelessly drawn to him. After a few tense moments, he let out a deep sigh and sat down, purposely on the other side of the room from her.

Eric must have taken it as a sign. He sat down beside Amelia on the floor and started rambling. "Okay, here's the Cole's Notes version. You're Mitch's soulmate. When he became a vampire, he lost his soul and it attached to you which created a bond between you guys. Sort of linking you together so he would be able to find you. That's why he could enter your dreams. When he bit you, it strengthened that link. Now he can feel everything you feel, hear all your thoughts, talk to you through his mind. But it's not just him; you can do all this, too. It has something to do with our sick mind control powers. It's pretty cool."

"I kinda already figured all that out, Eric. Why do I feel like you're holding something back?"

"Because he is," Mitchell said in a small, unsure voice. "But it doesn't matter. The rest is not important. I'll be careful." He ran his fingers through his hair and still avoided looking at her. "It's safer for you this way."

"As Eric said, it enhances his mind control powers over you," Luke continued, clearly ignoring Mitchell.

"Luke, stop it," Mitchell pleaded. "She doesn't need to hear all this."

Amelia studied him more closely and noticed his aura had changed again. *Was that normal?* she wondered. It seemed to change with his feelings. It was now a muddy forest green, and he was radiating jealousy mixed with guilt. "Actually, I think I do need to hear this." The clarity of her voice surprised her.

"No, you don't, Amelia." He looked up at her, finally, with pleading, sad eyes. "Just leave it. Why don't you go and rest. I think you've heard enough for now."

"Just like I predicted," Eric said, and promptly stood up and crossed the room. "The kaboom is coming. Just wait for it. She's about to blow."

"Shut up, Eric," Amelia snapped. Her face was hot, her neck was boiling, and her head was throbbing from her tightly clenched teeth. "I don't need to rest. What I need is the truth." She jumped up, too quickly, and a hot flash of pain ran through her head. Through all the commotion, she'd forgotten about the lump and it took her a moment to catch her breath.

"Come on, love, just sit down." Mitchell leaned back in his chair, letting his arms dangle off the side. "You don't need to get all worked up over this."

"I don't want to sit down. What I want is for someone to tell me what's going on." Amelia winced at a sharp, stabbing pain in her stomach. The pain moved from her stomach to her chest, then to her thighs and she doubled over, gasping for breath. "What's happening to me?" she screamed. All of a sudden, the pain was everywhere, like hundreds of knives jabbing deeply into her flesh. Her lungs felt as if they were collapsing, falling in, and she couldn't catch her breath. She dropped to her knees and screamed. She was burning from the inside out. It was like hot lava boiling within her, burning through her flesh, and she kept screaming in agony.

"Amelia," Angelle cried, her voice sounded panicked but oddly far away. Within seconds, she was hovering over Amelia, stroking her hair. Amelia screamed again. And again. Even to her own ears, it sounded horrible. Like a wounded dog. "Mitch, stop it. Just stop it."

"I'm not doing anything."

"She didn't want to sit. She didn't want to rest. Dammit!" Angelle looked outright horror-struck and started rubbing Amelia's back.

The pain started to slowly fade and Amelia stayed curled in a fetal position on the floor, panting and gulping in mouthfuls of air. After what felt like hours, she managed to sit up on her own and gently pushed Angelle away. She didn't want to be touched, not now, not by anyone. "What have you done to me?" Amelia gasped, hugging her knees into her chest.

Mitchell cast his eyes down and rubbed his face roughly. "I'm so sorry, love."

"Tell me what you've done," Amelia said through clenched teeth, keeping herself in a tight little ball, gently rocking back and forth.

"It's all part of the bite," Mitchell said so softly she barely heard it. "Like Eric said, it strengthens the link between us because we are already connected. It also gives me an edge of control. It's a way for me to keep you safe." Amelia looked up at him with wide eyes. He thought he was keeping her safe? "The pain you're feeling is my fault. With the stronger link, anytime you try to do something that I don't agree with you will feel it."

"You knew this would happen and you still did this to me." Amelia didn't say it as a question. He met her straight on, squarely in the eyes, but didn't say anything and she laughed. It was a harsh, broken sound, like plates crashing to the floor, shattering into little shards. "You know I think I could've handled the vampire thing, and I can deal with you being able to read my thoughts and never having secrets from you because frankly, I've never hidden anything from you anyways. What I can't accept is that you knew that biting me could hurt me and yet you did it anyways." She paused and looked at him fiercely. "You know what, never mind." She threw her hands up in the air. "I'm done. I'm leaving." She turned on her heels, straightened her shoulders, jutted her chin up, and with purpose walked away. Amelia had just reached the doorway when she felt the stabbing pain return in the pit of her stomach.

"Amelia, wait," Mitchell called. It was not a request, his voice simmered with authority and there was no mistaking it: he was demanding that she stop. She turned back to him with a defiant stare. He was standing now, looking like he didn't know whether to go to her or not. He looked uncomfortable and to her disbelief, that gave her a touch of satisfaction. It was petty and shallow, but she was glad he was feeling something.

"Don't," she said, keeping her voice in control. "You can feel it, right? You can feel what you're doing to me right now."

"Yes, sort of." Mitchell's whisper sounded hollow and raw, and somehow full of guilt and pain. He shifted his gaze to the floor, shifting slightly, back and forth, from right to left. "I don't actually feel the pain. Vampires don't feel pain the same as humans; it's just sort of uncomfortable. But I can feel how much you're hurting through the bond. I know you're in pain; I just don't feel it the same way."

Amelia felt cold. Cold and numb and disgusted. Uneasiness twisted her stomach into a knot, inching tighter and tighter every second. Not knowing what was coming, or if she would be able to make it out of the room, she swallowed hard, straightened her shoulders again, and took a deep breath. "And yet you still keep doing it." She smiled a humorless and distant smile. "I always thought you were just a figment of my imagination. I can't even begin to count how many times I wished you were real. I take all those wishes back. You're not a dream. You're real and nothing but a nightmare. I can't believe I ever thought I loved you." Without giving herself a chance to chicken out, she left as quickly as her legs would move.

Eric's whispered voice reached her just before she left the room. "Kaboom."

CHAPTER 16

Amelia made it to her room. She didn't know how; she really hadn't thought she would get there. Every step she took was like fighting against a raging current: drowning, and then coming back up for air, only to be pulled under again. The chain at her heart constantly pulled her back staggeringly hard, and a few times she just wanted to give up, run back to Mitchell, throw her arms around him, and tell him, tell him she was sorry and she loved him. But she couldn't. Amelia knew that wasn't an option. She didn't want to love him, she wouldn't, she was sure of it.

She closed her bedroom door and sunk to the floor in a soggy mess. Tears poured down her cheeks. "This can't be happening," she whispered to the empty room. Mitchell couldn't be here. Vampires don't exist. Her head was spinning, thoughts rushing in too quickly to understand and she felt cold, chilled to the bone. So cold that she thought she just might never be warm again.

How could he do this to her? There was just so much she didn't know and didn't understand. He'd bitten her. Did that mean she would become a vampire? She didn't think so. Amelia thought about every story she'd ever read or movie she'd ever seen. What was real? She knew they couldn't all be real. She remembered her first night; they had eaten garlic bread and they all went out in the sun. So was anything real? What could hurt them? What could she use against them? And did she want to hurt them?

Amelia leaned her head against the door and drew in a few shaky breaths. Soulmates. She didn't want to believe it. Soulmates weren't real. There was no such thing as the perfect person. One person for everyone and only one. It was a fairy tale. A romantic notion created only to help people get through the cold, hard reality of life. But she could feel it. They were connected and no matter how much she told herself that she didn't love him, it was inevitable. She did and she would even if it killed her.

Amelia wasn't going to let that happen. She'd fought too hard for too long. As if she'd hit a brick wall at one hundred miles an hour, she knew what she had to do. She had to get out of there, away from Mitchell, away from all of them. She'd known from the beginning they were all just too good to be true. They had been nice to her and she'd been so desperate for friends that she'd let her guard down, let them in, and they betrayed her. How could they keep this from her?

Amelia pulled herself off the floor, went to her closet, and grabbed her bag, stuffing clothes in frantically, not caring what, just whatever would fit.

Once it was jam-packed, she rushed to the bathroom to grab some toiletries. She grabbed a scrunchy, pulling her hair up into a messy bun, and winced at the pain in her head. Then she caught a glimpse of herself in the mirror and gasped. Her mark. It had changed. How had she missed that when she first woke up? Amelia ran a shaky finger along her mark and she suddenly knew what Angelle had been looking for, what the cop had been looking for. "Who do you belong to?" he'd asked her that first morning and he'd stared so hard at her neck she'd felt sick. But it all made sense now. *Mitchell Lang*, in script, had appeared, branded right below the soul's mark.

The pieces were coming together; suddenly, the picture was crystal clear. This was what that horrid little kid, Kandi, had been talking about. "He hasn't claimed her," she'd said last night. A wave of nausea overcame her. What did this mean? How did it happen? Flashes of last night came back to her. The burning. She'd thought her neck was on fire and it dawned on her that must have been when his name had appeared.

Amelia scanned her neck thoroughly in search of any sign of a bite mark. *Maybe this was just a vast, horrible nightmare*, she thought in desperate hope. She located the small pinprick mark where Mitchell had bitten her on the other side of her neck, almost completely healed.

The sound of her phone chirping the arrival of an incoming message brought her back from the painful memories. In haste, Amelia forced her eyes away from the mirror and searched for her phone. Forty-one missed messages, a mixture of voicemails and texts. Eleven of the texts were from Erin and she read through them quickly. They were all the same, just wanting to make sure she was okay. Some were from random people she didn't even know, or maybe she did know but she couldn't place them, and the last one caught her eye. It was from Tyler.

Worried about u. Can't get u out of my mind. Plz call me back. Need 2 know u r ok. Ty.

Amelia read it over and over, debating on what to do. Should she call him? Would Mitchell know if she did? Could he always read her mind? She needed to get away from the house; would Tyler pick her up? Before she knew it, her fingers were flying across the keypad, replying to his message.

Need to get out of here. Pick me up? I'll explain later.

Amelia waited for what seemed like an interminable period before her phone chirped again.

Be there in 5.

Amelia dropped the phone on her bed and rushed

around in a flurry of motion, grabbing the last of the things she would need. She didn't give herself time to think of what she was doing, because she knew, just knew, if she stopped to think, she would realize how stupid this was, bringing Tyler here, to a house full of vampires. She wasn't even sure she would be able to leave, but she knew she had to try.

Amelia knew the exact moment Tyler arrived and she also knew who answered the door.

Mitchell.

A surge of ugly, green jealousy ran through her, so hard and so vivid, it was almost as if it were her own feelings. The jealousy quickly turned to white-hot rage and Amelia snagged her bag and ran out of her room.

It wasn't hard to figure out they were in the foyer; all she had to do was follow the pull. She wondered if it would always be like this. Would she always be able to find him?

Amelia bolted into the foyer as if she had been shot from a cannon. When she let her eyes focus on the room, she froze just as fast. Tyler was up against the wall, Mitchell standing over him. Tyler was a big guy, and strong, but this close to Mitchell he looked small and he almost looked scared.

She rushed over, dropping her bag. She needed to get in between them. Mitchell wasn't touching Tyler, but his aura was black as pitch and the muscles in his neck were bulging with tension.

Amelia had only made it a few steps before someone grabbed her around the waist, and she shrieked. Forcefully, a hand was placed over her mouth to silence her and then she heard Luke's voice whispering frantically in her ear. "Amelia, stop. You can't get in between them. You shouldn't have called him."

Amelia struggled against him, kicking, biting, but nothing worked. Luke didn't move, didn't even stagger while she thrashed about. Sweat dripped down her neck, soaking into the collar of her sweater, and tears streamed down her cheeks, but she still fought. It was a mistake. She shouldn't have called Tyler. She needed to stop Mitchell before something happened. He hadn't moved, hadn't said anything, but his pale white skin was now flushed pink and he was furiously glaring at his adversary.

"Let her go, Luke," Mitchell said, so low that Amelia barely heard him. Instantly she was free. She tried to move, but her knees gave way and she tripped. Luke caught her and steadied her and held onto her shoulders until he was sure she wouldn't fall again. "Amelia, this boy said you asked him to pick you up," Mitchell said, still not taking his eyes from Tyler, who was looking paler by the minute.

Amelia couldn't speak. Her mouth was dry, her throat prickled. A secure arm wrapped around her and she shifted her gaze to see Angelle, her big brown eyes looking sad but somehow comforting. "It's okay, sweetie. You don't need to be scared."

Amelia cleared her throat, and with Angelle's support, she walked over to Mitchell and squeezed in between him and Tyler. Angelle stood close by, not interfering, but her closeness was comforting, nonetheless.

Tyler had been holding his breath, she realized, when a gust of wind hit the back of her neck and he sucked in air. Amelia tried to ignore him and focus on Mitchell. "Yes, I did," she said, looking him squarely in the eyes and was glad how strong her voice sounded. "I want to leave. I don't want this."

Mitchell reacted as if he'd been punched in the gut. The hurt on his face was almost too painful to look at and Amelia couldn't stop the tears from pouring, like shiny little streams down her face.

"Millie, what's going on?" Tyler asked from behind her and she ignored him, not wanting to make the situation worse. She could feel Mitchell's thoughts and knew the littlest thing could push him over the edge. He was struggling, fighting the overwhelming urge to lash out and hurt Tyler, maybe even kill him. The terrifying, nightmarish image of snapping his neck and ripping out his throat kept flashing into his mind. She felt Tyler's hand on her shoulder and she stiffened. "Millie, seriously, let's get out of here."

"Keep your hand off her," Mitchell growled. He took a step forward, in a blur, and before Amelia could stop him, she was behind him. "She's not leaving and you are not welcome here. There's the door." He pointed to the open door. "You better go before I do something she'll regret."

"Millie?" Tyler asked hesitantly; she could hear the tone of determination and she knew she would have to say something to get him to leave. The flashes of what Mitchell wanted to do to him were coming faster and faster and she knew he wouldn't hesitate to kill him if she tried to leave. It wasn't just her anymore. Now Tyler was in danger and it was her fault and she had to do something.

Amelia put a light hand on Mitchell's arm and wiggled her way around him. He didn't try to stop her, but she knew he would if she got too close to Tyler. His aura was flecked with red and green, coloring the black fog and the spots were jumping around, agitated. She let her hand drop from his arm and with a glance over her shoulder, she took another shaky step towards Tyler, trying not to move too quickly. "That's far enough," Mitchell snarled.

Amelia closed her eyes tightly, trying to stop the tears, and then focused on Tyler. "I'm sorry, Ty. I shouldn't have asked you to come. You need to go."

"Not without you." Tyler gave her a look, with beseeching eyes. "I don't know what's going on here, but you don't need to stay. Please come with me. Just get in the car."

You are not leaving, Amelia. If you try, I will hunt him down and kill him. Do you want his blood on your hands? Mitchell projected the thoughts loud and clear and complete with images that Amelia wished she hadn't had to have seen. She shuddered visibly and took a gasping breath.

"I can't go with you," Amelia choked out. "Please just leave." Tyler didn't move. He looked as if he weren't going to leave and she needed to get him out. She looked back at Mitchell. "I'm just going to walk him to the car."

After a long minute, Mitchell gave her a quick nod, signaling it was okay. "Luke, go with her." He turned away and left the room. He must have given some kind of signal that Amelia had missed because Angelle and Eric turned and followed him. From the looks she got from them, they clearly did not want to leave her.

As soon as Mitchell was gone, the color started coming back to Tyler's cheeks. Amelia grabbed him by the hand, pretending not to notice the flash of red in Luke's eyes and dragged him out of the house towards the car. How had she missed those eyes before? She didn't know, but she wished—truly wished—she could have stayed in that ignorant bliss. She could feel Luke following them, closely watching.

"Millie, you need to come with me," Tyler whispered, obviously aware that they were being followed. "You can't stay here. I don't care who he is to this stupid town, he can't force you to stay here."

Amelia didn't answer him until they got to the car. She opened the driver's side door and then looked at him. "I can't. I can't explain, but you need to go, Ty. I'll call you soon and I'm so sorry I put you in the middle of this." Tyler wasn't moving. He looked sad and scared and she wasn't sure what to do.

Hurry up, Amelia, Mitchell's voice blasted into her head.

"Ty, please, just go. He's not going to let me leave. I don't want them to hurt you." She put a hand on his back and pushed him towards the car. "Please," she begged. "I was wrong to call you. I'll be fine, but you have to go."

Amelia saw the resistance flee from Tyler's face and his shoulders sagged. Confused, she glanced over to see Luke standing in front of him, eyes foggy like milky glasses focused on Tyler's now expressionless face. "Thank you for stopping by to check on Amelia," Luke said, in a soothing and strong voice. "She took quite a spill last night, but she is just fine now."

Tyler gave his head a little shake and smiled at Amelia. "You had me worried." He got into his car and turned the key. "Glad you're okay. See you on Monday." He shut the car door and reversed out of the driveway, grinning at her the whole time.

"How?" she breathed, once Tyler was safely out of the driveway.

"I used persuasion," Luke answered, as if that was really an answer. He motioned for her to go in, but Amelia stood her ground waiting for an explanation. "Come on, kiddo." He smiled at her, that fatherly smile that used to make her feel warm and loved inside, but now it made her quiver. "Let's not keep Mitch waiting and make this any worse than it already is."

"How can you stand there so calm?" Amelia shouted at him. "You're supposed to be my friend."

Without warning, Luke scooped her up, tossing her over his shoulder, and started for the door. "This is your destiny, Amelia," he said. "You best get used to it because he's not going away."

Before she knew it, they were in the living room and Luke was setting her down on the couch beside Mitchell. Angelle and Eric were standing by looking as if they were caught in the middle of wanting to leave but needing to stay and Luke took up the armchair looking completely relaxed.

Amelia waited for someone to talk and the tension grew. It was as if everyone were waiting for something to happen, anything to happen, and finally when she thought she would burst from the stress, she broke the silence. "I would like to go to my room," she murmured, and waited. She could feel the turmoil bouncing around in him: anger, hurt, love, a dangerous mixture she didn't want to ignite.

"Not yet," Mitchell said. He took her hand and looked at her with sad, sullen eyes. "I'm sorry, love. I know this must be hard for you, but I want you to know I love you. I really do. I only want what's best for you." He paused for a moment, watching her, trying to gauge her feelings. She could feel him poking around in her head and could sense his hope that she would believe him.

That thought made her laugh unpleasantly, and she snatched her hand away from him, standing up abruptly. Amelia put on her best ice queen stare and fixed it on him. "What's best for me?" she spat. "You think locking me up here and threatening to kill my friends is best for me?"

"You were attacked last night, Amelia," Angelle said, deliberately stopping Mitchell before he could say anything. She crossed the room to her. "You were attacked by two other vampires. If we hadn't been there, you could have been killed. Even with your mark they still went after you." She reached out to brush some loose curls out of Amelia's eyes. "Adam and Kandi were banished from this town fifty years ago. We don't know why they're back." She sighed, a long and stormy sound. "Amelia, we're the oldest coven around these parts. If they went after you, there's a reason for it. No one would cross us, not here. They wouldn't stand a chance. He really is just looking out for you, sweetie."

Amelia turned her ice-cold eyes on Angelle. "Don't talk to me like you care. You're just as bad as him. I confided in you. I even told you about him and you acted as if you didn't know anything. Was your stupid dream story even true?" Hurt flashed across Angelle's face as she backed up. "You know, I don't even care." Amelia focused back on Mitchell. "I will stay here only because I don't want my friends to get hurt, but you should know that's the only reason I'm staying. I don't want anything to do with you or any of you." She glared around the room, making sure to focus her chilly stare on each one of them. "Now if you're done, I'm going to my room." And without waiting for an answer, Amelia stormed out, keeping her shoulders straight, and went straight for the refuge of her room.

CHAPTER 17

Amelia was a bundle of nerves. She paced her room for a full hour trying to come up with a plan, but she knew deep down there was nothing she could do. She cried, she yelled into a pillow, and then she paced some more.

Just after 7:00, Mabel brought in a bowl of homemade chicken noodle soup. Amelia tried to talk to her. She had so many questions. Did Mabel know about them? She was sure that the older woman wasn't a vampire. But Mable wouldn't talk to her. She just dropped the food and left. Despite her best efforts not to, Amelia gobbled the food down. She was starving and she ate it so fast she barely even tasted it.

When the sun set, the night started to play tricks on her. Lurking shadows filled every corner of her room, reminding her of all those horror movies she'd seen and what could be hiding under her bed or in her closet. Her fairy tale castle no longer felt like a fairy tale. It felt too big, and spine-chillingly creepy. And it really was filled with monsters, the fanged bloodsucking kind. Amelia got down, peered under her bed, and checked her closet. She was starting to feel really stupid when a gust of wind hissed through the open window, whipping the curtains around, and she jumped.

She let out a nervous little laugh and went to the window, pulling it shut. She was about to turn away, and start the restless, helpless pacing again when a movement caught her eye. She peered out into the cloud-covered night. Standing outside her window, on her terrace, was Kandi, her smoldering scarlet eyes staring in at her. Amelia recoiled and blinked and when she opened her eyes, Kandi was gone.

Keep it together, Amelia, she scolded herself silently. *It's just the night playing tricks on you.*

Deciding she needed to relax, Amelia went into the adjoining bathroom and turned on the taps filling the tub with warm, steaming water. She added a dollop of strawberry-scented bubble bath to the water, and lit some vanilla spice candles. Instantly, the room filled with their soft scent and she stripped off her clothes, tossing them wherever they landed. She took a deep calming breath, letting the aroma soothe her.

Amelia was just about to climb into the tub when she heard a little knock at the door, so soft that she almost missed it. And if she hadn't still been so jumpy she probably would have missed it, but she was so wired with jitters that every little bump was making her jump out of her skin. She snagged her silk housecoat from the hook, and went to the door, unlocking and swinging it open.

It was Eric. He had that mischievous twinkle in his eyes and he raised his finger to his lips in a *shhhh* gesture. He glanced surreptitiously over his shoulders and then without a word snuck past her into her room, moving with all the stealth of a cat burglar.

Amelia was speechless. She hadn't expected any of them to bother her, not tonight. She watched as he shut the door behind him and once that door was shut and he was standing in her room, and they were alone, she became hotly aware that she was in a thin little housecoat, completely naked underneath. She flushed.

"Did I wake you?" he whispered, still glancing at the

door as if he thought at any moment someone would burst through and catch him.

"Um, no. I was just about to have a bath. What do you want?" *Bath, crap!* She'd left the water running and rushed to go turn it off. When she got back into her room, Eric was lounging on her bed. "Eric, I think you should leave."

He looked surprised at her reaction. "What's up with you?"

"Really? You're really going to ask me that?" Amelia rolled her eyes. What was it about him that made her not want to stay mad? She should hate him. Throw him out. But there was something so... fun about him. Folding her arms and trying to keep an annoyed tone, she said, "Like I said, I was just about to have a bath so if you don't need anything, go away."

"Oh, okay, sure. Here." He slid off the bed and shoved a book at her, looking wounded. "Thought you might want to check it out."

"Thanks, I think." Amelia took the old leather-bound book in her hands and examined the cover. There was no title, just the soul's mark carved into the worn and weathered book. "It's the book. The one you told me about the first night."

Eric winked at her and smiled. "Sure is. Thought you might have some questions and since you don't seem to be about to ask them you should read this." He gave her another secretive look. "But don't tell anyone I gave it to you." He cupped her chin in his hands lightly and tilted her face up to meet his eyes. His gaze was intense and serious, and really, really, wrong. Eric shouldn't look serious. He was supposed to be fun and carefree. "Hey, Millie?" he asked, hesitating for a moment.

"Yeah," she breathed, lost in his eyes.

"I'm really sorry for kissing you and I'm sorry for leaving after. I hope you understand why now. I didn't mean to hurt you. It's just..." he fumbled over the words. "You don't belong to me and even though you're fighting it right now..." He huffed and gave her a torn and sad smile. "You love him. You won't be able to fight it forever and he really does love you." The carefree smile sprang back over his face and he headed towards the door. "Besides, I'm a slacker. You deserve better than me," he said, glancing over his shoulder at her and then he was gone, door clicking shut behind him.

Amelia stared at the door for a moment, shocked and befuddled. Her heart wasn't racing like it normally did when Eric was around. Was that because of Mitchell? Even thinking his name made her heart skip a beat, answering her silent question. Yes, yes, yes, it was all because of Mitchell. She was made for him, body and soul, and Eric just wasn't... right. After that flabbergasting revelation, Amelia looked back at the book in her hands, whose brittle, old pages exuded a faint scent of mold.

She opened up the book, gingerly flipping through the pages looking for an author, but she found none. She went back to the start. There was no table of contents or copyrights and the first page was entitled: *WARNING TO ALL HUMANS WITH A SOUL'S MARK.*

Amelia closed the book, wondering if she should actually read it. Would it have answers? Maybe it could tell her how to break the bond between them. Did she want to break it? She had so many questions and really wasn't sure if she even wanted the answers.

She padded back to the bathroom and set the book down on the tub ledge. Maybe she would just scan through it. It couldn't hurt. She took off her housecoat and slid into the tub, letting the hot water soothe her aching muscles, and closed her eyes for a few seconds. After a few calming strawberry filled breaths, she reached for the book, holding it up, well away from the water, and started to read.

What you are about to read is an overview of what you can expect before and after you are found. I speak from experience and can guarantee that you will be found. It may be in this lifetime or in one to follow, but you should know it is inevitable. You have been marked by a vampire's soul. The journey you are about to embark on will not be easy. At times, you may be blinded by love or overtaken by hatred.

From this point on you are no longer the master of your destiny. It is imperative for you to forget the notion that you have the power to control your own fate. Your path has been chosen for you and whether you like it or not always remember **YOU CANNOT RUN FROM DESTINY.**

That's not very encouraging, she thought, rereading the warning. She considered putting the book down and not going on. If it started out like this, it couldn't possibly get any better, but curiosity got the best of her and she kept reading.

A Brief History of the Mark

The first thing you should know is that soulmates are real. They are not just some romantic idea. We are made for one person and one person alone.

When it comes to souls, the alchemists were close to the truth. They believed that we are not born with a soul but only with sparks of spirituality and our purpose in this life and every life to follow is to find our souls. This is not entirely true. Our purpose is not to find our soul but to find the missing half. Our twin.

Since the beginning of time, souls have been divided equally amongst men and women. The theory is that we are destined to spend our lives searching for our other half, over countless reincarnations, in hopes to become one again.

With that bombshell, Amelia wondered how much weirder this could all get. Reincarnation wasn't possible. Of that, she was certain. She was more of a "big bang theory" kind of girl. She looked for the scientific explanation, and reincarnation was, without a doubt, not it. Halfhearted, or at least that's what she tried to tell herself, she read on.

The second and probably most important thing you need to know is that vampires do exist. The sooner you accept this, the better off you will be.

As for the mark, I have found records of it going back at least a thousand years. Throughout time, the stories have been altered, but they all hold a similar tale of a witch finding her lover dead—drained of blood by a vampire.

Heartbroken over her loss, the witch wanted to avenge her lover's death, so she stripped all vampires of their souls, casting them out to wander the universe. Once the souls were taken, she then cursed the vampires with an eternity of emptiness and condemned them to always be searching but in the end never able to find their souls.

What the witch did not consider is that nature always finds a way to maintain the balance between good and evil. This curse shifted the natural balance by creating a breed of soulless, bloodsucking monsters.

To rectify this disturbance, nature took over, gathering the lost souls and joining them with their human twins. The humans were then marked with the soul's symbol, giving the vampires a chance to find their souls. Through the mark, a bond formed between the vampire and their soulmate allowing them to keep in touch with their humanity.

In the pages to come, you will learn the stories of two individuals who wore the mark. By no means do we claim to be experts on this subject. We can only hope that our stories will help others with the trials and tribulations that are to come. Learn from our choices and let them act as a guide on your journey.

Amelia closed the book and let it drop to the floor. She had Mitchell's soul? How was that even possible? She guessed it explained the connection, but was it just his soul that was entwined with hers or was it more? Was he also her true love? That's what a soulmate was, wasn't it? The questions burned through her brain, swirling around in a whirlwind of puzzlement. The hunger for knowledge, to learn the unknown was taking control of her and she knew she just had to keep reading. She had to know more. What was happening to her? What was happening to him? What more was to come?

She pulled the plug on the tub, dried off quickly, pulled

on her pajamas, and took the book back out to her room. After snuggling up in a cozy blanket on the comfy chair, she dove back into the reading.

It was deeply engaging, and if she hadn't seen with her own eyes that vampires were real, it would have been a great story. But with her newfound knowledge, it all seemed just too real as she flipped the pages, reading as fast as her mind could absorb the words.

The dreams are not really dreams. It took me a long time to figure this out. My soulmate enlightened me after years of questions. Your vampire has many supernatural powers, one of which is mind control. With your link, they are able to not only control your mind but your spirit and soul. They can pull your spirit out of your body at will and bring you to them. This is why the dreams seem real. They are. You are really there.

Huh, made sense. Amelia had seen Luke do some kind of mind, brainwashing thing on Tyler. What had he called it? Persuasion. And she'd always thought that the dreams had felt like real life. Amelia tried to figure out the science behind it but only hit a bunch of brick walls. She didn't want to admit it, because, well, it was crazy, but the only explanation was magic.

He bit me today, only after I asked him to. He is scared that I will regret it, but I know I never will. I have never been so close to another. He loves me, of this I am sure. I can feel everything he feels, pulsing through me like waves of radiant light. We can speak without words now, communicating with our thoughts. Even when he is not at my side, I know that he is out there, thinking of me and wishing we were together. He truly is my soulmate and I thank the stars above that destiny has brought us together at last.

Amelia traced the words lightly with her finger. Maybe it wasn't all bad. She tried to imagine what it would be like with Mitchell. Could she let herself forget the monster she'd seen? The betrayal? The deceit? If she could, then maybe, just maybe, they could be… happy. As if her heart and soul knew what she was thinking, she felt a jerk, rough and forceful, around her heart that almost pulled her off the chair, compelling her to run to him. She took a few deep breaths, and pushed herself to read on, not wanting to admit that that's exactly what she wanted to do. The stupid starry-eyed ideas were quickly extinguished as she continued.

You must watch out for the bite. It will ruin you and it will only cause you a great deal of pain. I think she did it to me to try to help me accept her. I can see that now, but when it happened, it only made me hate her more. It strengthened the link between us and my thoughts, my decisions, everything that made me who I was, was no longer in my control. I spent most of my days writhing in excruciating pain. Any decision that I made that she did not condone caused the pain, burning from the inside out, collapsing my lungs so I could not breathe. She could not stop it and at the time, I believe she did not want to. They are all monsters first and foremost…

****

Amelia was startled awake. There was a noise… the soft click of her bedroom door. She bolted up to her feet, letting the book and blanket fall to the floor with a dull sounding thud. Her eyes were fuzzy, still half-asleep, and she blinked a few times to clear the sleepy haze.

Eric, green hair standing up (he obviously hadn't bothered to brush it) was standing at the doorway dressed in gray jogging pants and a sweater, grinning at her.

Amelia groaned, and plopped back down into her chair. "Now what?" she snapped, annoyed that he was back again. Hadn't he just left like an hour or two ago?

"Get dressed," he said, not bothered by her tone or her glare. "Time for your morning run. No one wants to deal with grumpy Millie today."

She stared at him blankly for a few moments and when

he just laughed at her, she glanced over at the window. The sun was just starting to peek over the tree line in a soft, orange glow. She looked at the clock: 6:45. No wonder her bones hurt and muscles felt so stiff. She'd slept sitting up in a chair all night.

Eric snapped his fingers and tapped his foot on the floor. "Come on, Millie. Everyone will be up soon so if you want to go you need to go now before his highness," he paused to give a dramatic eye roll and bow that could have given Angelle a run for her money, "wakes up and tries to forbid exercise because it's dangerous."

Despite her morning grumpiness, Amelia laughed. That was the one good thing about Eric. He could always make her laugh. "I'll be ready in a minute." She jumped up, grabbed a pair of light blue jogging pants, a T-shirt, and a matching light blue hoodie, and dashed into the bathroom to change.

In seconds, she was ready, shoes on, hair retied into a loose bun—so loose that it would probably fall out, but the lump on her head was still throbbing and the pressure stung—and she was padding her way across the room to the door. "Go out the patio doors," Eric said, stopping her just before she went out into the hallway. "Someone's moving upstairs." He glanced up at the ceiling, looking as if he were trying to pinpoint exactly who it was. Amelia also looked up, but she couldn't hear anything. *Maybe they really did have super hearing powers*, she thought and was about to ask when he continued. "We need to sneak out so keep quiet." He gave her a wicked smile. "And try not to think about where we're going. If he's paying attention, he'll know."

Amelia giggled and followed Eric out the back. They tiptoed down the steps of the terrace and slithered around the house, keeping close to it, out of sight of the windows. She focused her mind by reciting over and over the table of elements in the hopes that if Mitchell started to listen into her thoughts, he would assume she was studying.

When they made it to the front, all her excitement

vanished. She hadn't realized how open it was; a good twenty-five feet of wide-open lawn stretched out in front of her. If they tried to sneak across it, they would be seen for sure. She just knew it.

Eric must have noticed that she deflated like a popped balloon and grinned at her. "Do you trust me?" he asked in a hushed tone.

Did she? She didn't want to, that was for sure. What kind of a question was that anyways? And how could she trust him? Like, really trust him after everything that had happened over the last twenty-four hours.

Eric noticed her hesitation. She'd never been good at lying and her mother had always told her that she was an open book and her face always gave away what she was feeling. He sighed, a sad sound. "Millie, I'm not going to hurt you." He paused, gauging her reaction, and when she still hesitated, he continued, "I get it. I led you on. I'm a big jerk and I'm sorry. Really I am. I just..." He reached out and brushed his fingers lightly across her cheek and then a look of horror crossed his face and he promptly dropped his hand and his gaze. "It doesn't matter. We need to get past the trees and onto the street. You can't run fast enough to not be seen, but I can. If you'll let me, I can carry you across."

Everything after that happened in a blur. Mitchell started yelling at her through the bond, frantically looking for her. Amelia started to tremble and in a panic she hopped onto Eric's back, not wanting to face Mitchell yet, and Eric took off for the trees. In under a second, he was setting her down on the sidewalk.

Amelia was dizzy and her stomach queasy. She bent over, sucking in deep, calming breaths. Eric cleared his throat and rubbed her back. "We need to get moving if you want to get in any running time, Millie." Her head was pounding and Mitchell started yelling incoherently, words too loud and too panicked to really understand them. Her chest hurt and she couldn't breathe. She tried desperately to suck in air, but it was as if her lungs had collapsed and her throat had closed up and no air could get in. Amelia searched for Eric. She could hear him, his voice distant, but she couldn't find him. Little spots, all the colors of the rainbow, flickered across her eyes. Her lungs were burning and she was sure her face was turning blue. She needed air, needed to breathe. A stabbing pain, like a knife ripping into her stomach, sent her crumbling to the ground and she screamed, pushing out the last of her precious oxygen from her body.

CHAPTER 18

As quickly as the pain started, it vanished, leaving Amelia drained and breathless.

Mitchell's voice blasted into her mind, *Love, I'm so sorry. I didn't mean to. Are you okay?* He sounded so sad, so ashamed it brought the sting of tears to her eyes and her heart swelled, just a little. He could control it. He was trying to control the pain.

After a few more shaky breaths, Amelia cleared her mind enough to answer him. *I'm okay.* Even in her mind, the words sounded shaky and unsure and she was glad she didn't have to actually use her voice.

The link was silent for a long moment and she could feel him, poking around in her brain, sifting through her thoughts. It was the strangest feeling, one she wasn't sure she would be able to get used to. She knew the exact moment when he found her. The images of her in the blue jogging suit standing at the tree line flashed before her eyes and she felt him breathe a sigh of relief. *You went for a run,* he said, sounding bemused.

Um, yeah, with Eric. Amelia sent the thought to him hesitantly. Would he let her go? Would he order her back to the house? A quick flash of rage passed through the bond, but he quickly extinguished it and she knew how hard he was trying to keep his calm. When he didn't say anything, she asked, *Is that okay?*

Mitchell stayed silent for a minute and Amelia couldn't get a handle on his thoughts. They were just so muddled up it was hard to tell. When he answered her, it sounded tight and forced. *Fine,* he sent, obviously annoyed and angry, and she winced. He must have felt it because at that very moment, Mitchell sent a warm and sparkly burst of tenderness and then she felt him recede, drifting out of her thoughts, but still somehow staying on the sidelines.

"You okay, Millie?" Eric asked. He was kneeling in front of her, scanning her over with concern. "I'm really sorry. I didn't think he would freak like that."

Amelia forced a smile. "I'm good." She rolled up to her feet, feeling more stable with every passing second, and she did a few light stretches.

"You sure?" Eric asked, frowning. "Do we need to go back?"

Amelia felt every muscle in her body clench and she clamped her lips together in a thin line. *Was this how it was going to be?* she wondered. When Mitchell says jump, they all jump? "I'm sure and no, we don't need to go back." Her voice came out short with a hint of annoyance and she felt bad. This wasn't his fault. Eric was just trying to help her, get her out of the house, and she was taking it out on him.

To her surprise, Eric chuckled. "Glad to see having Mitch around hasn't sweetened you up any, 'cause I don't know what I'd do if I didn't get my morning dose of bitchiness from you."

Amelia glared at him, but it must not have been convincing because he just laughed.

The run helped, a lot, in fact, and by the time they got back Amelia was drenched in sweat—Eric, to her utter astonishment, was not—and she almost felt... okay. At least she did until she walked into the kitchen and the tension that filled the room forced her roughly back to reality. Eric must have felt it too because his joyous laughter stopped abruptly and his expression turned grim.

Mabel stood over the stove, making eggs. Her hands were shaking so bad that when she cracked the egg on the side of the frying pan it would split all the way through, splattering her hands with slivers of the shell and the goopy yoke. Angelle looked like a disaster. She was still in her pajamas—Winnie-the-Pooh shorts and tank top—her hair was dull and limp, as if she hadn't bothered to brush it, and she had no make-up on. Amelia had never seen her look so... unruly before. She was sitting at the island flipping through a magazine so fast, Amelia was sure she wasn't actually looking at it, but using it as a reason not to talk to anyone. Mitchell sat beside Angelle, gripping his coffee cup so tightly Amelia wouldn't have been surprised if it shattered in his white-knuckled hands.

Amelia, even though she tried to fight it, couldn't help but notice how sexy he looked, dressed in jeans and a button up blue and gray striped collared shirt, untucked and unbuttoned, showing off his firm and sculpted abs and chest. He looked up at her and smiled. It was a forced smile, she could tell, but her heart fluttered anyways. Mitchell was trying and that was all that mattered. Amelia gawked at him, physically unable to pull her eyes away. He was a powerful magnet and she a helpless piece of metal, and their mutual attraction was a strong, unbreakable force she knew she was powerless to resist. She wanted to hate him. She wanted to look away. But she just couldn't.

"Good morning," Luke called, strolling into the kitchen, not noticing or choosing to ignore the friction in the room.

Amelia sucked in a breath, realizing when the air hit her burning lungs that she'd stopped breathing and fire blazed in her red cheeks. *You're supposed to hate him*, she scolded herself, disgusted that she couldn't control the overwhelming urge to run to him and kiss him, touch him, just be close to him. With haste, desperately wanting a diversion, she rushed over to Mabel. "Let me help." Amelia took the egg out of Mabel's hand and retrieved a new pan—one that wasn't caked in eggshells. "Do any of you want breakfast?" she asked, glancing up. It dawned on her that she didn't know if they actually needed to eat or if they even liked the taste of food. Did they only need to drink blood? They had always eaten with her before but did they have to? Did they want to eat or did they do it just for her benefit? She didn't know and she didn't really want to ask.

Mitchell heard her thoughts and chuckled. Amelia bristled. Would she ever be able to have a thought without him knowing it? "We don't need to eat. The food provides us with no nutritional value, but it still tastes good." He set down his mug and glanced at Mabel, who was now in the fridge looking as if she wanted to climb in and shut the door. "Mabel, why don't you take the day off? You look like you could use a break."

Mabel slowly closed the fridge and made her way over to Amelia, taking her hand tightly. Her hand was cold and clammy, Amelia noticed, and she was trembling. "No..." her voice sounded shaky. Mabel cleared her throat and tried again. "No thank you, sir. I would like to stay with Millie."

Sir? Really? Amelia didn't get to finish the thought because Mitchell was angry again. It boiled through her like steam from a boiling pot of water and it was all directed at Mabel. It was becoming very clear that Mitchell always got what he wanted and wasn't used to people outright disobeying him—something Amelia found strangely comforting. At least it wasn't just her that he expected to be at his beck and call.

Amelia pushed Mabel behind her, and looking back, that was probably a bad idea. There was a collective gasp, hissing like snakes, from her roommates and Amelia saw their pale faces turn stark white. She hadn't seen him move, but Mitchell was suddenly in front of her, towering over her. She'd never felt as small as she did at that very moment. His crimson eyes bore into her and to her horror, his fangs snapped down, white and deadly.

She didn't know how she mustered the strength, but Amelia squared her shoulders, pushed her head back, and looked up, right into those terrifying eyes. "Back off, Mitch," she said in a lethal voice.

Mitchell laughed wickedly, reached out, and grabbed Amelia by the neck, lifting her off the ground. Mabel screamed and pounded her fists on him. She tried to pry his fingers away from Amelia's neck, but he just batted her away as if she were a pesky fly.

Amelia didn't struggle, she couldn't breathe, but she just stayed limp in his grip. Tears burned her eyes, but she didn't blink and focused her stare on him, willing him to realize what he was doing. She could feel the monster in him taking control. That's what he was, she realized, a monster. Was there anything human left in him? What had happened to the man from her dreams? The one she'd fallen in love with? Was he still in there? She didn't know, but she truly hoped so, because if not, if he really was just a monster, he could kill her now, and she would be happy. "Please," she choked out, unable to finish the rest, she sent the thought through their link, *Just kill me now. I would rather die than spend a lifetime with you.*

Blue flecked his blazing eyes for a quick second and he looked taken aback. His grip loosened enough for her to pull in a bit of air, though it burned all the way down to her lungs. His fangs were still down, and he looked like he was fighting the demon that wanted to kill her. She could almost see the devil on one shoulder and the angel on the other coaxing him back and forth between good and evil.

All of a sudden, Amelia was airborne, flying across the room. She crashed against the fridge with a clatter and a thick thud to the ground. A loud pop sounded and an intense, immobilizing pain shot into her shoulder. She looked down to see her arm limply dangling from its socket. Her shoulder had dislocated.

Amelia didn't focus on the pain long. The next sound was so loud and horrifying she was almost sick. The meaty crack of a fist hitting flesh and then the dry snapping of bone echoed in the otherwise silent kitchen. She watched in horror as Eric's lifeless body crumbled to the floor at her feet. She could feel the blood rushing out of her cheeks and her body went numb.

She didn't remember moving, but the next thing she knew, she had Eric's head in her lap and she was stroking his hair. Tears fell freely down her cheeks in a waterfall of despair. Commotion erupted all around her, yelling, crying, more fists and the same sickening cracks, but she drowned them all out.

Eric's perfect complexion had taken on a grayish tint and his skin was rapidly cooling, far faster than Amelia would have thought possible. She supported his floppy, crooked neck in one hand and continued caressing his hair. *No. He can't be dead. He can't be dead,* she thought over and over. *Not Eric. Please, no.*

Someone pulled her away, wrapping her in a hug. Amelia tried to fight it. She needed to stay with Eric. He looked so uncomfortable, his head resting on the cold marble floor at an impossible angle, but she couldn't break free. "This is going to hurt, kiddo," Luke said in her ear, just before she heard the loud bone popping sound of her shoulder going back into place.

Amelia squealed out in pain, paralyzed for a moment. Sweat beaded on her forehead and she bit her tongue to stop from screaming out. Luke held her tightly to him, gently massaging her shoulder until the pain receded to a dull throb. It took a few minutes, but as soon as she could she said, "Let go. I need to help him."

Luke didn't let go. "He's going to be fine, kiddo. You don't need to sit there crying. He'll be awake in a few minutes."

"You can't get rid of us that easily so stop crying," Mitchell snapped. Still in Luke's arms, Amelia glanced at Mitchell. He sounded so cold. She didn't know if her expression told him how she felt or if he heard her thoughts, but he softened. "I'm sorry. I didn't mean to snap at you, it's just…" he stumbled over the words and scrubbed at his face for a second. "You care for him. I can feel it and it hurts."

"Sorry?" Amelia shouted and Luke, startled at her outburst, let go. She stomped over to Mitchell, fists clenched into tight balls and jaw tensed. He was sitting at the island, leaning back in the wooden chair. "You're sorry for snapping at me? What about choking me? And correct me if I'm wrong, but I'm pretty sure you're the one who hit him hard enough to break his neck and all you can say is sorry for snapping at me." Amelia drew her arm back, opened her fist, and slapped him, with everything she had. She knew instantly it had hurt her more than him. Pain shot through her shoulder, and she realized that she probably should have used the other hand. Her eyes prickled, but he just sat there, looking at her, his face not even a little pink from where she'd slapped him.

"Are you done?" Mitchell asked coldly, and Amelia could almost see the ice frosting up around his heart. He kept his expression just as chilly as he glared at her and it made her want to cower away and hide in a corner. "I don't know what you want me to say, Amelia. I'm not sorry for hitting him. He's lucky that's all I did." He paused, collecting his thoughts, sorting through them and organizing them, and she tried really hard to ignore it, because hearing his thoughts was just… creepy. "He kissed you. He took advantage of you. He snuck you out of the house this morning after I gave clear instructions that you were not to leave." Mitchell was saying it all so matter-of-factly that it made her sick, revolted by his attitude that she was just a piece of property. "Whether you like it or not, you're mine. He knew that and he crossed the line with you. I've been trying to find you for more than eight hundred years. Even after I made contact through the dreams, it took me another five years to find you. So no, I'm not sorry for what I've done to him and honestly, you shouldn't be either."

"I wish you'd never found me," Amelia said through clenched teeth. She turned on her heels, crossed the short distance to Eric, and sunk down cradling his head, determined to be there until he came back.

CHAPTER 19

"What the hell is wrong with you?" Luke asked, finally dragging Mitchell away from the kitchen and shoving him into Amelia's bedroom. "You've got to pull yourself together, Mitch."

Luke slammed the door behind them and crossed his arms over his chest, guarding the door as if he were determined not to let anyone in or out.

Mitchell put his hands up in surrender and backed away from the door. Not that Luke could actually stop him if he wanted out, but the last thing Mitchell wanted was to hurt someone else. "What I need to do is leave. Put as much distance between us as possible."

Luke arched a brow and hardened his stare. "It's not that simple anymore. And even if you do leave, you know you won't be able to stay away."

Luke was right, Mitchell knew that, but he didn't like it. The bond wouldn't let them be apart, not any longer, and it was his fault. He crossed the room, sat down on Amelia's bed, and slouched wearily, resting his head in his hands.

Luke placed a hand on his shoulder and the bed dipped with the extra weight as he sat. "Look, I know it's hard. I've been there... at the beginning it was a constant battle with Lola, especially after she changed. She was a loose cannon, but we made it through."

Mitchell shook his head. "But look at what I just did. It's not just affecting her. All of you are suffering because I can't keep it together. You'd think I'd have more self-control after this long. And if the rest of them figure it out, all hell will break loose. I should never have brought her here. I knew she was different and still..."

"How is she different?"

Mitchell chuckled in disbelief. "Come on, Luke. I know you felt it."

Luke stood up and started pacing the rich hardwood floor. It didn't take long for the truth to hit him. He suddenly froze and looked at Mitchell, the color slowly draining from his face. "You're kidding! She can't be. It's... it's not possible." Creases indented his brow and he locked his fear-filled eyes with Mitchell's and whispered, "The curse..."

Mitchell's lips curved into a small and distant smile. "I doubt our souls stopped and said *wait* vampires and witches shouldn't be together. We're soulmates. Destiny's idea of a joke." A hollow chuckle erupted from his throat.

Luke broke eye contact, shuffling from right to left. "You know you can't blame Eric for all this. He told me about coming to you for help. You knew he was struggling with her here."

Mitchell rubbed at his face, guilt and shame rushing around him, making him feel sick. "I know. Dammit! It's like everything is spiraling out of control and I can't think straight." He took a few calming breaths. "She hates me, you know and I don't blame her. I don't know how to fix this. Maybe she'd be better off if I didn't exist."

"Don't," Luke snarled, not missing the hidden message behind Mitchell's words.

"I have to do something. Neither of us can continue like this. What if I can't stop myself next time?" Mitchell raised his eyebrows in question. "What happens then? She doesn't even know what she's doing. She doesn't realize that every time she gets mad she's throwing her power at me. When she throws it at me, I lose control. It's too strong. It hurts too much. The bond, the feelings, everything. It's just too much." Mitchell lifted his shirt to reveal reddened skin covered in welts and blisters.

Luke gasped. "She did that? Shit, it looks like burns."

Mitchell tugged his shirt back down and shrugged, "It's not too bad. It'll heal, but one of us is going to kill the other if we keep this up. I have to go."

Luke sat back down beside Mitchell. "You wouldn't just be leaving her," he whispered in a shock-filled voice. "What about Eric? He's your kid. Are you going to just walk out on him, too?"

"After what just happened, he'll be glad to get rid of me."

Luke shook his head in disagreement. "You're his idol. You know damn well he won't let you go." Luke's eyes drifted down to Mitchell's chest and then back up, filled with a new intensity. "We'll help her control it. We can teach her. You need to tell her what she is. She needs to know."

Mitchell thought about that, wondering if it would make any difference. Amelia hated him. He was sure of it. He could feel sparks of love from her but most of the feelings were blinding hatred. She even hated how sometimes she loved him. He knew he was grasping at straws, but maybe if she knew, they could fix it all together. With that thought, he smiled. "I will. Tomorrow, when everyone calms down, I'll tell her everything."

CHAPTER 20

It took fourteen minutes and nine seconds for Eric to come back, or wake up. Amelia thought that sounded better, less disturbing, that was for sure. She sat on the cold, hard floor with his head in her lap, her eyes constantly checking the big grandfather clock as it ticked away the seconds.

After the first five minutes, Luke had managed to calm Mitchell down enough to get him out of the room, but for some reason, his absence didn't help. Amelia could still feel him and the distance was unbearable. She had to intensely focus on not running out of the room after him. Why did she have to feel this way? She wished she could understand it, but she just couldn't. How could two people be tied together like this?

Amelia was so busy trying to forget about Mitchell that when Angelle spoke she flinched, having forgotten that she wasn't alone. "Mabel, you really should go," she urged. Angelle was sitting beside Amelia braiding her hair.

The older women looked at Amelia, her brow furrowed and arms crossed. She looked conflicted, Amelia thought, as if she wanted to run from the house screaming but was bound by a duty to stay. "I'm not leaving her," she said. "Amelia needs one of her own on her side through this."

One of her own? Amelia raised a questioning eyebrow, not sure what to say. "A human, Amelia. You need a human on your side."

Angelle sighed—long and sad—she looked genuinely hurt. "I wouldn't let anything happen to her. She's my sister." She ran her fingers through Amelia's hair, loosening the braid, and started again.

"Don't call me your sister," Amelia murmured. She wanted to move away from Angelle, but she didn't want to disturb Eric. "We're not sisters. A sister wouldn't betray me like you did. She wouldn't stand by and watch me suffer. You let me believe that I was crazy. I told you everything and you let me continue to think that it was a dream. If you really cared about me, really thought of me like a sister, you would have told me the truth."

Angelle's hands stilled on her hair, and Amelia risked a glance at her. A small tear slid down Angelle's cheek, leaving behind a thin, glistening trail. "I wanted to tell you. Please believe me. I really wanted to."

Amelia didn't want to care. She didn't want to believe it and she didn't want to accept that there was any excuse that would convince her, but she asked anyways. "Why didn't you?"

"It's complicated."

"You've got to give me something here," Amelia pleaded. She looked back down at Eric's lifeless form, ran her fingers through his hair, and caressed his cheek. "Give me a reason to believe you." Because, despite what her brain was saying, she really did want to believe Angelle.

Angelle stayed quiet for a moment, and the idea that she wasn't going to explain stung. Amelia really wanted to believe that Angelle was her friend, that she had some kind of rationale for hiding Mitchell from her.

Another silent minute passed and Amelia glanced at her. As their eyes met, the words suddenly came out of Angelle in a rush. "Mitchell is the oldest. That makes him the strongest. I can't fight him. None of us can. We wouldn't stand a chance. But it's more than that. He's a good man, Amelia. He's done so much for me. For all of us. So when he asked me to wait to tell you, I did. I owe him my life and all he wanted was for you to get a chance to settle in, make some friends, get used to us before we told you. He thought it would make it easier for you." When Angelle finished, she went back to braiding Amelia's hair distractedly. "If I thought for a second that you were in danger, I would've stepped in." She uttered the last words with such fervor that Amelia knew it was true.

"But you already let the worst happen, my dear," Mabel said, reminding them she was still there. "Have you forgotten about Derek? About all the pain and heartbreak that was caused by your actions. The very same actions Mitchell has taken?"

"Who's Derek?" Amelia asked.

Angelle ignored her, and suddenly the braid went from loose to pinching tight. She was just about to ask again, when Angelle hissed, "This is nothing like Derek, Mabel, and you know it. Amelia loves him. She doesn't want to admit it yet but she does and he would do anything for her."

"He's letting the devil take control of him," Mabel said. Amelia was thunderstruck. Sweet-tempered, motherly Mabel was glaring so hard at Angelle it made Amelia nearly cringe. Angelle's braid was so tight now that it felt like her hair was being ripped out, and the lump on her head was not making it any easier to stay still, but her desire to know more made her resist the urge to jerk away. "He can't be trusted with her," Mabel continued. "Not yet. And she needs someone to look after her. Someone who will stand up to him, not cower behind a magazine while he's choking her."

"Does she look hurt to you?" Angelle shouted. "Are there any bruises on her neck? Your family has been with him for seven centuries and you've been with him for sixty-one years now. Has he ever threatened you? Or put himself before anyone human or vampire?"

"This is different," Mabel said relentlessly. Amelia had

never thought of Mabel as a stubborn woman before, but she was now. "Remember how you felt, Angelle. She doesn't just hold his soul, she is his core. The connection between them is stronger than I have ever seen, even stronger than Luke and Lola. A connection like that can be dangerous. It plays with their minds. There is a fine line between love and hate and Mitchell is not used to anyone outright defying him. And our little Amelia is a strong one." She looked over at Amelia, pride illuminating her round features. "The light shines bright in her. If she keeps fighting him, and I'm sure she will, he may lose control. All it takes is a second and they will both regret it."

That's when Eric stirred. The conversation between the women stopped abruptly as his neck straightened, snapping and popping, and his eyelids twitched. "Mabel, grab some blood," Angelle ordered. She dropped Amelia's hair and pushed her back. "Sorry, sweetie, but he's gonna be hungry and I don't want him to make a mistake."

Mabel tossed a bag of blood to Angelle and then pulled Amelia back further. *Why?* Amelia was sure that he wouldn't hurt her. Not Eric. She watched with a mix of fascination and horror as Eric sprung back to life. One second, his eyelids were fluttering and the next he was on his feet, snarling savagely. Angelle held him easily with one hand, arms locked behind his back, and held the bag of blood in front of him, dangling it like a T-bone in front of a dog. Like an animal, he tore into it, sucking and slurping. It was bloodcurdling and nauseating, and if Amelia hadn't been so petrified, she almost certainly would have lost her cookies.

Halfway through the bag, Angelle released his arms while he continued to devour the thick, red liquid. His eyes slowly turned from fiery red back to their beautiful, vibrant green and his skin took on a light pink flush.

When he'd sucked the bag bone-dry, Eric pitched it into the sink and rolled his neck. The room echoed with a pair of stomach-churning cracks, like the snap of celery sticks.

"Dammit," he said and rubbed his face. "I hate it when that happens. Where the hell is he?"

No one answered him, so Amelia searched the bond—stunned at how normal it felt—to find Mitchell. "In my room," she answered. Eric looked mad. She guessed he had a right to be; Mitchell had broken his neck, but even though he was justified, she felt an insistent urge to defend Mitchell. "He's with Luke. He's sorry," she stuttered, hoping that may help.

"Like hell he is!" Eric yelled at her. "He's probably wishing I was dead. You probably wouldn't care much either," he spat at Amelia with so much hostility that she came close to bolting. She shuddered uncontrollably, mustering all her will to force herself to stay put and not reveal her fright.

"You know that's not true, Eric." Angelle put a hand on his shoulder. "Amelia sat here holding you the whole time. But you went too far with her. You know it. Seriously, what were you thinking getting in between them? Did you really think he was just going to let you stop him and walk away with her?"

"At least he tried to stop it," Mabel snapped.

Angelle rolled her eyes and huffed. "He wasn't going to hurt her." She sounded exasperated and defeated.

"She wasn't breathing," Eric countered.

Amelia watched the three of them yell at each other. She knew it was tacky, but she smiled inwardly. This was all for her. They cared. All of them. They were at each other's throats about what they thought was best for her. Then it hit her; they were fighting about her and that just wasn't okay. "Um, guys, I'm fine," she said, a bit louder than she'd hoped, and she felt her neck burn with a creeping blush. "I think Angelle's right. I really don't think Mitch wanted to hurt me."

"Amelia, you really need to take this seriously," Mabel cautioned, giving a stern look. "Mitchell's a vampire. He's a killer and you are pushing him over the edge whether you mean to or not."

As if he knew they were talking about him, Amelia felt Mitchell tune in. She knew right away, with an overwhelming surge of wildness, that Angelle was right. With the way things were going, it could get nasty between Mitchell and Mabel. "Mabel, thank you for your concern. It's really touching, but I'm fine and I need to deal with this on my own. I think you need to leave. Take some time off."

"She's right," Eric said. "If Amelia hadn't gotten in the way you might not have been so lucky."

"He's ashamed of the way he acted and I think he's scared for you," Amelia added because Mabel looked determined to stay. "He'd never forgive himself if something happened to you, Mabel." She wondered if that was actually true and then quickly dismissed the thought, not wanting to consider that Mitchell could be so monstrous.

Luckily, Mabel didn't notice her hesitation, and she visibly deflated. She bobbed her head in agreement. "You call me, dear. Call me every two hours. If I don't hear from you, I'll come back."

In no time, Amelia had Mabel safely in her car and when she drove away, Amelia felt as if a colossal burden had been lifted from her shoulders. *One less person to worry about.*

After some coaxing, Eric went to take a shower and get his head together. He wasn't himself yet, not that Amelia blamed him. He had just, in a sense, died.

With Eric taken care of, Amelia made a cup of instant coffee and plopped down at the island. Too much was happening. Too many feelings. Too many changes. She couldn't help but feel as if she were getting the short end of the stick again. Someone else was choosing her path and she was powerless to change it.

Tears dripped down her cheeks. She knew something had to be done, but what? Where should she start? Should she deal with the fact that vampires were real? Or that soulmates existed? Or that her soulmate was a vampire? Or what about the fact that it was all real and for some reason he bit her and now, because of that bite, they were linked together and she would never be able to do anything again without him knowing? There was no logical way to look at it. No mathematical equation to solve the problems. It was magic. She struggled with that hard, solitary rationalization.

"Wanna talk about it?" Angelle asked. She was rinsing the blood splatters from the sink that Eric had left behind.

"Yes," Amelia smiled weakly. "But I think I need to talk to him." Mitchell. He was the only one that could help her now. She knew that. Maybe they could come to some kind of arrangement. She doubted it, but she knew she had to try because she couldn't live like this.

"I'll go with you," she said, and Amelia was grateful to have the support.

As they walked in silence to Amelia's room, Amelia tried to figure out what to say to him. *Yes, I love you, but I hate you for making me feel this way*, just didn't sound right, because, well, she really didn't want to love him and from tip to toe she loathed herself—not him—for doing it. She wished there were some kind of switch she could just turn off.

Amelia braced herself when they got to her bedroom door. Coaching herself, giving a mental pep talk, not to act like a fool, not to run to him. He didn't deserve it. He wasn't worthy of her love. That was the brain wave that messed up everything. She hadn't noticed, but Mitchell had been eavesdropping, and he was ready for her the second she walked into the room.

Angelle went first, taking a seat on Amelia's bed beside Luke, and Amelia trailed along. The talking quickly exploded into a full-blown fight that dragged on for hours. They clashed on everything. It started out about important things, like why he took so long to find her, and why he'd bitten her. As their anger increased, it fueled the burning hatred Amelia felt. They argued about what he'd done to Eric, about how he had no right to make decisions for her, and the hostility continued to build. He told her that she hadn't actually won a scholarship. He was paying for her education, and the fake scholarship was just part of his master plan to get her to Willowberg.

When they dealt with the important things, they kept right on fighting. He picked on what she was wearing; telling her jogging suits didn't look good on anyone. She told him his hair looked stupid (it didn't—Amelia loved his silky, light brown hair). They even battled about the color of the sky—which now that she thought about it—they both had agreed it was blue but disputed it anyways.

Angelle intervened when Mitchell had revealed, in a very heated way, why there was a curfew. As it turned out, the curfew was only for humans because the vampires, who filled the entire street, used the gated complex as a hunting ground. They brought in humans at night, set them loose, and hunted. Not all of them did, Luke had said, not the ones she lived with, but some still enjoyed the hunt.

"I've heard enough," Amelia said, cutting off Luke's attempt to justify the animalistic behavior. Her head felt as if it would explode from information overload. She needed to be alone. She felt rotten and needed to think. The dried sweat from her run and the morning's madness had really taken its toll; she craved solitude, and a nice hot bath. "Please," Amelia started, and when tears stung her eyes, she stopped and scrubbed at them. "I need to be alone. Please... all of you just go away."

Amelia had expected Mitchell to fight her on it, refuse to leave, but when he didn't, she supposed that he must have been just as beat from all the fighting. The three of them left her without another word.

When the door shut, she flopped down onto her bed, buried her face into her pillow, and screamed out all her frustration. It felt unexpectedly good, and Amelia did it again and again and again until her throat was raw. Talking to Mitchell really hadn't gone how she'd hoped and now, she was left with even more questions... she was even more afraid.

Amelia rolled onto her back and stared vacantly at the ceiling. Her brain was fried. Since nothing was making any sense, she decided that soaking in the tub was the best thing. Clear her mind and start again fresh.

She slugged her way across the room and caught sight of her phone blinking on the table. She detoured to see what she'd missed.

There was a text message from Erin. It had just come in and she realized she must have missed the tone while screaming into the pillow.

Talked to Ty. U OK?

Amelia wanted to say that no, she really wasn't okay, but she didn't want to explain that so she answered: **Yep. Fine.**

Before she could set the phone down it chirped again: **Need to C U alone. Can we meet?**

Yeah, right, Amelia thought. Like she would be able to leave the house. She replied: **Not a good time. Family issues.**

Amelia waited to see if Erin would respond and a moment later, another message flashed up: **Tomorrow? Pick u up at 9 for class.**

Amelia quickly replied: **Ok. C U in am.**

Mitchell couldn't object to that, right? She had to go to school so what did it matter if one of her friends picked her up? She called Joe at the gate and let him know, then she poured a scorching hot bath, letting the heat and steam soothe away her worries, if only for a moment...

The peace didn't last long enough. By 4:00, Amelia was starving. She thought about ignoring it, but her stomach felt as if it were eating itself so she headed for the kitchen. She regretted it as soon as she got there. Mitchell was standing on the terrace with his arms around another girl, kissing her—on the cheek—but that didn't matter, he was still kissing her.

White-hot fury overtook Amelia, every muscle in her body went rigid, and she gritted her teeth. Her fists were clasped so tightly that her fingernails cut into her palms, but she couldn't seem to loosen them. *What the hell did he think he was doing?* A voice in her head hollered. *And who the hell was the tramp he was all over?* Mitchell knew she was there. He knew she was fuming and he was enjoying it. Amelia could hear the silent rumblings of his chuckle vibrating through her mind and it was infuriating.

The girl, whoever she was, noticed Amelia glaring and pushed him away. She came over to Amelia. "I'm Lola."

What a tramp, Amelia huffed silently. She was shorter than Amelia was, maybe by an inch, and she had the same perfect figure and flawless skin that all the vampires seemed to have. Her pixie cut blonde hair had a little fringe at the front and it looked great with her cute oval face. She was dressed stylishly—not like Angelle, more toned down—in a basic black knee length, pencil skirt, a black fitted long sleeved T-shirt, and a colorful rainbow-striped scarf arranged around her neck.

Lola must have spotted Amelia's fury—she was sure it was impossible to miss—she tilted her neck to give Amelia a full view of her mark. It was the same marking she had, the alchemy symbol for soul, but the name Luke Price was scrawled along the bottom. "You don't need to be threatened," she said, letting Amelia take a good long look before smiling back at her. "I belong to Luke."

Surprisingly, that didn't help and Amelia was disgusted with the jealousy—green-eyed and nasty—that was pulsing through her. She didn't want Mitchell. She didn't want anything to do with him, but she also knew she didn't want anyone else to have him.

Luke chuckled. "Maybe she'll come around sooner than we thought." He gave Mitchell a congratulatory whack on the back.

Amelia bristled, ashamed and cheesed off with her reaction. "Don't hold your breath," she nearly yelled. Luke and Mitchell doubled up with laughter. She gave Lola another glare and said, "Welcome home," then went to the fridge, swung it open, and gaped. It had been emptied of food except for a single shelf; the rest was heaped up with bags of blood labeled with the Willowberg Blood Bank logo.

"Get used to it," Mitchell said coolly. "We drink blood and I don't see the point in hiding it from you anymore."

"Whatever. Doesn't bother me." Amelia knew that was a worthless statement. He knew it was bothering her. It was revolting. Blood in the fridge? Did they have to flaunt it around her? Amelia took out a box of strawberries and went to the sink to rinse them.

"Why don't you guys take my things upstairs," Lola said. "I'd like to get to know her."

Wow. That was the last thing Amelia wanted. To get to know the tramp that was all over Mitchell. *Damn this crazy jealousy*, she thought. She didn't like it, not one bit. "Maybe some other time," Amelia said, dumping the clean berries into a bowl. "Kinda busy right now."

Amelia knew Mitchell was pissed off at her before he snapped. *Maybe there is something good about the bond*, she thought, laughing silently to herself.

"Amelia," Mitchell growled.

Amelia put on her best innocent little girl smile, glad she had put on clean jeans and a low cut white tank. She glanced demurely at him, batting her eyes. "What? I have a paper to write."

"That's okay," Lola said, cutting off Mitchell before he could get a word in. "I'm sure we'll have tons of time later. Come on, Luke." She smiled sweetly at Amelia, which Amelia thought looked unnatural and fake. Then Lola turned, her knee high leather boots clicking as she floated across the marbled floor.

Luke looked torn. He cleared his throat, obviously uncomfortable, and said, "Sorry, but someone needs to stay with them."

Lola stopped, and spun around. Her brown eyes flared. "You've got to be kidding me. I'm sure he can handle her."

"That's the problem." Luke shuffled from one foot to the other, looking anywhere but at Lola. "He's not handling her very nicely right now and she's…" he glanced at Amelia apologetically, "not making it easy."

It was at that moment that Amelia knew she'd just made her first enemy. The look Lola shot her made her quiver right down to the bones. The trembles rushed up her spine and prickled through her fingers all the way to her toes. The stare felt like it would never end. When it did, Lola left, leaving Luke to stare after her like a lovesick puppy.

Mitchell's glare was almost as insufferable. He wasn't mad, but he was clearly disappointed. How had she become the bad guy? Amelia didn't know, but it didn't feel good.

"Luke, it's okay. You can go," Amelia said, trying to fix his bleak look. "Really, I'll stay in my room and Mitchell…" she looked at him, not sure what to say.

"I'll help her with the paper," he said firmly.

Crap. That wasn't what she'd been anticipating. Amelia almost said no, but then she glanced at Luke again, saw the heartbreak radiating from him, and said, "Um yeah, I could use some help." Luke looked longingly at the empty doorway where Lola had gone, and Amelia was sure she could hear his heart shattering. It was written all over his face. She just couldn't imagine how they had stayed apart for the last two weeks. Not that she wanted to admit it, but she thought she just might die if Mitchell left now that she knew he was real. "Go, Luke," Amelia pleaded.

Luke looked at her. Really *looked* at her, making sure she was okay and then smiled. "Thank you." He shifted his gaze to Mitchell. "Both of you. I've missed her so much." Then he gave Amelia another serious, fatherly kind of look. "Eric and Angelle went out for some air so if anything happens, if you think you need help, yell. I'll hear you."

"She won't, Luke," Mitchell said, just as seriously. "You have my word." Luke nodded, his lips tilted upwards, and his hazel eyes gleamed with delight and then he left, with the speed, which Amelia now knew, only a vampire could have.

CHAPTER 21

One of the downsides of living in a mansion was how bloody long it took to get anywhere. The walk from the kitchen to her office felt like a death march, eerily silent and gloomy. Amelia couldn't seem to stop her thoughts—not that any of them helped. Each idea seemed to pop up and then just as quickly as it came, the thought swirled around, and then in a rush, disappeared, like water flushing down a toilet. What was she doing? Why did she agree to be alone with him? They hadn't been able to say more than two kind words to each other in a row in the last forty-eight hours, so how were they going to work together? The worst part of it was that Amelia didn't really want to study because the idea of being alone with Mitchell so close to a bed was doing things to her body that had never happened before. She felt alive and sick all at once. Her mind was telling her that he was a monster and he was just going to hurt her, but her heart—her foolish heart—was pulling her towards him, telling her that he was her destiny urging her to get closer.

If Mitchell had been tuned into her thoughts, he didn't let it show. Amelia had come to realize that it wasn't an automatic link from her mind to his. They had to pay attention or look for what they had missed. She could tell when he was spying, most of the time, at least when he wasn't distracting her, which was pretty much all the time. It was like a hum, a vibration in her brain when he was there. She wondered if he felt the same thing.

"Do you really need to write a paper?" Mitchell asked, following her through the bedroom and into the office. "Or was that just an excuse to be rude to Lola?"

Well, that didn't last long, Amelia thought. *Were they really going to start to fight already?* She sat down at the desk and switched on her computer. *What had Mabel said? "There's a fine line between love and hate."* Words of truth. Amelia had never been so emotionally confused before. Is this what love was like? Blistering hatred fused perplexingly with genuine love and devotion. Heart swelling and beating erratically one second; the next, black and broken? Why did anyone want to love?

"I didn't mean to be rude," Amelia said, keeping her eyes on the computer screen. "It just kinda happened."

"I know." Mitchell sounded so miserable that she couldn't stop herself from sneaking a look. He was leaning against the doorframe, arms folded, shoulders slumped, and tiny creases lined his brow. "I never thought I was the jealous type, but with you…" he paused, and rubbed at his face. "I don't know. It's as if I have no self-control. You make me crazy. You know that, right?" She did. She really did because he made her feel the same way. Granted, it was different because he didn't want to be cruel to her, she could feel that, but she didn't want to love him. Even so, she understood.

"Why did you bite me?" Amelia blurted. "You knew it would be harder."

"I was scared." Mitchell laughed—hollow and empty— and a slight smile touched his lips but didn't reach his eyes. "I thought I was losing you. Even when you were drunk, your eyes lit up when you talked about Tyler, the same way they did when you first realized you'd fallen in love with me. I hoped it would keep you with me." He chuckled. "You've always had a mind of your own. I should've known you would fight it. I guess I just didn't want to believe you could want anything else."

Wow. That was the most honest thing he'd ever said to her. Even in the dreams. He'd always been so strong. The rock. But now, in this moment, he seemed vulnerable. He'd been honest with her so maybe she should do the same. "I need time, Mitch. This is a lot to take in. Do you have any idea what it's like to find out your whole life has been mapped out for you and that you have absolutely no control over it?"

"Yes," he answered, but Amelia knew he didn't really understand. For hundreds of years he'd been in control. Dictating and leading.

"I really don't think you do," she said, slouching back into the chair. "I spent the last five years in therapy. I thought I was a nutcase dreaming of you. And you let me think it. You let me think I was crazy. Now... you've decided that it's time to be with me. What did you expect?" Amelia didn't wait for an answer and kept right on going. "Did you really think I would just open my arms and run to you? You gave me a fake scholarship. You moved me into this prison." She gestured around the room with a sneer. "Then when things didn't go how you planned you took away my free will. How could you do that to me? If you really loved me you wouldn't have."

Amelia could feel him clamming up, giving off a clear-cut vibe that said she had gone too far, so when he spoke she was stunned at what came out. "I thought I could control it, Amelia. Luke did. I thought I could keep the pain away. I don't want to hurt you. You're just so damned stubborn."

The vibe was getting stronger and he was getting more frustrated with every passing second. She knew that the honesty thing had to end before they ruined any progress they had made. "I really do have a paper to write, Mitch. It's due tomorrow."

"Do you want help?" he asked hopefully.

Yes, a voice in her mind hollered. She didn't want him to leave and the truth was she was sort of struggling with non-commutative rings. "It's okay," she said. "I'm sure you have things to do anyways."

Amelia felt the hum, and wasn't surprised when he said, "I'm pretty good at ring theory. I could try to explain it." He left the doorway, pulled a chair over to the desk, and took a seat.

Before long, they were deep into ring theory, and she got it. It seemed so simple when he explained it. His hundreds of years of experience endowed him with a wealth of knowledge. The paper was written in no time and even after it was done, they kept at it. Mitchell knew the theories inside out and Amelia was good at putting them to work, and they worked together like a well-oiled machine.

Amelia had squealed when she completed revamping his accounting software. Mitchell had been sure that one of his employees was skimming money from the coffee shop in town, but he was wrong. There had been a glitch in the system stopping income from 5:00 to 6:30 every evening from transferring properly. The squeal must have sounded like a scream because Luke, Angelle, and Eric barged in ready to save the day. Mitchell and Amelia laughed, leaving their friends confused at the sudden change in them, but in the end left them to continue.

By two in the morning, Amelia could barely keep her eyes open. The yawns were coming steadily, and her brain was reduced to mush; even the simplest calculations seemed tough and her irritation was mounting at her numerous mistakes.

Mitchell turned off the computer and closed the books they had scattered across the desk. Amelia tried to protest, but she was just too tired. "You need sleep, love," he said warmly, and without hesitation, he scooped her up and carried her to her bed.

"You know I can walk, right?" she asked, but she snuggled into his chest, glad she didn't have to.

"This is more fun," Mitchell smiled. He tucked her in and kissed her forehead. "You're adorable when you're tired and not arguing with me."

Amelia gazed up at him, eyes half closed and smiled. This was the Mitchell she knew. The guy she'd fallen helplessly in love with.

Intense warmth washed over her in waves and her heart quickened. The tenderness that came from him was heavenly, cocooning her in love. *Love*. It was a wonderful feeling, a feeling that she'd craved for so long. Mitchell bent down and brushed a loose curl from her forehead and before she realized what she was doing, she grasped his hand, planting little kisses on his fingertips.

Who would have known such a tiny gesture could be so... intimate. His skin burned under her lips and a tingling pleasure instantly raced through her limbs. Amelia glanced up, meeting his hungry, wistful blue eyes, and every bit of control she had vanished.

In one swift motion, she threw back the covers and launched herself into his arms, wrapping her legs around his waist, her fingers digging into his soft hair. Her hungry lips found his and she kissed him greedily. For a second, he didn't respond; confusion pushed through the bond and that confusion just made it all the more exciting. How amazing was it that they could feel everything? Know each other's thoughts, dreams, fears... And that ramped up her need to a whole new level. She flicked her tongue against his lips, and that was all it took to wipe away his confusion.

Mitchell's hands cupped her bottom, and he brushed his tongue against hers, deepening the kiss. Amelia threw her arms around his neck, holding onto him tightly as if her life depended on it. His hands roamed her body, running along her thighs, up her back, down her arms. His lips trailed along her jaw until they found an earlobe, and she moaned and gasped for breath from the sensation.

His hunger skyrocketed, and mixed with hers; it was overwhelming and wonderful all at once. With his lips still nibbling at her ear, he moved Amelia back towards the bed, lying her down and slowly, he lowered himself closer to her.

Amelia fumbled with the buttons of his shirt, desperately longing for him to get closer yet. With his help, she managed to get them undone and the shirt off him and then with her legs still around his waist, she flipped him on his back, straddling him, and let her lips and hands explore the new found skin.

Mitchell moaned as she flicked her tongue at his neck and his hand slipped under her top, pulling her closer. His lips, urgent and moist, found hers and he moved her back underneath him, pulling her top off at the same time.

His lips trailed down her neck, chest, and stomach and a flash of all the things he wanted to do with her raced across her mind. She gasped, and horrible warning bells went off in her mind. What was she doing? She was supposed to hate him. They didn't even know each other. She wasn't ready for this. But damn, she wanted it. Wanted him. She tried to ignore the bells, pushing them away. The last thing she wanted was to stop, but before she could get rid of the thoughts, Mitchell pulled back and faster than she could process the movement, he was off the bed, looking down at her.

"Sorry, you're right. That was too fast," he said, shame dripping off him. "I shouldn't have let it get that intense. I'll, um...goodnight." He nervously started inching towards the door, snagging his shirt and jamming his arms into the sleeves.

"Mitch," Amelia whispered. "Don't go." She wasn't sure why, but the last thing she wanted was to feel the distance between them. She didn't want to feel the pull and she didn't want to be alone. He searched her face, and she could feel the hum as he searched her mind. Amelia sat up and grabbed her shirt, pulling it back on and then locked her eyes on him. "I don't want to be alone."

He smiled brilliantly at her and if her heart could have wagged its tail, it would have. He closed the distance between them in a few short steps, touched his lips to hers with a light kiss, and then whispered. "I need a shower. I'll come back soon." And then, with another quick kiss, he left.

Wide-awake now, the idea of a cold shower sounded really, really good and Amelia jumped at the thought. After a quick burst of cold water, she pulled on shorts and a tank, ventured back out into her room, and curled up in bed. Not long after, Mitchell came back, freshly showered and in jogging pants and a T-shirt. Without a word, he cuddled in behind her, pulling her close to his chest and before long, Amelia drifted to sleep.

CHAPTER 22

Erin looked herself over in the mirror, fiddling with her pigtails and straightening the straps of her overalls. She sighed. She already looked guilty and she hadn't done anything yet. If *he* saw her, *he* would know something was up, and then she wouldn't be able to fix what was already in motion. And she had to fix it.

She dabbed on more cover-up, hoping to hide the raccoon eyes, and then took in a deep breath and bolted from her room, praying she could get out before anyone noticed her panic.

"Gotta run," Erin chirped, glad her voice sounded steady, racing through the house. She'd managed to stay away from *him* all night, but she was really starting to run out of excuses and she really hoped her goodbye would be enough to keep his suspicions at bay.

"Hold on a minute," *he* said, appearing from nowhere. "Where are you running off to?"

Erin stretched her cheeks into a sweet smile. "School. I promised to pick up Millie," she said, not bothering to look at him. She knew all too well that he would see she was hiding something and if he saw it, he'd check and if he checked he wouldn't let her leave. And if she didn't leave, then she wouldn't be able to help Millie.

Erin held her breath when he reached out and tipped up her chin. He searched her face and the soft buzzing started. *Shit,* she thought, trying to erase the corrupting thoughts from her mind but it just kept popping up. Desperation engulfed her; she couldn't get rid of it. He would find out and then...

She kissed him. Erin rolled up on her tiptoes and took his bottom lip between her teeth with a little nibble. "You are such a hottie," she whispered against his lips, praying the distraction would work.

He pushed her away, his black eyes boring into her, hard and cold. Erin trembled under his stare; had he already seen her plan? She wasn't sure, but the look he was giving her was deadly.

Her bottom lip quivered and his eyes flashed to it. He sighed and closed his eyes tightly for a second, then pulled her closely into his arms. "You're being careful, right?" Erin couldn't answer, she didn't want him to hear the tremors in her voice and she nodded against his chest. He kissed the top of her head lightly. "Good," he said, dropping his arms. "I love you."

"I love you, too." Erin kissed his cheek and then ran out the door before he changed his mind.

"Cover up that mark, Erin," he called after her.

"Yeah, I will," she called over her shoulder without slowing down. "I have cover-up in my purse."

Erin had never been so happy to be in her shiny red VW. She jammed the key in the ignition and the engine roared to life. She let out the pent up breath, tossed the car into reverse, and sped off, leaving a spray of loose gravel and dust behind her.

She drove in fear, waiting for the inevitable. He knew something was up. She was sure of it. So why hadn't he come after her yet? *Because he doesn't know,* she tried to reassure herself.

Once out of sight from the house, Erin pulled over. She

was shaking so badly she could barely keep the car on the road and she knew she needed to calm down.

After a few deep breaths and a double-check of the bond to be sure he wasn't listening in, Erin rifled through her bag for her phone. She hated to make the call, hated that she was betraying him and it made her feel sick.

But Amelia is innocent, Erin told herself firmly. She's nice, caring, and a friend. The thoughts reaffirmed what needed to be done. She didn't have to be like him. She wouldn't let the hunger for revenge ruin her like it had him. Not this time around.

Erin tapped in the number and hit call. The shrill ring of the phone was torture and she waited for Madame Crystal to answer. "Hello, Erin. I've been expecting your call."

An involuntary shiver passed through Erin. She hated the idea of psychics and witches. Wasn't a vampire soulmate enough? At least she knew how to deal with vampires. She took a deep breath, remembering Amelia's friendly smile, and said, "I need you to help my friend, Amelia. She's in trouble and she doesn't know she's a witch yet. She needs to be able to protect herself. It's all happening too fast and…"

"I know, dear," Madame Crystal said, cutting off her panicked rambling. "*His* plan has changed."

"Can you help her?" Erin asked, holding her breath. If Madame Crystal couldn't help, she'd have to figure out how to get Amelia out of town. She'd have to figure out how to hide her.

"Maybe, bring her to me as soon as you can," the psychic said and then she hung up before Erin could get another word in.

Erin let out her breath in a gust of wind. *Maybe.* That wasn't exactly what she'd been hoping for, especially after bumping into the psychic last week in the supermarket. She replayed the words Madame Crystal had said, "*You will meet a new friend and you can save her by bringing her to me.*" And now all she was getting was a "maybe"?

She bit her bottom lip nervously. Had the prophecy changed? She tried to call back. She needed answers, but the line just rang and rang and rang. After the eighth try, she tossed her phone back into her bag and swore under her breath.

The sky opened up and rain pelted down, pinging against her car. Erin scrubbed at her face, took a deep breath, and then put the car in drive. *At least "maybe" is better than "no,"* she told herself, trying to see the positive in a bleak situation. Now all she had to do was figure out how in the world she would get Millie to Madame Crystal.

CHAPTER 23

Morning dawned, gloomy with rain. Amelia rolled over dreamily and took a deep breath. Mitchell's sweet, clean scent lingered in the air. Amelia opened her eyes to sneak a peek at him, and she was disappointed to find that he wasn't there. *Work. He must have gone to work,* she thought with a yawn, and closed her eyes, listening to the tapping rhythm of the rain.

Suddenly, the rumbling thunder shook the windows and, stunned, Amelia bolted out of bed. Wide awake now, she noticed her alarm clock was blinking; the power must have gone out. She snagged her phone off the nightstand: 8:46. Crap. She'd slept in and Erin would be there to pick her up in fourteen minutes.

Amelia took the quickest shower on record, cursing under her breath. Mornings sucked, life sucked, and it was pouring rain.

She got dressed in record time, pulling on a pair of low rise jeans and a gray hoodie. She could almost picture the look on Angelle's face at her choice in clothes, and it made her grin. No time for make-up or to dry her hair—not that it mattered—it was raining. Amelia piled the curls high on her head and secured them with a jumbo butterfly clip.

Amelia had just stuffed her books and the paper that she had written with Mitchell into her backpack when her bedroom door swung open, cracking against the wall. She spun around, dropping her bag with a clunk, to find Mitchell barging in and he was not happy. If looks could kill, Amelia was certain she would be dead.

"It's called knocking," she snapped. "I know it's probably a foreign concept to you, but it's when you rap your fist on the door and then you wait for someone to answer it."

He glowered at her, unimpressed. "Where do you think you're going?"

"To school," she answered, returning his glare. Two could play at this game, and Amelia knew she had a killer, *screw-off look*. "I told you I've got a paper due today."

"You're not going, Amelia. We need to talk."

Amelia grabbed her bag, puzzled at the sudden mood swing. She wasn't in the mood for his crap, not in the morning, so she slung her bag over her shoulder and shuffled towards the door. "We can talk later. Right now, I'm going to class. Erin's waiting for me."

"Who the hell is Erin?" Mitchell growled, staying on her heels.

A wave of jealousy rushed over her and for a second Amelia thought it was her own. Their emotions jumbled together, like a tossed salad; it was getting harder and harder to figure out whose feelings belonged to whom. She gritted her teeth, certain it was him, and kept right on moving. "Seriously, Mitch. Get a hold of yourself. Erin is a girl. She's a friend and she's driving me to school."

"You're not going," he yelled, and Amelia winced at the sharp stab of pain in her chest. It took everything she had, but she managed to keep moving, head down, concentrating on making her legs work. It felt as if she were attached to a bungee cord and every step she took away from him, the cable tried to snap her back. She made it to the foyer with Mitchell right behind her.

"Dammit, Mitch," Angelle cursed, appearing from nowhere. "You need to stop this. She's not ready."

"This is none of your business," he snarled. Amelia got a flash of a dangerous thought; he wanted to hurt Angelle and she stepped in between them. She wasn't going to let him hurt one of her friends, not again, not like Eric. The uneasiness in her gut faded. "Amelia, stop it! You are acting like a spoiled brat," he yelled in her face.

"Why? Because I'm trying to go to school?" she retorted bitterly. "It was your idea in the first place. You're the one paying for it."

"Don't push me." His eye flickered, streaking red.

Amelia sucked in a steadying breath and pushed on. "Or what? What more can you do to me?"

"Whoa, let's take a breather here," Eric said. Amelia hadn't seen him come in, but he was now in between them. Bad idea. She knew Mitchell wouldn't hit her, but she wasn't so sure about what he would do to the rest of them.

"Back off, Eric," Mitchell said with a lethal undertone. "This doesn't concern you."

Eric didn't seem bothered. He gripped Mitchell's shoulder. "Dude, you need to chill. You can check in on her anytime you want."

The blast of a horn sounded and Amelia glanced at the door then back to Mitchell. "I'm going, Mitch. If you really want to stop me then stop me, but I've made up my mind so you'll have to hurt me again." She went for the door, twisted the knob then looked back, meeting his crimson stare. "Go on, stop me. I dare you," she said so coldly that she felt the chill rolling off her tongue. Then she left, slamming the door as loudly as she could.

Amelia made it to the car with little discomfort. She could feel how mad he was but that he was trying to keep it under control, and she was grateful. It was pouring down in sheets and the last thing she wanted was to collapse on the soggy grass writhing in pain.

"Morning," Erin chimed when Amelia got into the car.

"Who's the hottie?" She was wearing her usual, overalls and a fitted long sleeved T-shirt. Amelia was starting to doubt that Erin owned anything other than overalls. Her hair was in its normal style—stubbly pigtails.

"No one noteworthy."

"I'm sensing a lover's quarrel." Erin shifted the VW in reverse. "But that can't be right because I'm pretty sure you were at my house making out with Ty last Friday."

Why did everyone have to be so chatty in the mornings? Amelia wondered. It was a phenomenon that she would never grasp. She huffed. "Look, I've had a rough couple days," Amelia said sharply. "You said it was important that we talk alone, so what is it?"

Erin giggled, apparently enjoying her crankiness. "Chill out and trust me for a minute. He could be snooping."

"What are you talking about?" Amelia asked, but as soon as the question came out, she already knew what Erin was talking about. Mitchell. Amelia wanted to scream. Another one of her so-called friends knew the truth and had hidden it from her. "You know about the mark." Her tone was caked with animosity.

Erin snuck a quick look and focused back on the stormy road. The splattering rain on the windshield was loud and Amelia almost missed what Erin said next. "I'll explain as much as I can, but first, I need you to see if he's listening. He can't know about me."

Amelia closed her eyes and rummaged around for any trace of Mitchell. She could feel him, but the sensation was murky and distracted so she was pretty sure he wasn't spying. "I don't think he's paying attention," she said after a few moments.

Erin loosened her white-knuckled grip on the steering wheel and a pent up breath gushed from her lips. "So I'm guessing the hottie is Mitchell Lang. He must've been pissed about Ty."

"That's definitely an understatement," Amelia groaned. "How'd you know about me?"

"I was going to tell you. I tried at the party, but your entourage of bodyguards ruined that plan. I'm marked, too." Amelia spun her head around and examined Erin's neck. The mark was there and for the life of her, she didn't know how she'd missed it. Erin must have guessed her confusion and explained, "I usually cover it. I know what you're going through and I thought you could use a friend. You know, one that's not all..." she mimicked fangs and then replaced her grip on the wheel. She looked so relaxed about the whole vampire thing it made Amelia realize how wrong it all was. She'd been so wrapped up with Mitchell being real and that he bit her, that the vampire part seemed like the least of her worries, but now, it was hitting her with staggering force.

"How can you be so calm about this? Don't you get how impossible it is?"

Erin shrugged, keeping her eyes on the road. "I grew up with them. Tristan took me when I was just a baby. I guess I just don't know anything else. It must be hard just coming into it."

"How do I stop it? How can I get rid of him?" Amelia's voice came out more scared than she'd hoped for and she took a few soothing breaths.

"You don't," Erin said matter-of-factly. "You can't break the bond between souls. I'm actually a bit surprised you made it out the door this morning. He didn't look impressed."

Erin turned into the parking lot at the University and found a spot. "I didn't think he was going to let me leave," Amelia admitted. Erin handed her an umbrella. "It was touch and go for a minute, but I don't think he actually wants to hurt me. Once I stood my ground he backed down." She opened the car door, popped the umbrella open, and jogged to the shelter of the school. Erin trailed behind a moment later.

Erin shook her umbrella, flicking water drops everywhere, closed it, and then did the same with Amelia's umbrella. "You're lucky. Tristan never backs down from our fights."

Amelia rolled her eyes and held the door for Erin. "You call this lucky?"

"I know you're pissed right now." Erin dropped her voice to a whisper as they walked through the hallway. "He was probably a big controlling jackass. They usually are. And in case you missed it, Mitchell kinda rules the vamp population here so he's used to getting his own way. But he's your soulmate and whether you like it or not you can't help but love him. You can't get away from him. Even if you die, you'll just keep coming back and he'll keep finding you. Reincarnation sucks."

"Reincarnation?" Amelia yelped, and then quickly checked herself as heads turned in their direction. *Another reason to hate Mitchell*, Amelia thought; it was his fault that anyone even noticed her. "You can't be serious."

Erin kept walking, keeping her voice low. "This isn't my first life with Tristan. I was murdered fifty-three years ago. It took a bit to come back, but here I am. It's kinda strange. I can remember everything from my past life. Tristan says that it's because a soul never forgets."

"This is insane," Amelia hissed. "First vampires, and now you're telling me that you've died before and you've been reincarnated."

Erin shrugged. "Welcome to my life."

"Why can't Mitchell know about you?" The suspicion was evident in her voice, but Amelia didn't care. So far every friend she thought she'd made since she arrived had stabbed her in the back and Erin wanting to hide just seemed strange, especially if Mitchell, in fact, ruled the town. Shouldn't he already know about her?

"It was another vampire that killed me." Erin stopped just outside the door of their class and the look she gave Amelia made her want to cry. "Someone Tristan trusted. He thinks that the fewer vampires that know I'm marked, the safer I'll be. He'd freak if he knew I was hanging out with you."

"Then why are you?" It seemed like a good question, but once it was out of her lips, Amelia wished that she could take it back. Erin might have hid this from her, but it was for her own protection, Amelia was sure of it.

To her relief, Erin hugged her. "Like I said, you need a friend." She released her embrace and winked. "Also, I heard you were smart and I need someone to copy off of. This whole math thing isn't my forte."

Amelia laughed, rolled her eyes, and they snuck into class taking a seat in the back, just as the professor started talking. Glancing around the room, Amelia was surprised she'd never noticed before, but now as she looked at her classmates she could tell them apart. There was the group at the front on the right that looked timid and bunched together. She knew, almost instinctively, that they were the locals and she was pretty sure they knew about the vampires. They had been overly welcoming and had tried the hardest to please her. To her left, in the middle, was Fiona, surrounded by a bunch of shiny and fake-looking magazine cut out girls—marked or vampires. Amelia could see glimpses of exposed marks on some of their necks and realized with a start that Mitchell must have made them cover them for her benefit. Then there were the out-of-towners. Those were the ones who were strictly here for school and knew nothing about the dangers that lurked in the town. They were the ones that had spoken to her because of the hype surrounding her, but nothing more.

CHAPTER 24

Amelia never ever thought she would think it, but school sucked. She could think of a million different places she would rather be and it was deeply disturbing that each place involved Mitchell.

He wasn't paying attention to her and it felt as if it were a deliberate effort to stay as far out of her mind as he could get. It hurt. It *really* hurt, and she found herself trying to see what he was doing. Amelia let her mind drift. Shutting out the droning professor, ignoring the students' muted whispers, and extending her mind.

She reached a wall of blinding, shimmering light, and then she found him. Mitchell was sitting on her bed, holding a photo, and he was crying. Soft tears slid down his cheeks, and little droplets wetted the surface of the photo. His thumb glided over the tiny puddles, pushing them off the glossy page.

She focused on the photo. Who had made him so sad? A rush of anger pierced in and she just knew that she would kill the person who had hurt him.

It was her.

Mitchell was holding a picture of her. His soft murmurs drifted to her ears, "I love you, Amelia. I'm so sorry, love.

I'm sorry." He set the photo down and rubbed at his face.

A hand touched her forearm. "You okay?" Erin whispered.

Instantly, Amelia was back in the classroom just in time to hear the professor announce a pop quiz. It took a moment and a few deep breaths and then she put on her best cheery smile and nodded.

Erin wasn't convinced. "You're crying."

Amelia hadn't noticed, but as soon as Erin said it, she could feel her prickling, puffy eyes and her damp cheeks. She kept the smile, wiped at her eyes, and said, "Allergies."

Erin didn't believe her for a minute, but luckily the TA handed them the test and that kept her from pushing the subject.

Amelia finished the test in twenty-three minutes. It was a breeze, solely on ring theory. Thanks to Mitchell, she was sure she had aced it. She mouthed a silent *washroom* to Erin, who still had a few questions to answer, shouldered her backpack, and went to hand in her completed test and paper.

She snuck into the washroom just outside the lecture hall. A few girls, locals she recognized but whose names escaped her, stopped talking as soon as she walked in. Amelia had a feeling that she'd been the topic of their gossip. It was pretty obvious from the way they clamped up and scurried out of the washroom.

Great. What had she done now? Last week they would have chatted with her. They would have wanted to know what she'd done on the weekend, how she'd liked the party.

Amelia dumped her bag and slammed the stall door hard, causing it to bang back and nearly smack her in the face. She had just flushed when the washroom door banged open and a familiar voice called her name.

Fiona. Her voice had a ring to it that signaled authority and status. Amelia held her breath and listened. The last thing she needed was to have another face off with the Barbie Squad. She just wasn't in the mood, not today, not ever. "Did you know the little tramp was all over Eric, too? It wasn't just that trash Tyler."

There was a collective gasp. "Eric, really?" That was Jessica, Amelia was sure of it. "Mitchell's going to kill them. Does he know?"

"Sure he does," Fiona said, followed by a cruel laugh. "It's not like she's hiding it. He deserves better. Too bad Kandi and Adam didn't finish her off at the party. He'd be better off without her."

Go out there. Stand up for yourself, Amelia's nagging conscience urged. She knew Fiona was a witch, but she had never thought her to be that bad. Did she really just say it was too bad that she hadn't died? Amelia found herself holding her breath as they continued. She crouched onto the toilet seat and made herself into a small ball, hoping they wouldn't notice she was there.

"So it's true," Amber gasped. "They came back to town?"

"They did and it's a good thing, too," Fiona said. Her voice sounded forced, as if her lips weren't moving, Amelia could almost picture her painting on a devil-red lipstick. "Someone needs to get rid of her. Mitchell's a mess. He put out another notice to all the vampires. We're supposed to watch out for her. He's making us her babysitter. And can you believe that he threw me out last night?"

"He what?" Jessica and Amber said in unison. Why would she have gone to him anyways? Amelia didn't know, but a sick feeling was creeping in.

"He threw me out. With Amelia here he won't give me the time of day. He's acting like the last hundred and twenty years didn't happen."

"What are you going to do, Fiona?" Amber asked. "What if he makes you leave? You're young and, no offence, but you haven't added much value except for warming his bed."

"I'll figure something out. Amelia won't last. There will be an accident. I guarantee it. Then he'll come running back to me."

No. No. No. No. He wouldn't. He couldn't. Fiona and Mitchell? Not possible. *Dammit! Why do I even care?* Maybe she knew Amelia was there. Maybe Fiona was just talking to get a reaction from her. But if that were true, then why, why would she admit that she was planning on an accident? What kind of accident? Was she really planning on getting rid of her, just to get Mitchell? What was so great about him anyways?

"Justin said he's not hunting either," Amber said. "He said that Mitchell is considering banning it because she doesn't like it. And he's drinking the bagged crap." *He is?* Amelia thought. She hadn't really thought about it and had tried not to because the whole blood thing turned her stomach. "She's not even giving it up for him, but she'll slut around with Eric. I bet she's even letting him bite her."

Amelia heard the door open again. "Yo, Millie. Hurry up," Erin's voice carried, bouncing off the walls.

"Wrong room, freak," Fiona snapped. "Get out."

Fiona sounded vicious, and Amelia knew she had to get out there. She sucked in a breath, hopped down off the seat, and opened the stall.

Amelia had never wished she had a camera as much as she did at that very moment. All three girls froze horrified, wearing the same expression as if they had just seen a ghost. Amelia laughed, a cold, humorless laugh, but on the inside, her nerves were shot and she was petrified. She pushed her shoulders back, held her chin high, and walked over to the sink to wash her hands. She risked a quick glance at Jessica and was relieved to see the sad look in her eyes. Fiona and Amber were mean girls, but Jess was sweet and Amelia really did like her. "Watch it, Fiona," Amelia said coldly. "Accidents do happen and like your friends said, you have no value to us."

Amelia knew right away that she had gone too far. Fiona's eyes flashed and her fangs slid down, terrifying. "Look who's gotten all high and mighty," she hissed.

"News flash, Amelia, Mitchell rules this town. Not you. You are nothing."

Erin cleared her throat. The look on her face clearly said she was struggling to stay strong. Her mark was still showing and Amelia now knew how important it was for her to stay hidden, so when she spoke, drawing the attention to herself, Amelia's whole body went cold, and she visibly shuttered. "Hey, Fiona, you're getting pretty careless. Bet you're wondering how you missed her heart thumping away." Fiona's horrifying eyes focused back on Amelia and she could see the exact moment that Fiona realized what Erin was saying. "Isn't it funny how the bite changes everything? So if you didn't notice her that must mean you want to hurt her. Mitchell probably heard everything you just said, too. Better run home and pack your bags. You are so done here."

Without warning, Fiona charged at Amelia, fangs bared, and for a quick second she thought she was going to die, but just as quickly, tiny Jessica charged, pinning Fiona against the wall. Erin and Amber screamed. Fiona flailed, kicking and struggling, and Amelia stood still, frozen. "Fiona," Jessica snapped, her voice low and deadly. "Stop struggling. I have three hundred years on you. You don't stand a chance." Fiona thrashed about for another second and then she went limp, fangs folding back into her gums, and eyes returning back to a golden hue, which was of little comfort. Jessica kept a firm grip around her neck and glanced over her shoulder at Amelia. "She will be dealt with, Amelia. You have my word."

Amelia nodded, unable to do anything else, and watched as Jessica escorted Fiona out of the washroom, Amber running along behind them.

Once the door was shut and Erin pulled in a few shaky breaths, she asked, "You okay?"

"Just fine."

"Good, 'cause I have something for you that you probably won't like." Erin handed her a black rose. "Adam stopped me just as I was coming in. He said you need to go to Madame Crystal for the answers to your questions. He said that there's a way out and Madame Crystal was the only one who could help you. And he said she could tell you what happened to your parents."

Amelia took the rose, twirling it around and around, head spinning with questions. Holding it was just as bone-chilling as the look in Fiona's eyes. "Who's Madame Crystal?" she asked in a small voice.

"She a quack. Calls herself a psychic."

Amelia gave the rose one long, hard look and then tossed it in the trash. She sunk down to the floor, resting her head between her knees. "I'm not going to a psychic."

Erin crouched down in front of her and waited until Amelia finally looked up. "I think you should, Millie. She might be able to help. Fiona's after you. You keep getting these black roses and with Mitchell..." she paused to think. "I just think it couldn't hurt. Maybe she can help." She shrugged. "Besides, this could be your only chance. We've got no chaperones and with what just happened the sooner the better. So get your skinny little butt off the ground and let's go."

****

Why in the world had she agreed to this? Amelia wondered as she followed Erin up the steps towards the flashing neon signboard that read, "Witch and Psychic." Vampires, fine she could deal with it, but witches and psychics? This was crossing the line.

The morning's downpour had stopped, except for a few sprinkles, and a thick fog covered the ground, eerie and unnerving. Amelia was relieved to see the sun desperately trying to peek out from behind the clouds and she couldn't help but hope that maybe, just maybe, the sun would shine and lift away the thunderstorm that had settled over her world.

Other than the bright neon lights, the place looked normal. It was a small house in an older part of town with a white picket fence and grass green shutters on the windows. Erin went first, opening the whitewashed door. A bell chimed, announcing their arrival, and Amelia followed her in.

"Amelia Caldwell?" Madame Crystal, Amelia assumed, said. She was dressed in jeans and a T-shirt, contrary to Amelia's expectations. She was young, maybe thirty, with long, knee-length jet-black hair. "I've been expecting you. I thought you would have come sooner."

"If you're really a psychic wouldn't you have known that I wouldn't be here until today?" Amelia glanced around the bare room and noticed the pile of suitcases against the wall. There were three chairs around a rickety card table in the middle of the room, but otherwise, the house was packed up. "You going somewhere?"

"Yes, once I help you, it'll no longer be safe for me here, and your message was delayed," Madame Crystal said and took a seat at the card table. "You should have received the rose at the party. How is your head by the way?" Amelia was unnerved by the unexplained depth of her knowledge.

"Erin, we should go," Amelia said. This was nuts. This woman couldn't help her. "I changed my mind. This is a waste of time."

"Shut up, Millie," Erin snapped. "Madame Crystal, the message she got said you could help her. Can you break the bond?"

"Slow down, Erin," Madame Crystal said with a laugh. Erin was overly animated, like always. "I can't break the bond between souls, but little Amelia can."

"What the hell is that supposed to mean?" Amelia asked. She could feel the annoyance bubbling up and she took a deep breath, hoping to calm herself. The last thing she wanted was to draw Mitchell's attention and after the Fiona thing, which she was sure Jessica would be telling him about, she knew it was only a matter of time before he tuned in.

"Look deep inside, Amelia," Madame Crystal said. "You have always known you were different. It's time you learn why."

"Millie, just sit down and listen to her," Erin urged. Amelia couldn't believe that she was actually falling for this crap, but the look on Erin's face showed she was hanging onto every word.

Madame Crystal's blue eyes focused on Erin and she smiled, a sad sort of smile. "She is not the only one who needs guidance today, Erin. Please sit as well. I will start with you."

"Yes, ma'am," Erin said, and sat down, folding her hands in her lap.

Amelia couldn't believe what she was seeing. Was Erin really falling for all this? "Your life line has grown shorter since the last time we spoke, Erin. The choice you made today will come at a great cost. Trust the enemy. Your friends are not as they seem. Only your enemy can save you from yourself."

"I don't understand," Erin said, and looked over at Amelia, lost and confused.

"You will when the time comes," Madame Crystal continued. "Your friend will show you the truth and you will know what must be done. Memories can be deceiving, little one. We block what we wish not to see."

A sullen, fearful expression covered Erin's face. Amelia couldn't stand it. She needed to do something, get them out of there. She marched over to Erin, grabbed her hand, and pulled her off the chair. "Erin, don't listen to her crap. Come on, let's just go."

"Your parents' death was not an accident," Madame Crystal said softly, and Amelia stopped. "Have you ever wondered why you were not killed?"

Amelia whirled around, glaring daggers at the 'so called' psychic and yelled, "You don't know anything about my parents!"

Madame Crystal was unfazed by her outburst. She kept

her eyes focused and the sad smile on her lips. "Oh, but I do. You were tied to a chair, bound and gagged, and forced to watch while a man stabbed them. He left you to watch as they bled out onto the floor. Why did he leave you alive?"

Erin's hand went cold and clammy in her grip and Amelia shot her a look, making sure she was okay, before she answered, "He said it wasn't my time yet."

"Why not?"

"Shouldn't you already know that?" Amelia spat. All the painful memories were suffocating. She'd spent years trying to figure out why he hadn't just killed her. Terrified that he would come back to finish the job. It had taken years for her to accept that he was a psychopath. There was no other explanation. She wanted to leave, get out of there and never see this woman again, but she just couldn't move. There was some part of her that needed to hear more. Erin must have noticed because she pulled Amelia over to the table, pulled out a chair, and they both sat down.

"I do. Your parents were sacrificed in order to bring you to Mitchell."

"Are you telling me he had something to do with their deaths?" Amelia asked, but all the fight had left her voice. It wasn't possible. He wasn't there. And there was no way that Amelia would believe he would do something that horrible, not to her, she was sure of it. "Mitchell wouldn't do that."

"All the guilt and anger," Madame Crystal said. Erin squeezed Amelia's hand to reassure her. "It's black and dangerous, Amelia. You need to control your temper."

"Control my temper? You've got to be kidding me. You sit here and act like you just told me some wonderful insight to my parents' death. Am I supposed to be impressed? It wouldn't take much to find out how they died or that I was there. It was all over the news. You're just some fake." Amelia tried to stand up, but Erin firmly held her in place and gave her a pleading look. She didn't want to hear this. It was all too close to the truth and Amelia had fought too hard to forget.

"Amelia, I know how hard this must be for you to hear, but we really do not have time for you to wallow in self-pity. Think about it. When did the dreams start?"

"The night before they died."

"Their death was all part of a plan to get you with Mitchell. You're in grave danger, Amelia. Now that he has found you, the time is coming for your reunion with the killer. Your only chance to stop it is for you to accept what you are: a witch. Now that you are eighteen, you can access your gifts."

A rush of heat settled into Amelia's cheeks and she gritted her teeth. "Are you completely insane?" she uttered, her rising anger just waiting to erupt. She bolted up from her chair, shoving it back and letting it clatter to the floor. "There's no such thing as witches!" Amelia reached out to Erin, grabbing her wrist and yanking her to her feet. "We're leaving."

"I cannot let you do that, Amelia," Madame Crystal whispered.

Suddenly, a violent shock surged through Amelia's hand, as if she had grabbed hold of an electric fence, and she dropped her grip on Erin. Out of the corner of her eye, a glimmer of light drew her attention. Amelia gasped. A halo of bright, golden light striped out in ribbons from the psychic. Before her eyes, Amelia watched dumbfounded, as a pistol formed in Madame Crystal's hand, and she pointed it menacingly at Erin.

"Neither of you are leaving," the psychic hollered, hand trembling around the gun. "You will not survive this if you do not listen to what I must tell you."

"What the hell are you doing?" Amelia shrieked.

"I'm sorry, but you need to accept what you are," Madame Crystal said, her voice shaky.

"Millie," Erin whispered, "Just do what she says." Amelia glanced at Erin's fear-stricken form, the gun just inches away from her head.

Amelia took a deep breath. "Put the gun down," she said in a deathly undertone. "I swear if you hurt her, I'll have every vamp in town after you in a flash."

Madame Crystal laughed nervously, turned the gun onto Amelia, and pulled the trigger. The world around Amelia seemed to freeze at the metallic click of the bullet leaving the chamber of the gun. Before she knew what she was doing, a burst of steaming energy settled in her stomach and in a split second she yelled, "Immobilize!"

Erin screamed. Amelia pushed on the hot energy that had gathered in the pit of her stomach and watched as it shot out in a rainbow of colors towards the bullet. The air around the silver bullet pieced together, as if building up a wall, and the bullet's velocity slowed, before clattering to the hard wood floor. Amelia dropped to her knees panting.

Madame Crystal sighed in relief and smiled wide. "I'm sorry to go to this extreme, but we really didn't have time to use a more conventional method of drawing out your power."

"Holy shit," Erin breathed.

Madame Crystal ignored her and pushed on. "There is much I need to tell you, but we have a lot of work to do first. Mitchell is a good man, but he has no control when it comes to you. His love blinds him. You need to block him out. You may be able to break the bond later if you choose, but that will take work. For now, we will need to block his connection."

Amelia pulled herself off the floor, snagged the chair that she'd knocked over, and plopped down. "I'm not a witch," she said, but even to her own ears it didn't sound believable. She could feel a sudden burst of energy coursing through her veins. It was comforting, like warm tea with honey. It reached from her toes to her fingertips. She'd felt it once before, on her eighteenth birthday, but she'd brushed it off, thinking it was just the flu.

"Millie?" Erin called and gave her shoulder a little shake.

Amelia didn't respond, she just kept her eyes fixed on

Madame Crystal, searching her face for answers. "We do not have time for you to get used to this information," Madame Crystal said. She got up from the table and disappeared through a doorway, returning a minute later with a small clear bag. She pulled out a white candle, set it on the table, and lit a match. "The white candle is for purity of mind." She held the match to the wick and the candle came to life, flickering in a high flame, and then settling to a soft and steady glow. Then she pulled out a bundle of dried leaves and set them alight. She blew out the flame and let them smolder. "We will burn the sage to cleanse your spirit. Breathe deeply and let it work."

Before she knew it, Amelia was breathing in, deep full breaths of the bittersweet smoke. The herb spoke to her and her body tingled with pleasure. She could feel the light shooting out in little sparks from her fingertips. "I can't do this," she whispered in between a lungful of the cleansing herb.

"You must. It is the only way to keep Mitchell safe. The less he knows, the safer you both shall be. He will understand when the time comes. Now repeat after me." Madame Crystal took her free hand, Erin clenched the other, and Amelia repeated the phrase word for word.

"Single candle burning bright, shield my mind with your light. Let my thoughts be private once more, cleanse my spirit to its core. So I ask. So it shall be."

"Did it work?" Erin asked as soon as the last words left Amelia's lips.

"I don't know. I can still feel him, but he's…" Amelia paused, closed her eyes, and reached out to him; a rush of panic left her breathless. His thoughts were jumbled, scared. And then he confirmed it. Mitchell couldn't feel her and he thought… she was dead. Her cell phone rang, ear piercing loud, and all three of them jumped.

"Turn it off, Amelia," Madame Crystal said. "Don't answer. We don't have much time. Your bond with him is stronger than most because of your powers. It is also what has made you so conflicted." Amelia hesitated and she stared at his name flashing on the call display. He was so scared, so worried, it took every ounce of willpower she had to ignore the call and turn off her phone.

Madame Crystal continued, "You must leave before they find you here. There is danger in your future. Many wish you harm and will seek to destroy you. The one you love most will be the cause of your death. But be warned, he is also the only one who can save you. Revenge is for the weak. When the time comes, you will need to forget the past and forgive those who have harmed you. Only then will you be able to forgive yourself. If you choose to be weak, you will sacrifice those you love. Now go. Take these books and learn the craft. Your life depends on it." She shoved a stack of old journals into Amelia's hands and pushed her and Erin towards the door. "You were never here. He must not know that I helped you sever the link. Please understand if Mitchell finds out I am the one who helped you, my time here will end."

"Wait," Amelia gasped as she was shoved out the door onto the porch. "What does all that mean? What about Mitchell? Will the spell wear off? When will the link come back? Why can I still feel him?"

"All your questions will be answered in time. Now go." The door was closing on Amelia's face and she shoved her foot in just in time to stop it.

"But what do I tell him? What if I don't want to keep him out?" Amelia asked frantically.

"Look inside yourself, Amelia. When you are ready, you will know how to bring him back. Now please go. I must leave before it is too late for me. Be safe and trust only those who are worthy."

Amelia moved her foot and the door slammed. She stood there, staring at the closed door until she heard the engine of a car rumble to life. A white Honda sped around the back of the house, and squealed onto the road, Madame Crystal at the wheel.

CHAPTER 25

"Did you really shut him out?" Erin asked, as the taillights of the Honda disappeared around a bend in the road.

"Yes." Amelia was shaking. She was trying to wrap her head around the impossibility of what just transpired. But as impossible as it was, she knew deep in her heart, it was all true.

"You're a witch." Erin took Amelia's hand, lacing their fingers together. "I'm probably going to sound crazy, but I didn't believe in witches. Weird, huh? I can handle vampires, but this witch thing is just... I don't know." She was rambling and she was trembling. Amelia could feel it vibrating through her like a plane in turbulence.

"I know." What else could she say? She'd thought the exact same thing. Her head was swimming and Mitchell—Mitchell was about to send out a hunting party. She could hear him rallying the troops. Jessica was there. Amelia closed her eyes, trying to piece together what she was seeing. His thoughts were broken and hard to piece together. It took her a few minutes to figure out what was going on. Fiona had gotten away. Mitchell thought Fiona had killed her.

Amelia dropped her bag. Keeping a tight grip on Erin's

hand, she crouched down and fished through her bag for her phone. She found it, switched it on, and called Mitchell. He answered on the first ring. "Amelia?" His voice sounded frantic.

"I'm okay, Mitch," Amelia said. An overwhelming flush of relief washed over her, warming her cold and trembling fingers. He was silent, and she could feel him pushing against the link, trying to feel her. "I'm coming home," she continued. "Call off your hunt. I'm okay." She hung up before he could say anything else.

"What's happening?" Erin asked.

Amelia was numb. It was as if her body was shutting down. She could feel the chaos and her brain was trying to convince her that her world was ending, but she just couldn't bring herself to care. "Erin, I need you to take me home." Something had changed in her and it was as if her emotions had been turned off.

"Is that a good idea?" Amelia looked at Erin, who appeared like a scared little child. Her eyes wide and red from unshed tears, her normally tanned complexion white as paper. When did this happen? Erin was the strong one. She usually had no fear or at least hid it well. And then, Amelia suddenly realized that even though she could see how terrified Erin was she just didn't care. Her friend— maybe her only friend—was terrified and she didn't care.

"Yes," Amelia answered, a blank expression on her face, matching her lifeless sense of self. She dropped Erin's hand, walked to the car, and climbed in. Erin hesitated, and for a minute, Amelia thought she wasn't going to follow, but then she grabbed Amelia's bag and the journals that Amelia had dropped and got into the car.

They didn't speak during the ten-minute drive to Amelia's house. Neither of them knew what to say and the silence was peaceful. It gave Amelia time to figure out what to do next. She didn't know what would happen when she got home. Now that Mitchell knew she was okay his anger grew black. He was sure that she'd done something, but he didn't know what it was.

Amelia made Erin drop her off at the gate. She didn't want to risk Erin, especially since every vampire in town had been called and were all at her house. Amelia promised to call her later, shoved the journals in her backpack, shouldered it, and went off to face the music.

As soon as she reached the driveway, Amelia felt Mitchell pick up her scent and suddenly, he was in front of her, wrapping her in his arms, kissing her cheek, forehead, and every inch of her face. She let him examine her from head to toe and when she felt that he was sure she was okay, she took a step back. "The bond isn't broken. I can still feel everything." Then she turned away and headed for the house, Mitchell trailing behind her.

You can still hear me? he asked silently.

"Yes," she replied. "And don't ask me how because I don't know." Amelia climbed the steps and reached the front door. She was just about to turn the doorknob when he stopped her, holding her tightly to his chest.

His voice sounded cold and broken. "You're lying to me, Amelia. You know exactly what happened. You may have blocked me from your mind, but I have your blood in my system and you hold my soul. I can hear the frantic beating of your heart and you always hold your breath when you lie."

Mitchell's lips trailed along her neck and his fangs came down scraping against her skin. "You will not bite me," she murmured and closed her eyes. He licked her neck, sending a tantalizing chill down her spine. *Damn him!* She didn't want to feel this way. But every part of her body was yearning for him. And it chilled her that part of her actually wanted him to bite her.

"You're mine." His lips vibrated against her sensitive skin as he spoke. She could feel herself relaxing into him, and her body was calling to him. She was about to take it back and tell him to do it when he continued, "I can do what I want with you and it's time that you learn that." His lips continued to trail along her jaw to her ear. "If you try to fight me, we'll just see how much of the bond you were able to destroy. Are you willing to see if the pain is gone?"

"You should be happy," Amelia said, the image of Fiona popping to her mind, giving her a newfound strength. "Now that I've blocked you out you're free to play with Fiona."

He was turning into the monster. Amelia could feel his black anger swirling with red-hot rage. His fangs pressed against her neck, the pressure increasing, and she could feel the pinch. *He's enjoying this*, she realized, disgusted. He was trying to do it slowly so she could feel his fangs slide into her skin. He wanted it to hurt. He was trying to teach her a lesson.

Amelia stiffened. Every muscle in her body wound tight. Her anger was taking over and mixing with his. She could feel a burst of warm energy building in the pit of her stomach, yearning to be set free. It was waiting with anticipation, building bigger and stronger, waiting to explode like a loaded gun. She focused her mind on it, pulling it all together into a bullet of white fire. She pictured a gun, the blazing bullet in the chamber, and pulled the trigger.

Mitchell let go and Amelia watched as he crashed through the door, breaking it off its hinges, and slid into the house, across the foyer floor. He jumped up in a blur, crimson eyes blazing, and in a flash, he was grabbing her again. Amelia closed her eyes and focused on the heat, and like a flash of lightening, Mitchell was back on the floor, crashing into the wall.

A collective gasp hissed through the room like a nest of rattlesnakes signaling an attack. Amelia's eyes snapped open, and she was oddly undisturbed by the frightening sight before her. Every vampire in town stood behind Mitchell, fangs flashing and eyes blazing. A few of them advanced on her. Mitchell was staring at her as if she had six heads and had grown snakes for hair. For a moment, Amelia thought he was going to let them attack her and she pulled on the energy, preparing herself for a fight.

Amelia could feel the drain and knew she wasn't strong enough to hold off the ones moving in on her. She looked at Mitchell, pleading with her eyes, and held her breath. Would he call them off? Would he let them kill her? His aura was shifting faster than her vision could register and she could tell that there wasn't one stable emotion in him.

It was a surreal feeling, watching her life flash before her eyes. Her mother's smile, her father's voice, and Mitchell. The first time they kissed. The first time he said, "I love you." All the laughter, all the love, it surrounded her, lifting her up, keeping her strong. The thoughts filled her heart with sunshine, and flowers, and kittens, and everything wonderful and beautiful. How could memories of him bring her strength? *Because he's you,* a voice in her head whispered. *He's your other half. He's your light. He's what makes you whole.*

Amelia shoved the thoughts from her mind. She wouldn't use his strength against him. She just couldn't. She felt squeezed, as if she were being pushed from all sides at once, as Mitchell tried to get in and take control. Amelia kept her gaze on him. If Madame Crystal was right, Mitchell would be the cause of her death, and there was no doubt in Amelia's mind that she was right. But she wouldn't go without a fight.

"Mitchell," Amelia said in a strong voice. "It's about time that you know what it feels like to have no control." The air around her shimmered, like diamonds in the light, as she spoke the words, and before she knew what she was doing, Mitchell screamed out. It was a scream so bone-chilling and ear splintering that the windows shook.

Amelia tried to pull back the light. It was soaring from her, sparkling and shifting like a kaleidoscope. What was she doing? She needed to stop it. She hadn't meant to hurt him, not like this.

Someone touched her shoulder. "Millie, you need to stop," Angelle said in her ear, scared and sad. "You're killing him."

Killing him? Amelia could see it now. She could see the little sparks igniting over his skin and the smell of burning flesh drifted to her nose. A part of her, a very small part, wanted to let him die. Madame Crystal's voice rang out, "Revenge is for the weak."

"Stop," Mitchell gasped. His voice, small and scared, spoke clearly to her heart, urging her to help him. Amelia blinked, shook herself like a wet dog shaking off water from its coat, and watched as the flecks of red from his eyes faded, turning back to the glorious color of a clear, blue sky.

Mitchell was looking at her as if he had never seen her before. *Why?* He sent the question silently and it made her feel sick. Amelia knew what he meant. She knew he was not asking why she hurt him, he understood that. He wanted to know why she would try and kill him, and that, that she couldn't answer. Amelia looked at him for an interminable minute. Everyone else in the room faded; for that minute, it was just the two of them.

Amelia took in a deep cleansing breath, and let her gaze focus on each vampire individually. "I'm going to my room," she said, surprised at the authority in her voice, and even more surprised at the horrified looks on their faces. Was she the monster now? "I suggest you tend to him since you can all see I'm more than capable of looking after myself." Amelia turned on her heels, head held high, and glided down the hallway.

"Millie," Angelle called after her.

Amelia looked back, a quick glance over her shoulder. "Take care of him for me." Angelle nodded and then Amelia slid into her room, shutting and locking the door behind her.

CHAPTER 26

"This is a waste of time," Amelia said crabbily and tossed another journal to the floor. Two dreadful days had passed since she almost accidentally (she thought) tried to kill Mitchell. He hadn't come to see her and she couldn't blame him.

Somehow, she'd managed to lock herself in her room—literally. It was some kind of magic, that much they had figured out but what kind no one knew. The doors opened, the windows opened, but no matter what they tried, Amelia couldn't get out and no one could get in. It was as if there were an invisible dividing wall of thick plastic enveloping the room. Anywhere she pushed, it would sag, then spring back into place.

"Don't worry, sweetie," Angelle said. She was standing at the door patting down the wall, determination plastered on her face, as she tried to find a weak point. "We'll figure this out."

"Hey, Angelle," Eric called from the terrace, pretending to help, but in truth he really wasn't doing much. Amelia didn't care because she swore his laughter was the only thing keeping her remotely sane. "You're getting good at that mime impersonation. I bet I could rent you out for parties."

Angelle shot him a look. "You're such a dumb-ass."

Amelia glanced over at Angelle and she burst into a sidesplitting laugh. Angelle really did look like a mime, especially with all the drywall powder caked on her face—her thought that taking out a wall might work proved incorrect. The laugh earned her a nasty look from Angelle, and a skin-tingling chuckle from Eric. "Will you guys shut up?" Amelia said, trying her best to sound annoyed and cover-up how ridiculously funny her friend looked. "Trying to focus here." She snagged another one of the journals from Madame Crystal and pretended to read.

"Don't be such a killjoy," Eric said. "You've gotta admit she's gifted." Amelia giggled again and he winked. "You could be part of the act, too, Millie. You could use your witchy talents and put her in an invisible box. Then all we'd have to do is sit back and watch her try and get out. Easy peasy. The cash will just roll in."

"Totally throwing a wrench into your plans," Angelle said. "You're so not renting us out." Musical laughter floated from her lips. She grabbed a wrench from the stack of tools she'd used to knock out the wall and she chucked it through the room, straight at Eric. It connected, smacking him in the chest, and Amelia was certain she heard the dry crack of bones breaking.

"Ouch!" Eric rubbed at his chest. He pushed on a rib that was sticking out, making his black T-shirt look like a mini tent, and it crunched back into place. "Hey, cupcake, it's an expression." He was laughing, a huge grin on his face and Amelia was sure she would never get used to that. Her chest hurt just thinking about it. "Doesn't mean you literally need to throw a wrench, and you called me the dumb-ass."

"You guys are both dumb-asses," Amelia shot back. "How did you do that?" They looked at her blankly for a second. She jumped up and rushed over to the door putting her hands up feeling along the blasted wall. "The wrench! You tossed the wrench and it went through the room."

Angelle's eyes went cartoon-wide and she squealed in

delight. "This is awesome." She snatched up a hammer from the pile and slowly, she inched it into the room, holding the end tightly. The wall shimmered around the wooden handle and as Angelle's hand reached the edge of the force field, it snapped shut, chopping the handle in half. She snatched her hand back, the wood clattered to the floor, and she huffed, looking fiercely at the invisible wall as if she were trying to burn a hole in it. "That sucks."

"Mitch's gonna be super stoked. I never thought about trying to just pass something in," Eric said. He was standing on the terrace looking at the broken hammer, utterly baffled. After a moment, he gave his head a shake and grinned at Amelia, eyes twinkling with mischief. "Bet you're starving. I'm gonna make you something awesome. Be right back."

Amelia tried to object. Eric didn't have a great track record when it came to the kitchen, and the last thing they needed was another disaster. But it was no use, Eric had already vanished. "Millie, I should go tell Mitch," Angelle said, shuffling her feet back and forth. "See if he has any ideas."

"Why bother? He won't care." Amelia knew it sounded like she was pouting. She'd never admit it, but she missed him like crazy. Tuning into his thoughts didn't seem to cut it. More than anything, she wanted to see him, touch him, or just be close to him. Staying away was a deliberate attempt on his part, Amelia was sure of it, and it was like a kick in the teeth. The chain around her heart that tethered them together was pulled tight, inducing a constant, relentless tugging. She was glad that she was used to it enough now that it didn't pull her off balance anymore, but it was still maddening. The worst part was she knew without a doubt that it wouldn't stop until they were together. She'd never really believed the old saying, *Absence makes the heart grow fonder*, but to her dismay, it was another ludicrous saying that was dead on.

"Jeez, Amelia, you really need to figure out what you want from him. You told Mitch you needed time and obviously..." Angelle rapped her fist against the barrier so hard it trembled, shimmering like disturbed water. "You need it. He's really trying to give you what you want. You made your bed, now you're gonna have to lie in it."

Amelia watched, speechless, as her friend disappeared. Since talking to the stupid psychic, she'd been trying to find any possible reason she could to blame Mitchell for everything that had happened to her. Especially since he refused to come and see her. Could he really be staying away because she'd asked for time?

Amelia didn't know how long she'd been in a daze when a metallic clank brought her back. She glanced at the door and saw Lola, kicking a tray of food over the threshold. "So you're a witch." She leaned against the doorframe watching Amelia.

"Screw off, Lola." Amelia huffed and crossed her arms. "I can't deal with your crap right now."

Lola rolled her eyes. "Stop moping around and feeling sorry for yourself," she said dryly. "This poor-little-me act is pathetic. Life could be a lot worse."

Worse? How could it get worse? "Easy for you to say. Just leave me alone. You don't understand." Amelia shuffled over to her bed and plopped down. She snatched up a journal and started reading, hoping Lola would take the hint.

She didn't. "Clearly I understand." Lola pointed at her mark. "I just chose to make the best of it. Most people would kill to find their soulmate."

"Guess I'm not most people," Amelia said haughtily and shot Lola a *screw off* kind of look. Amelia didn't really mean it. In all honesty it wasn't the soulmate part that was the issue. It was his irrepressible possessiveness.

"You're tearing apart my family," Lola shouted and slammed her fist against the wall. "I'm not going to let you keep doing it. I've never seen them so taken with anyone."

"Not my fault," Amelia retorted. "I tried to leave, but he won't let me."

"You're acting like a spoiled brat. You're lucky to have

someone like Mitch. He loves you. All of this is for you."
She waved around gesturing to the house. "This is the
stupid castle from your dreams. You loved it so much that
he bought it. You need to get over yourself."

Amelia swallowed hard, fighting back the tears that were
prickling her eyes. "He doesn't love me. I'm just a vessel to
him. He needs me, but he doesn't love me." Amelia
glanced at Lola, face closed and cold. "Just leave me alone."

Lola threw up her hands, exasperated. "I really don't get
why you hate me so much." She paused and gave Amelia a
hard stare, and then she huffed. "Not that I care 'cause you
definitely are not number one on my must-be-friends list,
but I'm just trying to help you. And if you think Mitch has a
temper, you haven't seen anything yet. If you keep this crap
up, you'll be sorry."

Amelia drew in a deep breath and puffed out her chest.
"Are you threatening me?" she asked in a lethal tone.

"No, not a threat—a promise." A wicked smile
stretched out on Lola's lips. "You can't pick your family,
Amelia, remember that." Lola glared at her for a long, hard
second. "You need to figure out how to let down whatever
wall you've put up because if you keep making Mitchell
think you hate him, he might actually let you go. Is that
really what you want?"

Amelia couldn't answer. She wanted to yell, *No, that's not
what I want,* but she just wasn't ready to admit it. Not yet.
Maybe never.

Lola huffed when Amelia stayed silent and then finally
stalked away. With her gone, Amelia shut the door to her
room and then curled up in bed, burying herself in the
mounds of pillows.

She couldn't help but wonder if she would ever be able
to really love Mitchell again, love him like she did in the
dreams. She wanted to love him. Everything in her yearned
for him. But he was a different person now. And so was
she. Back when it had all been just a dream, when the
unstable emotions of the bond hadn't been affecting them, it

had been perfect. *Well, almost perfect,* Amelia thought. *Aside for the just a dream part.*

Amelia let her mind drift, recalling her favorite dream with Mitchell, the dream when she realized how much she loved him.

Something covered her eyes, soft and silky. Her heart pounded in her chest painfully fast with a mix of excitement and fear. Had she fallen asleep? She wasn't sure. The last thing she remembered, she'd been sitting on her new bed, in her new foster home reading a book.

If she'd fallen asleep then maybe… "Mitchell," Amelia called.

"I'm right here, love," he whispered in her ear, his warm breath sending shivers down her spine. Amelia sucked in a breath, filling her lungs with his sweet, tangy scent. Her heartbeat became erratic and butterflies filled her stomach.

"Why do I have a blindfold on?" Amelia asked, leaning back against his muscled chest. A warm, tingling sensation filled her body from the touch.

"Because I have a surprise for you." His voice, deep and velvety, wrapped around her and her knees went weak. His soft lips brushed against her cheek and he chuckled softly. "Do you want to see the surprise?" he whispered against her cheek.

Amelia couldn't make her voice work so she nodded her head and the silky blindfold vanished. She gasped, not believing what stood before her. "The castle from the story Mom used to read me," she breathed, taking it all in. The stone clad castle, with high turrets and balconies from every window was exactly how she'd imagined it would be. "You remembered."

"Of course I remembered," he said, taking her hand and lacing his fingers through hers.

Amelia shifted her gazed from the castle to his breathtaking, sky blue eyes. His lips curved and her breath caught in her throat. "What are we doing here?" she asked, not sure of what else to say.

His smile grew wide, reaching his eyes. "I bought it for you."

Bought it? For just a second, Amelia's heart completely stopped beating. How had she gotten so lucky? She just couldn't understand. She felt as if she were floating, but all too quickly, reality came crashing in and the hard, cold truth filled her with despair; it's just a dream.

Mitchell cupped her face in his hands. "Do you love me?"

"With all my heart and soul," Amelia answered, and for the first time, she realized that she really meant it. She loved him. She loved the way he looked at her, like no one else mattered and she was the only person in the world. She loved the way his lips curved into a smile and the little creases that always showed at his eyes. She loved how he always seemed to know the right thing to say. She loved his deep, English accent, the way it cocooned her every time he spoke. And she loved the way he made her feel, the way her heart beat when he was near, the electricity she felt at his touch, and the nervous butterflies he always caused in her stomach.

Mitchell leaned forward, brushing his soft lips against hers, sweet and warm. He smiled down at her, eyes hungry. "Do you believe in soulmates, love?"

Amelia knew there was no such thing as a soulmate. She knew that this was just a dream and that he wasn't real, but she couldn't stop the words from falling from her lips. "I wish you were my soulmate."

****

The days passed by, and Amelia just let them go. She slipped into a near-catatonic state. Her friends called to her, even Lola tried to get a response, but her dazed stupor remained. Completely unresponsive. Too much had happened. Amelia had never imagined that her world could end twice in one lifetime, but in fact, her world was ending again. Overwhelmed, she let herself shut down. It was all too much. She was a witch. The love of her life was a vampire.

It was Tyler who brought her back to reality. When she heard his voice at the door, she thought she was imagining it. He couldn't be in the house. Mitchell would never have allowed it. "Millie, can I come in?" he asked, and Amelia watched in confusion as the doorknob turned and the door cracked open.

Amelia opened her mouth, and then closed it when no

sound came out. Was she dreaming? The look on Tyler's face told her he was trying not to scare her. "Mitchell asked me to check on you." He inched his way into the room. "We've all been worried about you."

The bed sagged when Tyler sat down. *This has to be a dream,* Amelia thought miserably, knowing she still hadn't figured out how to break the stupid lock on her room. She gazed at Tyler wondering why she would dream of him. Why not Mitchell? Because really, Mitchell was the only person she wanted to see, but she knew that was her fault, too. If she hadn't broken his connection, he would be here, not Tyler.

He looked tired, Amelia noticed, really tired. She reached out to touch his cheek, still not believing that he was really there, but just before her fingers touched him, a low growl rumbled through the air. Amelia snapped her head towards the door, looking for where the sound had come from.

Mitchell.

He stood in the doorway like a fallen angel, glorious and deadly. Before she gave herself time to think, Amelia was off the bed running towards him, arms open. She threw herself at him and was instantly flung back when she hit the invisible wall. Mitchell put a hand up and said, "I can't come in, love, and it looks like you still can't come out." He shook his head and looked at her with gloomy eyes. "What have you done?"

"I didn't do anything," Amelia shouted and threw herself at the door again, frustrated. The beginnings of tears settled in her throat and her voice cracked. She glanced back at Tyler and then longingly at Mitchell. "How is he even here?"

Mitchell looked at her, torn and broken. They locked eyes and Amelia desperately tried to tell him how much she loved him through the link. But with each thought she sent, she felt it bounce back, like an email undelivered.

"Millie," Tyler said, drawing her attention. "What is all

this?" He held up a stack of paper and started to read, "*There is danger in your future. Many wish you harm and will seek to destroy you. The one you love most will be the cause of your death. But be warned he is also the only one who can save you. Revenge is for the weak. When the time comes, you will need to forget the past and forgive those who have harmed you. Only then will you be able to forgive yourself. If you choose to be weak, you will sacrifice those you love.*" Tyler looked up at her, wide eyed, and then flipped through the pages. "You wrote it over and over."

"Give me that," Mitchell barked from the doorway, keeping his eyes fixed on Amelia. "You should have told me you'd had a vision, Amelia. I need to show it to Luke."

Amelia took the page and carefully passed it through the barrier, making sure she didn't touch it. She thought about telling him it wasn't a vision, but she couldn't tell him about Madame Crystal, so instead she remarked, "How could I tell you when you never bothered to come and see me?" He took the page. "Didn't you miss me at all?"

For just a second she could see how much he was hurting and his pain washed over her with such force that she staggered back. But the moment ended too soon and the steel vault closed in around his heart. With a fleeting glance, he took off in a blur of motion.

****

An hour later, Amelia and Tyler were on the floor, journals and the warning spread out in front of them. "How much do you know?" Amelia asked. She closed another journal, finding nothing that could be used to break the lock she'd accidentally placed on the room.

"Too much," he replied. "Way too much. Mitchell filled me in." He looked over at her, giving her a lopsided grin. "So, he's your soulmate."

Amelia laughed and man did it feel good. "Really? You know about vampires, you know I'm a witch, and you picked up on the fact that I have a soulmate?"

Tyler shrugged. "I was kinda hoping I had a chance with you. That piece of info seemed important."

Wow. Amelia knew he liked her, but really, that was important? Tyler was cute and sweet, and for a quick second Amelia wondered what it would be like to be with him, forget about Mitchell and run away with Tyler. A blush crept into her cheeks and he chuckled. She began flipping through another journal. "I just don't get it," Amelia said, frustrated, eager to change the subject. "How were you able to come in?"

Tyler closed the journal he was looking through and leaned back on his elbows. "Maybe we're looking at this wrong." He took the warning and started reading it again. "I'm guessing Mitchell is the one who will cause your death and the one who can save you. Maybe this whole lock down has something to do with self-preservation. Maybe I could get in 'cause I'm not a threat."

"I think he's right," Mabel said, and both Tyler and Amelia spun around. "Obviously, I'm not a threat either." She ventured into the room balancing a tray of sandwiches and sodas. "I thought you guys might be hungry." She set the tray down on the coffee table and perched on the edge of one of the chairs in front of the fireplace.

"Mabel!" Amelia squealed. She bolted up from the floor and smothered the older woman in hugs. "What are you doing here?"

Mabel laughed and hugged her tightly. "Mitchell called me. He's very worried about you, dear." She kissed Amelia's forehead and then pried her off giving her a motherly look. "Both of you eat up." She gestured to the tray of sandwiches. "I think it's time that someone tells you about Derek."

Amelia stood in front of her like a rock, refusing to move or to eat. She could tell by Mabel's expression that whatever she had to say it wasn't something that she was going to like.

Mabel must have seen the stubborn expression because she smiled, a distant smile, and said, "Derek was marked for

Angelle. Did you read the book Eric gave you?"

"Um, yeah," Amelia answered. "But there was no ending. It just stopped after the bite explanation."

Mabel nodded. "The book was written by Derek and Lola," she explained. "After Derek died, Lola couldn't finish it. It was a great loss for our family."

"How," Amelia choked on the words. She swallowed and tried again. "How did he die?"

"Take a seat and eat your sandwich, dear. You too, Tyler, and I'll start from the beginning." Mabel crossed her ankles and folded her hands in her lap, waiting for them to comply. For a moment, Amelia thought about crossing her arms, jutting out her lip, and refusing to eat, but then she looked at the peanut butter and jam sandwiches, her belly rumbled, and she realized she couldn't remember the last time she ate. She sat on the other chair, snagged a sandwich, and wolfed it down. Tyler followed her lead and popped open a can of soda.

Mabel waited until Amelia finished her first sandwich and started into the second before she continued with her story. "Angelle found Derek by accident. In that life, you were a barmaid. Angelle was helping Mitchell track you down. They had tracked you to a small pub just outside of Scotland, but when they arrived, you had already moved on."

"This isn't my first life…" Amelia breathed, not as a question, but a statement.

Mabel shook her head. "You have an old soul. It's a little different for supernatural beings. As a witch, you're blessed to always come back to the same family. You have always looked the same, had the same parents, everything about you stays the same in every lifetime."

"That's awesome," Tyler said, but Amelia wasn't so sure.

Mabel smiled and continued with her tale. "When Angelle and Mitchell got to the pub they found Derek instead. Sadly, vampires were more than he could handle. He was terrified of her. It broke her heart."

"So she bit him," Amelia said. "He's the one who said the bond was a curse."

Mabel nodded, a short bob of the head. "Angelle thought that biting him would bring them closer together. She had hoped that with the increased link between them he would see that she wasn't a monster. But young Derek was very stubborn." Mabel paused, drawing in a breath. "I told you once that there is a fine line between love and hate."

Amelia snagged a soda and took a few long gulps, giving herself time to think before she said, "I remember."

"Sometimes it's so thin you can't see the difference. The bite gives the vampire more of an edge because they already have the power to manipulate our minds. In most cases we're the weaker species, but I don't think that's entirely true with you." Mabel beamed at Amelia with pride. "I don't understand the magic behind it, but it has something to do with our blood mixing with theirs—this links any human to them, but with the soul bond ..." she sighed and her eyes glistened. "Angelle realized her mistake and turned him into a vampire, her equal, to stop his suffering. But after the change, he couldn't accept what she had forced him to become and his hatred grew. In the end, Derek killed himself."

"But he'll come back, right?" Amelia asked. "Maybe he'll be okay with it next time."

Mabel stayed quiet for a moment and Amelia took another sip of her soda, letting the sugary syrup soothe her fears. When Mabel finally spoke, breaking the tense silence, her voice was distant, as if fighting against an unbearable pain. "No, he won't. Humans come back because we have souls. Our souls stay intact in death. For a vampire, it's different. Their souls leave them and find their mates. Since Angelle is a vampire, when his soul found her it joined together and ended the circle." Mabel reached over and took Amelia's hand, eyes glittering with tears.

"Are you saying that the only way to break our connection is for me to become a vampire and then one of us has to die?" It couldn't be true. There had to be another way. Then an idea came to her. Did she even want to break it? She couldn't imagine what life would be like without Mitchell.

Mabel must have seen Amelia's inner conflict and she squeezed her hand reassuringly. "What I'm telling you is that Derek's the only one who managed to break the bond and it didn't turn out so good for him." She searched Amelia's face. "Do you hate Mitchell so much that you could not spend your life with him?"

"I don't hate him," Amelia said, amazed at the passion in her voice.

Mabel sighed, a long, gusty sound. "Then you fear him."

"What if she's not scared of him?" Tyler said and both women shot him a look. Amelia had been so involved in the story that she'd completely forgotten he was there. He put up his hands. "Just hear me out. You almost killed Mitchell, right? So what about the other part of the warning? The revenge is for the weak part. What if you're doing this so you won't hurt him?"

"Do you really think it's that simple?" Amelia asked.

Tyler shrugged, stood up, and paced, thinking. "Maybe this whole warning is about you accepting Mitchell. Maybe the death part is you becoming a vampire. It would make sense you know. He kills you, but then he also saves you by changing you." He shot a questioning look at Mabel. "Vampires are the undead, right?"

"You're a very bright young man," Mabel said, getting up from her chair and walking towards the door. "I think we need to let Millie have some time to think. Please bring the tray with you, Tyler. You can help me clean up."

"Wait." Amelia jumped up from the chair and rushed forward. "Don't go. Please, don't leave me in here alone."

"Amelia, you have the power to leave whenever you wish," Mabel said wisely. "As the prophecy said, look inside yourself. You will know what you need to do."

Tyler picked up the tray and collected the dirty dishes,

stacking them up. "Ty, don't go!" Amelia pleaded.

Tyler grinned, and his eyes sparkled with amusement. "Don't worry, Millie, I'm not leaving. Mitchell moved me into one of the guest rooms until you get better. Your house is sick." He elbowed her in the ribs and winked. "Take your time figuring all this out. I don't mind hanging around."

Amelia shot him a look that she hoped said she was not impressed. She must have missed the mark because he laughed and left the room.

Amelia glared at the door. *It's not fair,* a voice in her head shrieked. Being a witch really wasn't helping much. Shouldn't she be able to wiggle her nose, point a finger, and get out like Sabrina the Teenage Witch? She tried, embarrassing herself at the absurdity of the sight—the nose wiggling didn't work.

Amelia was just about to give up when the ear-piercing ring of her cell phone went off; she rocketed upward, a good foot off the ground.

Shaking off the jitters, she let out a nervous giggle and went in search for her phone. On the fifth ring, she found it under the masses of pillows on her bed and answered it just in time. "Hello," she squeaked, breathlessly.

"I've been calling you for days," Erin's panicked voice blasted through the phone. "Pack a bag. I'm coming to get you. You need to get out of town, *fast.*"

"Take a breath, Erin. What's wrong with you?" Amelia perched on the edge of her bed.

"I can't explain. You just need to trust me. You're in serious danger and you've gotta get as far away from here as you can," Erin blurted in a frantic frenzy.

The hairs on the back of Amelia's neck rose and a biting chill encased her skin. "You're not making any sense." She glanced back at the door and a flood of scorching fury washed over her. "And I can't leave. I kinda locked myself in my room."

"Unlock the stupid door and get ready," Erin snapped.

Amelia wished it was that simple. She gritted her teeth and put all her energy into calming down, because she really didn't want to snap at her friend. "That's not what I meant. It's some kinda magic. I can't get out and none of the vamps can get in." She knew she sounded bitter, but she was pretty sure she earned the right to be.

"Shit," Erin puffed.

Amelia heard something that sounded like glass shatter over the line. "What's got you so freaked?" she asked cautiously.

Erin ignored her. The line was so silent that Amelia was sure that the connection had been lost. She was just about to check the screen when Erin said, "I guess that's actually kinda perfect."

Amelia couldn't hold it in any longer. "Erin!" she yelled. "Tell me what's going on."

"I can't explain just please don't leave your room until you hear from me. I'm really sorry, but please believe me… I didn't know. But I promise I'll fix this." The words came out in a tear soaked stream.

"Fix what? What's going on?" Amelia yelled, but it was too late, Erin was gone, and the wretched beeping of the cut-off call was all that was left.

****

Hours passed by and Amelia watched helplessly as the sun set and the darkened sky came alight with glittering stars. A shooting star streaked by, and she closed her eyes to make a wish.

"Amelia," Mitchell said from the doorway, and she turned around. She hadn't heard him and wondered how long he'd been standing there. Her heart fluttered, skipping and jumping, and she felt the now familiar tug, urging her to go to him. Was she just getting used to him? A week ago she would have known he was coming. It was distressing to think that they might be drifting further apart.

Amelia smiled, lighting up like a spotlight, but he kept his expression serious, nearly blank. "I talked to Mabel," he said. "I've done a lot of thinking on this. I just want you to know that if you really want to break the bond, if you really don't want to be with me…"

"Mitch, it's not…" Amelia cut him off and took a small step towards him. She'd never felt so helpless before. He needed her and she couldn't get to him and it was all her fault.

His frown deepened. "Just let me finish." He looked so miserable that it broke her heart and a sting burned at her eyes. "You know what happened to Derek and Angelle. Well, I could change you if you want and once you're a vampire, I'll sacrifice myself. I'll do that for you, if it's what you want."

"Mitch…?" Amelia couldn't believe what she was hearing, and for a second she was blinded by a flash of red-hot rage. Did he really believe she wanted him dead?

"You don't need to say anything," he sighed. "I just want you to know that I'll do it for you. Think about it, love." He smiled a small, sad smile and then turned his back on her.

The anger bubbled up, boiling over. Amelia's face felt hot, and her neck and her entire body, as if she'd been consumed by flames. They licked up the back of her neck, flickering hotter and hotter. "This isn't as black and white as you're trying to make it, Mitch," she seethed through clenched teeth. "You just don't get it."

Mitchell kept his back to her and said, "I get it." She could hear him take a few deep breaths and his aura started to flicker, gray, darker, darker, black. "We bring out the worst in each other. Look at us. I broke Eric's neck. I wanted to kill Tyler." The blue veins in his neck bulged and he balled his fists. "I can't control myself when it comes to you. And you… You almost killed me."

"I don't want to live without you." The words seemed so wrong and so right. With everything they'd been through in the last few weeks, Amelia had let all the anger drag her down, but she genuinely meant it, unable to conceive of not having him.

Mitchell spun around, eyes blazing, and Amelia gasped as his fangs popped down. He smashed his fist against the barrier that kept them apart. "And you obviously don't want to live with me." The words were snarled.

"Dammit," Amelia yelled. "We're supposed to be a team," she raged. "Stop trying to make all the damn decisions. Did you ever think, just for a second, if you had asked me what I wanted it may have been different? You took the choice away from me. You forced all this on me. I'm sorry if I'm not handling it well, but what the hell did you expect?"

Mitchell softened, and his eyes slowly changed back to blue, fangs disappearing. "I expected you to love me as much as I love you." Then, before she could say anything else, he was gone.

Amelia ran after him, bouncing off the wall, which shuddered on impact. She banged her fist against it until bruises started to show and her arms were too weak to keep going. Amelia racked her brain trying to figure out why she couldn't leave, to locate the missing pieces. She'd forgiven him, forgiven all of them. She'd accepted him. She'd chanted, lit candles, tried everything, but nothing worked. What good was it to be a witch if she couldn't even get out of her own room?

Her head hurt. Her whole body hurt, and exhaustion weighted her down. Mentally, emotionally, and physically. Amelia leaned against the stupid invisible wall, cursing under her breath. She sunk down to the floor and rested her chin on her knees, staring blankly out the glass doors into the night.

She was missing something, but what was it? What was stopping her from getting out? Madame Crystal had said that when the time came she would know what to do. If this wasn't the time, then when? How much longer would she have to be stuck in here and away from him?

Amelia closed her eyes and the tears slid down her face, soaking into her already sweat dampened T-shirt and she let her mind drift to Mitchell. He was in the library with her family—they really were her family—and she smiled at the thought. Even Tyler was there. They were all working together, peacefully, trying to find an answer to the question that none of them knew. "Mitchell, you need to think this out," Tyler was saying. They were looking at each other as if they'd been friends for years. *When had that happened?* "I don't think Millie wants you to die. Didn't you see the way she lit up when you were at the door? If that's not love, man, I don't know what is."

"I just don't know if there are any other options," Mitchell said. He sounded tired as if he'd already tried everything else. "If we keep this up, we'll end up killing each other."

Amelia heard something, a banging, or knocking, and she was jerked out of Mitchell's thoughts, back to the lonely room. Her prison. She glanced around, thinking Mabel had come in, but there was no one. She was still alone.

She was just about to let herself drift back to Mitchell when a motion light flicked on just outside her door. The banging came again; a soft thud, thud, thud and Amelia darted up from the floor. There was something, a ball of some sort, bouncing off the French doors. She couldn't make it out and she ventured over, swinging them open.

It took Amelia a lengthy minute to figure out what she was seeing. The thing hanging from the balcony above was so beaten up it was almost unrecognizable. It was the blonde pigtails that finally made Amelia's brain register what it was—Erin, dangling from a rope. She was gagged, hog tied, and bleeding from so many different places that there was barely any trace of skin through the red smears.

"Erin!" Amelia cried and rushed forward, despite her horror at the sight before her.

CHAPTER 27

A surge of hot power sparked in her veins and Amelia hit the barrier at a sprint. She didn't know if she could get out, but she had to try. When she hit the wall, it was as if she were wrapped in plastic wrap and she couldn't breathe. It closed in around her, sagging and straining against her and like elastic, it tried to shoot her back in.

Erin was trying to tell her something, but Amelia couldn't hear it through the gag. Her voice was coming out in spurts of mumbled, distorted sounds.

Suddenly, like a bubble bursting, Amelia crashed onto the terrace in a crumpled heap. She scurried around, pulling herself up, and lunged for Erin.

Erin's muffled and choked voice was barely audible and Amelia fought with the gag that had been tied and duct taped in place. It seemed to take forever before she was able to get it off and when she did, Erin shrieked, "Run, Millie! It's a trap."

Amelia was struggling with the ropes that bound Erin's legs and arms and was about to tell her to stop moving, when, right at that moment, something solid pounded her on the head. She staggered, then collapsed to the ground.

Erin screamed. Amelia tried to get up. Erin needed her.

Erin was in trouble.

Amelia scrambled to her feet and then everything around her went dark. A rough canvas bag was wrapped around her head. Erin was still screaming, but Amelia couldn't understand what she was saying. Someone grabbed her, tossing her over a shoulder in a fireman's carry. She kicked and pounded her fists against her attacker.

A burst of wind whipped around her as her captor picked up his pace, running, and then suddenly, Amelia was tossed onto hard-ridged plastic and the sound of metal grinding on a track slammed through her ears. Tires squealed and she rolled, crashing into the wall of the vehicle, as the driver took a turn at a speed that made it wobble, teetering on two tires before straightening back out.

Strong, cold hands grabbed her arms, and the burning pinch of a needle stabbed into her vein. Amelia tried to kick and rip her arm away, but it was no use. At that moment, she knew it was a vampire holding her down. Fiona? No, not Fiona; it was a man, she was sure of it. The hand holding onto her was too big.

A warm burst coursed into her, as whoever was holding her pushed down on the plunger injecting (God only knew what) into her. The drug took hold over her quickly and within seconds Amelia felt as if she were covered in wet, heavy tar. The hand let go of her and she tried to move her right arm, but its sudden heaviness weighted it down.

The next thing Amelia knew, she was opening her eyes. A thick, moldy garbage smell, like rotten meat, drifted up her nose, and she gagged. She tried to cover her mouth, but her hands wouldn't move. Rope rubbed tightly against her wrists. She lifted her head up. She wasn't alone.

Amelia blinked a few times. Her eyes couldn't seem to focus. One second she saw ten people, the next fifteen, and then five. No, three. There were three people. Adam, she recognized him instantly, and a flash of the party came back to her. That rancid smell; she should have known that was him.

"If you're thinking of using magic, it won't work. The drugs will keep you too disoriented for you to gather enough power," a man said. He was tall and lanky, wearing black on black. Black jeans, black shirt, black leather jacket. Even his eyes and hair were midnight black.

"Who are you?" Amelia screamed, fighting against the rope that tied her legs and arms to a wooden chair. She lost her balance and the chair flipped backwards, and she smacked her already bleeding head onto the hard concrete floor. *I'm going to have major brain damage if I don't stop hitting my head,* she thought and then fought against a building giggle. She silently scolded herself for the stupid thought and blamed it on the drugs.

Kandi stood over her, cackling, eyes blazing and fangs down. She grabbed Amelia by the hair lifting her and the chair back up. "Don't you remember him, Amelia?" she asked. "It hasn't been that long since you saw him last."

"What are you talking about?" Amelia cried. Kandi yanked at her hair again and then crouched in front of her, licking the blood off her fingers. Amelia's blood. All of a sudden, Amelia thought she was going to be sick and she sucked in a few breaths, trying to keep the rising bile down.

"Kandi," the man snapped, pulling Amelia's eyes away from the girl sucking and licking her fingers. "Step away. You'll have plenty of time to enjoy her later." Then he grabbed a chair, placing it in front of Amelia. "I'm a bit hurt that you don't remember me. Especially after all the trouble I went through to make this a spitting image of the night we met." He smiled a toothy smile and Adam and Kandi laughed. "I really thought Erin had ruined my plans when she took you to that psychic." He shrugged. "I guess she turned out to be useful after all." His eyes flashed red and his smile widened. "All your bodyguards thought you were so safe."

Amelia forced herself to look around the room. What was he talking about? Who was he? What did he want with her?

The concrete floor, cold against her feet, and the concrete walls with no windows felt suffocating. She was in an unfinished basement. To her right were scattered paintings leaning haphazardly against the walls. Bright, water-colored landscapes and oil portraits. Amelia blinked, trying to clear her blurry eyes. She felt as if she were looking through a dirty, finger-smudged glass.

Slowly the paintings came into focus. "Where did you get those?" she gasped. They were her paintings, all of them. She snapped her head around to the left and a bolt of dizziness threatened to pull her into the dark. Her easel was set up and an unfinished painting of Mitchell rested against it. It was the painting she'd been working on the night her parents had died. Across his face was a deep brownish dirt line. Blood. Her father's blood. This basement was set up exactly as her basement had been the night they died, right up to the way she was tied to the chair. The painful memories came rushing in and Amelia looked at him, really *looked* at him, and she recognized him. The man who had killed her parents.

"I think she's starting to remember," Kandi giggled, clearly enjoying Amelia's confusion and panic.

"Where's Erin?" Amelia asked. "What did you do to her? If you hurt her, I'll kill you." She felt completely discombobulated, dizzy, weak, and heavy. The man laughed and it sounded loud and drawn out. What had he given her? She felt as if she were drifting in and out. A moment of focus and then it was gone.

"Now this brings me back," he said and leaned in towards her. Close enough that Amelia could smell his sour breath. "You were more worried about your parents than yourself five years ago and now here you're tied up again and worrying about Erin."

"Leave her alone," Amelia said, trying to wiggle out of the ropes again. A pair of firm hands squeezed her shoulders, holding her in place. "Why are you doing this to me? Why now? Why didn't you just kill me then?" Amelia screamed. She felt hot and cold all at once. Nothing made sense and the damn drugs were playing with her mind. She felt a burst of power, some focus, and then dizzy. No matter how hard she tried, she couldn't get it together. She tried to reach out to Mitchell, but even the link was foggy and she couldn't see what he was doing. Did he even know she was gone? She yelled out to him, trying to let him back in, but nothing. It was like listening to a static-filled radio station. She was really starting to hate herself for ever listening to that stupid psychic. Madame Crystal, Amelia was certain, had caused more harm than good.

"Did you really think I did this all just for you?" He leaned back in his chair, putting his hands behind his back, and grinned at her. "You are just a means to an end." He sat there staring at her, black eyes burning a hole in her, and then, out of the blue, he shot up cursing, at least she thought it was cursing, in a language Amelia did not understand. His white complexion turned ghostly, and then, he crumpled back onto the chair, leaning over and gasping for breath.

"You okay, Tristan?" Adam asked, patting him on the back.

Tristan? Where had she heard that name before? *Come on, Amelia,* her inner voice urged. *Put it together. You know this. Tristan. Tristan. Oh my God.* "Erin belongs to you," she said in a small, shaky voice, not really to him, more to herself. If Erin was his, then that meant Erin had set this up. She'd helped him. Erin had known all along about her parents, about Mitchell, about everything. She hadn't really been hurt and she'd lured Amelia out to her death.

He laughed, not a nice laugh. "Yes, Erin's mine. Or was." Tristan stood up slowly and ran his hands through his greasy black hair, and then he shrugged and glanced at Adam and Kandi who were standing by him, waiting anxiously. "Erin's no longer with us. At least I won't have to lie to her anymore. Mitchell just killed her."

"Oh well," Kandi said with a malicious smile. "I wasn't a fan of Erin 2.0. But third time's a charm, right? Maybe you'll get lucky next time."

*Dead. Did he really just say Erin was dead? And Mitchell...
Mitchell killed her? No. He wouldn't,* Amelia tried to convince
herself. But she knew, deep down, that if Mitchell thought
Erin had hurt her he wouldn't think twice about killing her.
"Why are you doing this?" Amelia asked and realized she
was crying when she heard the tears in her voice.

"Don't cry, Amelia," Tristan said. He reached out to
brush her tears away and before she thought about it, she bit
him. She bit hard, almost hard enough to draw blood—but
not quite. His eyes flashed and the florescent lighting
glistened off his fangs. In a quick, fluid motion, he slapped
her. Amelia screamed out in pain. She was sure her
cheekbone had cracked from the impact.

Adam and Kandi lunged for him, tackling him down to
the ground. Amelia tried to follow them, but it was a useless
effort. She couldn't keep up with their speed. They were on
the ground, and then they weren't. They were behind her.
The three of them were moving so quickly that when she
looked to the sounds of the scuffle they were already across
the room. "Tristan, stop," Adam grunted. Somehow, he'd
managed to get Tristan into a headlock. "You've waited too
long for revenge. What's the point if you kill her before
Mitchell gets here?"

Amelia wasn't entirely sure why, but the thought that this
was all for Mitchell enraged her. "Mitchell has nothing to
do with this!" she shouted.

"Mitchell has everything to do with this," Tristan snarled.
"Everything that has happened to you, to your parents, it's
all because of Mitchell." Adam let him go and Tristan
slithered across the floor like a snake. "Your loyalty to them
is disgusting, Amelia. They've all hurt you. Mitchell, Erin,
Angelle. They knew all about you. But you're still trying to
protect them. It's pathetic. Get a backbone."

How could he talk about Erin as if she were just some
piece of junk? Amelia couldn't wrap her head around it.
They were bonded, or had been. "What did you mean when

you said you wouldn't have to lie to Erin anymore?" Amelia played the story Erin had told her over and over in her mind, and the pieces just seemed to click together, like a jigsaw puzzle. Erin had said she'd been killed by a vampire and Tristan, Amelia was certain, was that vampire.

"Finally." Tristan clapped his hands in excitement. "I thought you were never going to ask the right question." He seemed to have calmed down, but he was still pacing the room restlessly. His fangs were still flashing and his eyes still blazing. "Erin and you might have been good friends in another lifetime. You guys are so much alike. So inquisitive and so loyal. Her loyalty is what killed her twice and yours will be the reason for *your* death." His tone became softer, almost caring as he spoke of Erin. Amelia knew she had to keep him talking about her. Maybe it would stall him, give her some time to get out of this mess. The flickers of raw power were coming to her in bursts now and Amelia was pretty sure the drugs were starting to wear off. She just needed more time. Tristan sat back down in front of her and his lips started to curve upwards.

"You killed her," Amelia said, and Kandi and Adam laughed. They were standing behind Tristan watching her like a hawk. "Erin thought it was a friend, but it was you."

Tristan's smile grew wilder and his eyes blazed brighter. "I knew you were a smart one. It was an accident," he shrugged. "Mitchell's fault."

Another burst of warmth sparked in the pit of Amelia's stomach. She focused on it, pulled it together into a ball of fire and just as she gathered it, it smoldered away, as if a bucket of water had been dumped on it. A flash of white-hot rage hit her; for a moment, Amelia thought it was her own anger, but it faded in and out, hot then warm. She closed her eyes tightly, focusing on the feeling, and she saw Mitchell's contorted, grief-stricken face and then it was gone.

Amelia glared at Tristan. "So you blamed her death on Mitchell. You told her it was him," she said, gauging his reaction. An instant replay of Madame Crystal's advice to Erin flashed through her mind, "Memories are not always as they seem." His eyes blazed brighter and she knew instinctively she was on the right path. "Why?"

Amelia caught a movement from the corner of her eye just as Kandi yanked on her hair, bending her neck almost to a breaking point. "He's taking too long," she said in a whiny voice. "The bond is strong with them. I can smell it. Let's just kill her now. He'll suffer just as much."

Amelia kept her eyes focused on Tristan and for a minute he looked like he was considering it. The thought passed clearly across his face and she was sure this was the end. *Was that a bad thing?* She wasn't sure it was. It would stop her suffering. It would set Mitchell free and if she was gone, he wouldn't have to go on with his stupid suicide mission. She was pretty sure Tristan didn't know that she'd blocked their bond, so if he killed her, maybe Mitchell wouldn't even feel it.

Adam noticed that Tristan was considering the idea and he was suddenly untying her wrists, kissing and licking the inside skin over her veins. Kandi's tongue darted out, licking her neck, dry and prickly, like a cat's tongue. Amelia quivered and bile rose up her throat. *Think about something else. Focus on happy thoughts,* a voice in her head coaxed. But it was no use. The only thing that crossed her mind was that Mitchell didn't know how much she really loved him.

The pinprick of fangs pressed into her wrist. Amelia closed her eyes, held her breath, and shouted as loudly as she could through the bond, *I love you, Mitchell.*

CHAPTER 28

"Tristan," a familiar, but somehow too bitter, voice rang through the room. "You've always underestimated me. I think it has to be your biggest weakness." Amelia thought she was just hearing things and she kept her eyes closed. The voice sounded so much like Erin's, but it couldn't be. Erin was always animated, bubbly. Never cold. And she was dead.

Unexpectedly, Amelia's neck swung up like a slingshot and Kandi's lips were gone. She opened her eyes just in time to see Tristan hurl himself at her and Adam dropped her wrist. From behind, she heard the dry snap of bones breaking and Tristan leapt over her. He wasn't lunging at her, Amelia realized, and gulped down a scream. He was going for whatever was behind her. She swiveled her head around to see Erin rip Kandi's head clean off, blood spraying, splattering in a line across Amelia's face, and the sound—wet and meaty—of flesh tearing made everyone freeze, like marbleized statues.

"I never liked her," Erin (but not Erin) smirked, Kandi's head dangling from her hands, her lifeless body at Erin's feet. She shot a look at Adam and tossed the head to him, as if she were pitching a ball.

Amelia was incredulous. Little, harmless Erin. All the cuts and blood gone. It was impossible. Erin had looked almost dead, a pulpy, meaty mess, dangling in front of her room from a rope, but now... now her sharp features were smoother, lustrous, and flawless. Her tan was gone. Her eyes were radiant rubies. Amelia was so taken aback at what she was seeing that she didn't notice that Adam was coming out of his haze until Erin said, "Yo, Mitch, um, little help here would be nice."

Adam was closing in on Erin, like a lion stalking its prey. Tristan stood still, gaping, and Amelia bolted into action, struggling to untie her legs. She'd just managed to get the ropes off and pull together a surge of white-hot iridescent light, a display of radiant colors like a rainbow flashing in her line of vision, when Tristan grabbed her by the neck and smashed her hard against a wall, effectively extinguishing her concentration.

Amelia heard grunting to her left. She struggled to see what was happening, but she couldn't move. Tristan held her tightly and lifted her a few inches off the ground. She couldn't breathe. Her eyes felt as if they would pop out of their sockets from the pressure and her face started to throb. "I'm really going to enjoy this," he growled.

"Put her down!" Mitchell barked, from somewhere in the room, out of sight. "This has nothing to do with her."

"Sure it does, old friend," Tristan said, keeping his scorching gaze fixed on Amelia. Stars flashed in front of her eyes and she struggled, trying to get a breath. "If I kill her, then I'll kill part of you. It's wonderful how this soulmate crap works." Amelia was sure her face was turning blue and she wasn't sure how much longer she had. Her lungs felt as if they were about to burst, and he tightened his grip on her neck, crushing her air pipe further. "It took you long enough to find her. I'd thought killing her parents would have been enough to draw you out, but I guess it all worked out in the end."

"I'll kill you," Mitchell growled.

"Kind of the point." Tristan chuckled. "I kill her. You kill me. All the problems solved. I won't have to live like this anymore and I get my revenge. It's the perfect plan. I've been dreaming of this day for fifty-three years."

"I know the truth, Tristan." Amelia was pretty sure it was Erin speaking, but everything was starting to sound distorted and the world around her was taking on a grayish tone. "Funny how your manipulation just disappeared once I changed. I know you planted my memories of Mitchell killing me. You can't blame him anymore."

"Shut up, Erin," Tristan spat. He loosened his grip around Amelia's neck and she sucked in a ragged breath. He shifted his gaze for a quick second to Erin and Amelia noticed a glassy look in his eyes.

"I will not shut up," Erin said, sounding desperate, and then Tristan's grip constricted again around Amelia's throat. "You need to stop this. Mitchell saved you. You would've died if he hadn't changed you. It's not your fault. And, hey," Erin paused, and Amelia could just imagine her snarky look and striking a pose. "I came back. It doesn't need to end like this. Stop blaming yourself. You were new. You lost control. It's not your fault."

Tristan uttered something, but to Amelia it just sounding like mere fuzz. She could barely make out Tristan's form standing in front of her and she could no longer feel Mitchell, not even a trace of the chain that connected them. She felt cold, as if a gusty burst of a winter's storm engulfed her, and her vision was murky, full of shadows. Then, everything around her went dark and she was falling, tumbling in a pit of wretched darkness.

****

"Amelia, what are you doing here?" Mrs. Caldwell said. "You shouldn't be here." Her airy and soothing voice wrapped around Amelia, easing her fears.

Amelia snuggled her head into her mother's lap and she

smiled. Her mother always smelled like just-washed laundry, fresh and soft. "I just had the craziest nightmare, Mom. It was horrible. You and Dad were dead and I was a witch and there were vampires."

"Oh, sweetie," Mrs. Caldwell said, and played with Amelia's hair, braiding it and then loosening it to braid again. She sounded sad, and a bit agitated, and very, very distant.

Amelia sat up and looked her mother over. She was wearing her favorite white flannel nightgown. "Mommy, are you okay?" Amelia asked. Mrs. Caldwell was frowning, and Amelia couldn't remember ever seeing that before. Her mother never frowned. She always said it caused too many wrinkles. "Oh, my sweet, sweet child," Mrs. Caldwell cooed, and rested a hand on Amelia's cheek. "You were not dreaming. You are a witch, Mitchell is a vampire, and your father and I are..."

"No! No, no, no," Amelia screamed, cutting Mrs. Caldwell off. "Where's Daddy? I want to see Daddy." Frantically, she scanned the room for her father and she gasped. Just a moment ago, she'd been sure she was in her parents' room cuddled up on their bed, but the image was fading, and now she found herself sitting on a fluffy ball of... *cotton candy?* Amelia hesitantly let her fingers drift across the soft and silky surface. She peeked over the edge and saw her body, covered in blood, lying on the cold, hard floor, and glanced back at her mother. "Am I dead?" she asked in a small, unsure voice and then pinched herself as hard as she could and winced when it hurt.

"In a way, yes, but not really," Mrs. Caldwell murmured, pushing a loose curl out of Amelia's eyes. "At least not yet. You're in limbo. The air spirit warned me that you were not coping well and sent me to help you."

"Air spirit?" Amelia asked lamely, totally befuddled, and a little scared.

"Yes, sweetie. That's the element our family is closest to. You can think of him as your guardian angel." Mrs.

Caldwell opened her arms and Amelia went for the hug. She kissed the top of Amelia's head and smoothed back her hair. "I've been watching you over the last weeks. I'm so sorry this has been so hard for you."

As if she were hit by a tidal wave, the reality of what had happened in Amelia's short life was absolutely crushing and with the comfort of her mother's arms, she cried. Deep heart-wrenching sobs emerged so quickly that Amelia could hardly catch a breath and her mother held her, rocking her gently. "All this time you knew," Amelia choked out through the sobs and pushed back slightly, just enough to meet her mother's eyes. "You knew about Mitchell. You knew I was a witch. Why didn't you tell me?"

Mrs. Caldwell brushed the tears from Amelia's cheeks. "The gift doesn't manifest until you turn eighteen, and I've learned over the years not to tell you too soon. You've never taken the news about vampires or witches very well."

"How long have you been my mother?"

"A little over twelve hundred years. Mabel was telling you the truth. Witches always come back to the same family. It's one of the joys of being supernatural."

Suddenly, Amelia felt an overpowering rush of euphoria; excitement bubbled up and she could feel the eager expression stretching across her face. "So you and Daddy will come back? We'll be a family again?"

"That's up to you." Little creases littered Mrs. Caldwell's brow and her lips tilted downwards. "Our purpose over the last eight hundred years was to reunite you with Mitchell. He's your true family, dear."

"No. This can't be real. I'm still having a nightmare." Amelia fiddled with her hair, wrapping a long curl around her finger so tight that it throbbed from lack of circulation. For a moment she let her mind wander and she thought about just how odd that was. If she was dead, or sort of dead, why could she feel her pulse? Amelia gave her head a little shake, glared at her mother, and said, "If you're telling the truth, then why don't I remember the past?"

Mrs. Caldwell smiled. "Oh, sweetie. If you only knew how many times you've asked me that. Not everyone remembers their past lives. But with your gifts, you can access it if you want to. I can show you how. It will help you make the choice that is laid out for you."

A choice? How many more choices would she have to make? The last few really hadn't turned out so well, obviously; she was kind of, sort of, dead. Maybe, just maybe—not that she would ever tell him—Amelia was starting to think that Mitchell biting her and taking that one thing from her wasn't such a bad thing after all. "What choice?" Amelia asked, discouraged.

"You can still go back to him, if you want." Almost in unison, her inner voices screamed *yes* and *no*. "The spirits will give you another chance at this life. Or, if you so choose, you can wait until the next lifetime and, with your father and me, we will help you find him again."

Amelia scooted back to get a good look at her mother because her mother's tone clearly conveyed that it would not be a simple *everyone is happy* decision. "So you're saying if I stay dead then you guys will come back? We can be a family again?" She tried hard to keep the burning hope out of her voice, but she was pretty sure she hadn't succeeded.

Mrs. Caldwell confirmed Amelia's suspicions with her heartbreaking reply. "Yes, dear, but you need to understand that at some point you'll have to let us go. We were not meant to stay on earth for an eternity. Our path was to help you discover your own." Mrs. Caldwell held out her hands, "Take my hands. You need to ask the air spirit to show you what you have repressed." She hesitated for just a moment and then Amelia took her mother's hands, marveling at how firm and solid they felt. "When you're ready, I want you to concentrate on the heat that's pumping in your veins and say: Past lives that have gone astray, show me."

Amelia took a few deep breaths to stop the tremors that shook her to the bone. She wasn't sure if she really wanted to see whatever her mother had to show her, but she also knew she had to. After a moment of indecision, in a clear and strong voice she barely recognized as her own, Amelia said, "Past lives that have gone astray, show me."

The air between them shimmered and then turned to a foggy gray. An image formed in the center, like an animated charcoal sketch, cloudy and smudged. A young girl with long curly hair scrunched under a bonnet walked with her head down and shoulders stooped. She stopped at a small door above which hung a crucifix. She hesitated for a moment and glanced back. Until that moment, Amelia hadn't been certain of whom she was watching but she was now. Staring at her through the murky image was herself, the soul's mark, clear as day, imprinted on her neck.

"Thou have come to the right place, child," a voice from behind the door called and the girl from the image turned back, opened the door, and stepped in.

She closed the door behind her and sat down on a small bench style chair, arranging her dress and folding her hands in her lap. Then she looked through a small meshed area in the wall and said, "Father, I am frightened. A man came to me in my dreams."

"When did he first come?" the priest, Amelia assumed, questioned. She could just barely make out his lips in the cloudy image.

"The night my parents passed," the girl replied in a shaky voice.

There was a long silence, then a deep sigh. "I have feared you would be taken." The rustling of clothing filled the air and when the priest continued, he let his voice rise to a holler. "You wear the devil's mark and the devil hath found you."

Suddenly, there was a commotion, crunching glass, wood snapping, and voices roaring, accusatorily chanting over and over, "Witch!" The door flung open and Amelia screamed.

Then, as if someone had taken a brush, the image was wiped away to gray and another illustration started to form in the center. Smoke billowed around her face and flames licked up a post. The girl in the image was bound to the post and hundreds of spectators stood watching with fervor. The chanting was deafening: "Burn the Witch!"

Amelia watched in horror as the memories kept flashing as vivid as if she were reliving the moment. Her skin sizzled against the heat and the rancid smell of her flesh burning turned her stomach. "Make it stop," she cried, unable to pull her eyes away. "I don't want to see anymore."

The image became more intense, and the face of her past self contorted with detestation. The view shifted to show what she was looking at: Mitchell. He stood motionless, tears smudging down his cheeks. The view shifted again to show herself, flames licking up her neck, touching at her chin. A chain emerged from her heart and Amelia followed the line. The spectators were gone, smudged away, and the chanting had decreased to a whisper. On the other end of the chain was Mitchell. He buckled, and as if the life was sucked of out of him, crumpled to his knees. He let out a cry, snarled and distorted, excruciating and filled with anguish. He watched, powerlessly, as she was consumed by the inferno.

The image blurred and faded. The air shimmered and slowly her mother's grief-stricken face came into focus. "This was the turning point for you. It was in this lifetime that you put up the wall to shield yourself from your past. It wasn't until you were so anguished by our deaths that Mitchell was able to break through." Her mother laughed cheerlessly. "You need to understand, sweetie, our deaths, your father and I... it needed to happen to bring you and Mitchell together."

"I don't believe that," Amelia whispered. "I need you, Mommy."

Mrs. Caldwell smoothed away the shiny trail of tears spilling down Amelia's face. "You've been given not only one, but two miracles. You can do so much good with these gifts. The witch who cast the soulmate curse had never anticipated that one of her own would be implicated. She acted in haste, not thinking of all the possibilities. But you're not powerless to him. You're stronger than you think. You, my sweet child, are his equal. Together you can help others. With your magic and his clout in the vampire world, you can stop all the pain and suffering. You can change the curse to a glorious gift for all those who it has befallen. You can right the wrongs of our ancestors."

"Work together?" Amelia shook her head, and a new sting came to her eyes. "Mom... he hates me. He doesn't want me."

"Oh, Amelia," Mrs. Caldwell said and made a *tsk* sound. "You know that's not true."

Amelia almost giggled. Even in death, her mother knew when she was lying. She racked her brain for something, anything to say that would sound believable. "Well, he wants to hate me and he doesn't want to be with me anyways. He said he was going to kill himself so he wouldn't have to be with me."

Mrs. Caldwell raised her eyebrow and crossed her arms over her chest. "He said that, did he?"

Amelia huffed. "No. He thinks I don't want him." She would never understand how her mother always knew what she was really feeling. She guessed it was another thing in life that could be chalked up as magic. That thought shocked her, though, because just yesterday she would have chalked it up to a mother's intuition, but today magic seemed right on the mark.

"I see." A small smile appeared on Mrs. Caldwell's lips and her eyes sparkled. "I know this has been hard for you. But you need to ask yourself, do you love him?"

"More than anything, but Mom..." Passion rushed through her veins and Amelia jumped up, pacing back and forth. She clenched her fists into little white balls. "We fight. We fight like crazy. We can't even be in the same room without wanting to kill each other."

Mrs. Caldwell laughed. "That doesn't surprise me. You're both very stubborn. Let me guess, he keeps making all the decisions for you and you don't like that."

"Exactly..." Amelia said under her breath. "He's just so... so... infuriating!" She loosened her hands and plopped back down into her mother's lap. "He thinks he knows best. He acts like he's some kind of king or something." Mrs. Caldwell laughed again. "Stop it, Mom. This is serious."

"True love is never easy and if my memories serve me correctly, he was a king in his human life. Come to think of it, I believe he still is a king of sorts amongst his kind. Mitchell has been on this earth for a very long time." She brushed her fingers under Amelia's chin and tilted her head up to meet her eyes. "Don't you think it's possible that he really does know what's best for you? He just may not always say it in the best way. You need to be patient with him, dear. After he watched you die, it changed him. Imagine what he must have felt. All the strength of a vampire and he could do nothing to help you. And it's been a long time since he's had to deal with someone so young. You know that feeling you get when he's around?"

A rush of emotion filled Amelia as she tried to find the words to explain how it felt. Her heart fluttered and a pleasant light-headedness swallowed her up, the way it always did at the thought of Mitchell. "Yeah, like I'm being pulled to him. It's like there is no one else in the world when he's there." She knew that was right, it wasn't even an approximation of her true feelings, but the words escaped her. Her love was ineffable.

Her mother seemed to understand and smiled. "Well picture that times ten and that's what he's feeling. As a vampire, he has heightened emotions. And dealing with teenage girls is not easy for anyone, especially someone as hot-headed as you." She brushed a tear from Amelia's cheek. "To be honest, I kind of feel sorry for him. You've always been a handful and so impulsive. I know you try to think logically like your father, but when there's no logic you let your emotions run wild." Then she got serious. "The world needs you, Amelia. Mitchell needs you." Mrs. Caldwell waved her hand delicately across the fluffy cotton. "Look," she said, and pointed below.

Amelia glanced down and saw herself, motionless in her bed, Mitchell sitting beside her holding her hand and caressing her cheek. "How long have I been gone?" Hadn't she just seen herself in the grungy basement crumpled on the floor and covered in blood?

"Almost a full day," Mrs. Caldwell replied. "Time passes differently here. You need to decide before it's too late to go back."

"How am I supposed to do that, Mom?" Amelia yelled. "If I go back then I'm basically signing away your life. If I stay, then you and Dad can come back."

"We're ready to rest," Mrs. Caldwell said quietly, as if she were scared to push too hard. It made Amelia think about Eric and the ticking time bomb. Did everyone think she was on the verge of exploding? A small giggle tried to escape, but she repressed it. "We've both lived long full lives and it's time for us to move on." Her eyes twinkled as if she were inviting Amelia to share a secret and her voice took on a magical, fairy tale kind of tone. "And remember, you're a witch. You have a connection with the spirits. We'll always be here for you. All you need to do is call."

Amelia was completely and utterly speechless. How was she supposed to believe that they didn't want to come back? How was she supposed to be able to call her parents? It made no sense. If it was possible, why hadn't her mother come before? Amelia couldn't even begin to count how many times she'd wished to see her parents.

"You wear your heart on your sleeve. I can see it so clearly, all your hopes and dreams. All the hard stuff's over. All you have to do now is look forward to the good stuff." Mrs. Caldwell smothered Amelia in a hug and kissed her cheek. "Amelia, you have so much good to share with the world. Your friend Erin needs you. She's suffering, and you can ease that pain."

"I understand," Amelia said, eyes wide as she gazed at her mother. Would this be the last time they would see each other? She knew, almost instinctually, she had to go back. Her mother was right. She had a chance to do good, to help people, and to be happy. She tried to think of something epic to say. How many people got a chance at a second goodbye? But she was drawing a blank, only uttering, "I know what I have to do, I just don't know how to say goodbye to you."

"It's never goodbye. Not for you, sweetie. The body may die, but the soul never does. We'll always be here. All you need to do is open your heart and you'll know how to find us. Look inside yourself."

"Mom, you sound just like that ridiculous psychic." Amelia tossed up her hands, exasperated. She knew she was stalling. She didn't want the moment to end, but she couldn't help it and she raged on. "Madame Crystal said I'd know how to let Mitch back in and I can't figure that out. How am I supposed to find you or help Erin if I can't even repair the bond with Mitch?"

"Open your heart. All the answers are there just waiting for you to find them." She gave Amelia another big hug and a wise, all knowing kind of smile. "It's time to go back. Always remember, I love you my sweet, sweet child."

CHAPTER 29

The sunlight glittered through the windows like ribbons of gold, twirling and weaving, casting the room in a glory of light. For a quick second, Amelia's heart stopped. Had something gone wrong? She was almost certain she was dead, because she'd never envisioned such splendor in such a simple thing as the sunlight before. Surely that meant that her time was over, she'd taken too long to decide and the spirits had done it for her.

Then she saw Mitchell. He sat beside her bed, staring blankly out the window, a single tear streaming down his cheek winding like a river. When the sunlight touched it, it sparkled like the shiny flecks of a diamond. His aura shone brightly—lemon yellow—and mixed with the sunbeams he looked indisputably angelic.

Suddenly, the floodgates opened and his pain, his worries, his fears, everything came crashing into Amelia. She gasped, instantaneously realizing that he thought she was never coming back. He was sure he'd lost her and that pain, the idea of losing him was more than she could bear.

When she gasped, Mitchell swiveled to meet her gaze. Hastily, he rubbed at his face and gave her a weak smile.

"You're here," Amelia croaked.

Pain and disappointment flashed in his eyes, and she knew he'd misunderstood. "Sorry..." Mitchell said—hollow and empty. "I'll go." He hesitated for a moment, looking her over, and then stood up.

"No." Her voice cracked and she cleared her throat. "I'm glad you're here. Is everyone okay? Erin? Is Erin okay?" Amelia tried to sit up and when she couldn't make it, Mitchell helped, propping pillows behind her. He fidgeted, fluffing them up, rearranging the mounds of cushions, smoothing out the sheets. With the way he was avoiding looking at her, it was obvious that something was horribly wrong. Glints of Erin surfaced in his thoughts, but as quickly as they flashed up he pushed them down. A rock hard lump formed in Amelia's throat and she swallowed hard, fighting against the tears that threatened. "Mitch... please... please. You have to tell me they're fine."

"They're alive," Mitchell said. He tried to keep his tone light and if not for their emotional link, she may have believed him. But as it was, she could feel that he was hiding something from her, something that she was sure she didn't really want to know.

"But...?" Amelia asked. Panic tinged her voice and she imagined the ghastly fates of her friends—her family.

Mitchell sighed and his expression took on a hard and closed air. "Don't worry, love. You need rest."

"Stop trying to hide things from me and tell me what happened!" she shouted, and smacked her fists onto the bed.

"Amelia..." he pleaded, fighting the anger that flickered in his eyes at her outburst.

The all too familiar fury started bubbling up in both of them, his mixing with hers, creating a thunderstorm of rage. Amelia clenched her fists and focused hard on keeping an even tone before she spoke. She took a deep breath and locked her eyes with his. "Listen closely, Mitch, because I'm only going to say this once. If you want it to work between us, you need to stop trying to make all the damn decisions.

You think you're protecting me, I get it, but you're not. I'm not trying to say it'll be easy. So don't kid yourself into thinking it will be. We're both stubborn and frankly," she smirked, "I know that I'm always right and you're always wrong. It'll be a lot of work, but if you're willing to try, so am I."

Amelia couldn't help but smile. For just a second, strong, closed Mitchell looked lost and confused. He gave his head a thorough shake and his lips curved the slightest little bit. "Did you just say you want to try?" His brilliant eyes shone blue like a clear summer's sky and a sudden surge of bliss wrapped around her like a cozy fleece blanket.

Amelia took a moment to enjoy the love and devotion that poured off of him, soaking it up like a dry sponge. She tried to send the same feelings to him, wanting him to feel what she felt, but as she gathered them up and pushed she hit a wall—the wall that she had placed between them. Amelia squeezed her eyes shut, frustrated with herself for ruining the magic between them, and then forced it out of her mind, because she knew that was the least of her worries right now. She fixed her stare on him. "That's what I said. Now tell me, what's wrong." She crossed her arms. When he didn't answer she yelled, "I'm serious, Mitch. Tell me!"

Mitchell sighed again. This time long and drawn out, the air slowly pushing from his lips; he was stalling, Amelia was sure of it. He shuffled awkwardly around the bed tucking her in like a sausage and then, when she could hardly breathe from the tight blankets, he said, "Erin's not doing well. Tristan got away and he's been calling to her through the bond. I had to lock her up so she wouldn't run after him."

Calling her? He still had control? A knot twisted in her stomach. This couldn't be happening. Amelia let her gaze wander the room, allowing her self-pity to get the best of her. All she wanted was to come back from the—almost—dead, see Mitchell, fall in love again, and live happily ever after. "I don't get it," she said through clenched teeth.

Then she felt ashamed. It wasn't like her to put herself first, and it just didn't feel right. And Amelia had to admit that she was the one who asked about her friends, so she knew she needed to suck it up and put her life on hold—again— to help them. "I thought with her being a vampire he wouldn't have that kind of control."

Mitchell ran a finger along her cheek. "They're still bonded, love. She still feels the pull and it's not something that's easy to fight. It's kind of like us. Even though you've shut me out, I can still feel your presence. I can still feel that pull, as if you're tugging a rope that's attached to my heart." He plopped back down in the chair and rubbed at his face, as if he were trying to banish away his pained expression.

It was a great feat, but Amelia managed to ignore his heartbreaking look and push on. She needed to know what had happened if she would have any chance at helping her friend. She dug into her memories, trying to piece together the drug-hazed conversation she'd had with Tristan. "Tristan said you killed her. He thought she was dead. What happened?"

A distant look settled on Mitchell's brow and small creases marred the soft skin around his eyes. "I came back to tell you I was sorry about our fight, but you were gone. I thought..." he paused, and Amelia watched as his Adam's apple bobbed with a bunch of quick swallows. "I thought you left me. I wouldn't have blamed you if you did." He reached out and caressed her cheek, letting his fingers slide down to her neck, lingering on her mark. "But when you weren't there, I lost it. I don't know if our family will ever forgive me." A frantic string of images passed through his mind and his jaw twitched as he fought them away. "Tyler was the one who found Erin. Tristan had left her to die."

Amelia waited for him to tell her more but when he didn't, she said gently, "So you changed her. You saved her life."

"I almost didn't. I wanted to kill her." His eyes flared and streaked with red and then he blinked, casting it away.

He let his arms drop, dangling to his sides and the creases on his brow turned to crevices, deep and sharp.

Amelia waited, afraid to say anything that might shut him down, because, whether she liked it or not, at times Mitchell could be worse than a teenage girl in the mood swing department. *Was that a vampire thing or just him?* she wondered.

After a few moments, he met her eyes, and his face lit up with excitement. "Amelia, can you help her? Is there a spell or something? You could break it like you did with me."

"I didn't..." Amelia started, and then quickly stopped. *Didn't what?* She was about to tell him that she hadn't broken their link but she had. She knew it was time that she stopped lying to him and took the responsibility for her actions.

He must have read it on her face because he said, "It's okay. I guess I didn't give you much choice."

It was at that moment that she knew, no matter what, she had to figure out how to fix what she'd done to them. But first, she needed to help Erin. "Help me up, Mitch. I need to see her."

****

Amelia was absolutely appalled to find out that her castle dream home actually had a dungeon and that dungeon was where Mitchell had locked up Erin.

"You left her in here," Amelia seethed, glancing around and taking in the barbaric room. She felt as if she'd stepped through a time portal and was teleported back to the Middle Ages. The rough and jagged stone walls were caked with what looked like centuries of grime and were splattered with dark spots that she knew, disturbingly, was blood. Thankfully, when she glanced at Mitchell, he looked just as unsettled. "I tried locking her in one of the upstairs rooms, love. She broke out."

"What was this used for?" Amelia asked, looking over a

contraption that hung from the ceiling. She had a frightening thought of someone hanging upside-down, the leather and chains tightening and pulling until limbs ripped off, and she cringed and trembled. Before Mitchell could help add any nightmarish ideas, she tossed up her hands and said, "Never mind, I don't want to know."

At that moment, she heard Erin's voice traveling down a dark and dingy corridor. "Millie, finally, you need to get me out of here." Erin's call surrounded Amelia, slithering around her like a tangled nest of hissing snakes. The words echoed, bouncing off the walls, and it felt as if they were trying to slither into her mind and pull her in. Her goose-pimpled skin prickled as the pimples turned into full-grown bumps. "I know you're there, Millie," Erin hissed when Amelia didn't respond. "I can smell your sweet, sweet blood pumping through your veins."

Amelia took a step back and jumped a foot off the ground when she bumped into Mitchell. He held her, rubbing small circles onto her back, and she fought to catch her breath. "Amelia, it's not really Erin talking. She's letting the demon take control. You should know that we had to restrain her as well so she wouldn't hurt us or herself."

Amelia opened her mouth, but the only sound that came from her lips was a scared little whimper. She swallowed hard and shook her head even harder, hoping the fears would fly out from the force, and then she gave herself a stern mental pep talk. *You're a witch. You have nothing to be scared of. Erin's your friend and she needs your help. Keep it together, Amelia. You can do this.* When she was sure her voice would work, she locked eyes with Mitchell and asked, "What do you mean restrain her?"

"You'll see. Just promise me you won't do anything rash. She's not thinking clearly and you can't trust her. She's not the Erin you knew."

As if he could feel how cold and scared she was, Mitchell sent a warm, bubbly sensation of strength through the link, letting her feed from his power, and then he turned from her and padded his way towards Erin.

Amelia reluctantly followed, weaving through the hallways. It seemed as if every few steps they took they ended up at a fork, small corridors leading off every which way. A few times, Amelia could have sworn they had already passed by a cell or a doorway, and she was glad she was not alone. It was like walking through an otherworldly web of torture, and with every turn, she fought the urge to run back the way she'd come. She fought her imagination, attempting to reassure herself the whole way that this place was never used. But no matter how hard she tried, she couldn't shake the idea of feeble humans running in the maze of hallways as their ruthless predators stalked them, playing with them like helpless little mice.

"Millie, hurry up," Erin howled, breaking through Amelia's overactive imagination. "Don't listen to that dumbass boy toy of yours. He doesn't know what he's talking about. I'm fine. Just get me out of here."

Mitchell veered to the right, down another dark and moldy smelling passageway, before stopping abruptly. Amelia collided into his back and she stumbled. Before she could hit the ground, he steadied her with an unearthly speed and grace.

It took a moment for her eyes to adjust to the dim, flickering light, but when they did, a feeling of sickness overcame her. "My God, Erin," she cried and rushed forwards. Erin was tied up helplessly in a tiny cell with barely enough room for her small body to fit into. Two chains hung from the ceiling cuffed to her wrists and her ankles were chained to the stone floor. Amelia shook the metal bars, but they didn't budge. She spun around, hands on her hips, and glared at Mitchell. "Mitch, open this cell."

"I'm not opening it until she can control herself," Mitchell said, the all too recognizable cold expression on his face. The very expression he used with her any time he was about to fight her on something.

Amelia bristled, ready for the battle. She was just about

to throw a tantrum when Erin piped up, "He's a lunatic, Millie. Please get me out. I'm so hungry." The last word was a drawn out hiss that sent a chill racing down Amelia's spine.

"Can you help her, love?" Mitchell asked softly. "Can you do the spell you did with us?"

Amelia glanced back at Erin and deflated. "I don't know if that will help. What I did... I mean..." she stuttered. "Well, it only blocked your connection. I can still feel everything. For me, it's almost like nothing has changed. I don't know how to severe the bond completely."

"What about just reversing it? Can you block her from seeing him?"

Amelia thought about that for a minute, but the cold, hard reality hit her. "I don't think that's a good idea," she whispered, reluctant to say it at all. "If I do that, then we have no way of knowing where Tristan is or if he's planning to come back. Right now, we have an advantage. If the link stays, then we'll know every move he makes."

Amelia stared at Erin, who was now growling and yanking on the chains. "If I can just take away the pull, we can let her go. I guess I need to mask her thoughts, too. I wonder," she paused, scratching at her head. "What if I can make it look like she's searching for him. Maybe that will be enough to trick him into thinking she's coming."

Her mind was swirling as the ideas tumbled forth faster than she could process them. She took a few calming breaths and tried to find a center. Suddenly, as if the knowledge had always been a part of her, what she had to do became clear.

Amelia took Mitchell's hand, closed her eyes, and focused on the memory of the power—hot tea and honey. The sweet, steamy power sputtered, shining unsteadily. It smoldered, then flashed up again, and blazed. It swirled around her and she let it pull on Mitchell's strength to feed the firestorm burning deep within.

Mitchell tried to pull his hands away, but Amelia held

tight using her magic to keep him still. "What are you doing?" he asked unsteadily.

"I need your power, Mitch," Amelia gasped and fixed her pleading gaze on him. "I need your help."

For a quick second, Amelia thought he was going to keep fighting her, but then he nodded. "I'm going to pull on your persuasion. I need you to focus and push it to me," she said.

Amelia drew from Mitchell, feeling his persuasion join with her, strengthening the blazing power that coursed through them both. She drew in a breath and chanted, *"Mold a twin and link the bond,"* over and over. Erin's snarls grew more savage and the chains rattled as she tried to break free.

Mitchell grunted and staggered. "You're taking too much." His voice was barely audible and his complexion was graying fast.

"Help me." Amelia wheezed and panted. "Don't fight it."

Amelia could feel the life draining from him and his struggles to break free became less and less. She heaved on his powers, merging them with hers and continued the chant.

Mitchell struggled for breath and staggered again. Erin's sickening laugh filled her ears. "It's no use, Millie. You aren't strong enough," she hissed.

Amelia continued to chant, *"Mold a twin and link the bond."* Her knees began to shake and she struggled to stay upright. She kept her eyes fixed on Mitchell and suddenly, as if he had a second wind, Mitchell straightened up and began to chant with her.

"Mold a twin and link the bond," they chanted, their voices strengthening with each intonation.

The jingling of the chains and Erin's snarls were deafening, but they continued to chant in repetition. Amelia focused all her energy and forced herself to speak clearly, enunciating every syllable. Mitchell squeezed her hands tighter. Erin screamed out, cursing and snarling, the sound echoing around the cold stone walls. A metallic sound of chains snapping rang out and another bloodcurdling scream penetrated Amelia's ears. She broke the hold on Mitchell and rushed forward just as Erin crumbled to the ground, whimpering.

CHAPTER 30

"I can't believe that worked," Lola said, in a slightly smug and disbelieving tone. Mitchell gave her a disapproving glare and she snuggled in closer to Luke, as if she were trying to hide in his arms. Her face was marked with a mix of amazement and fear and she kept a close eye on Amelia.

The whole gang—new members, Tyler and Erin included—had gathered in the kitchen, which seemed to be the unspoken meeting place to hear about the spell Amelia had used on Erin.

"I don't get it," Eric said, scratching at his head. "Are you saying there's another Erin running around somewhere?"

Angelle groaned and shot him a look that clearly said *You're such a moron.* "She created the illusion of another Erin."

"So there aren't two of them?" Eric asked, perplexed, and glanced around the table, as if he were hoping to find someone else who shared his confusion.

Amelia laughed a pleasant, good-feeling laugh. It seemed as if every time she'd laughed lately it was out of nervousness, but this laugh was genuine. "Okay, let me try this again," Amelia said. She'd told Eric five times now and he still wasn't getting it. "I'll try to keep it simple. I used Mitchell's mind control, um, talents, and mixed it with my witchiness. Using both our strengths, I was able to make an imaginary Erin. I planted fake thoughts in the imaginary Erin. Then, so Tristan will still think he has a bond with the real one, I cut the cord," Amelia gestured using scissors to snip the cable, "that connected them and attached it to the imaginary Erin. I left the mind-reading part intact for Erin so she can still hear his thoughts, but now, Tristan will only hear and feel the fake ones."

Eric smacked his hands onto the table. "I knew it. There *are* two Erins!" Then he hopped up from his chair and went over to examine the mouth-watering concoction Mabel was whipping up.

After everyone had a good chuckle at Eric, Mitchell said, beaming, "You guys should have seen her. She was amazing."

Erin huffed. "Amazing? Really not that amazing. It was torture. I feel like she cut me in half."

"I kinda did." Amelia blushed and then cursed under her breath. Really, after all the near death experiences she'd had since moving to Willowberg, she was still blushing? She glanced at Mitchell. He was looking at her with so much love that it made the blush turn beet red.

"Dude. What the hell happened to you?" Eric interrupted her moment. "Weren't you all death to Mitch two days ago?"

"Did you just call me 'dude'?" Amelia laughed. She couldn't help but marvel at how much everything had changed. Eric was leaning against the counter in the exact same place, giving her the exact same breathtaking smile he had on the first day she'd arrived and it was barely fazing her now. He was still hot—Amelia had to admit it—but next to Mitchell, well, Eric just didn't compare.

"Eric." Mabel smacked him on the head with a wooden spoon. The room erupted in laughter and she had to shout to be heard. "Get off my counter and sit down." She then waited for the laughter to die down before asking, "Who wants food?" Amelia, Angelle, Eric and Tyler promptly raised their hands.

"Bacon and eggs," Angelle chirped her request.

"I make killer scrambled eggs," Eric said. Unimpressed, Mabel gave him another whack with the spoon. "What?" he asked, attempting to look innocent.

"You're not helping, so get over there and plant your butt on a chair." Mabel raised the spoon as if she were going to smack him again. Eric chuckled, put up his hands in surrender, and slid into a chair.

Mitchell draped his arm around Amelia's shoulder and she settled back in her chair. Blissful warmth spread through her as she looked around at all her friends chatting easily and she let herself enjoy the feeling for a moment.

Yesterday she wouldn't have believed it, but it looked like everything was working out. Even Tyler looked happy—maybe a bit too happy—Amelia noticed. She watched as Tyler and Angelle stole fleeting glances at each other.

Amelia wanted to probe at them, see if a new romance was in the air—she was pretty sure there was—but in the end, she bit her tongue on the questions and asked, "How did Tristan get away?"

"That was my fault," Tyler said bashfully. "I tried to stake him when he was choking you and I kinda missed his heart." He grinned. "Seriously, not as easy as the movies make it look. He dropped you and took off."

Even Amelia couldn't help but laugh with the rest of them. Tyler looked so bewildered. It was as if he hadn't imagined that his heroic attempt to save her wouldn't work. She laughed until her sides hurt and tears came to her eyes. When she finally caught her breath she asked, "What about Adam?"

Her question silenced the laughter, and Luke's thoughtful hazel eyes focused on her. "We really don't know, kiddo. He snuck out when we were trying to keep Tristan from

Tyler after the little…" he picked up a fork and mimicked a staking motion over his heart, "*incident*." Then he gave Erin a hard stare. "I don't think you should go anywhere by yourself for now, given the whole Kandi thing."

The room went eerily silent and Amelia couldn't help but think they were giving Kandi a moment of silence. She hadn't been a fan of Kandi's, but she let herself wonder if maybe, just maybe, it was Tristan's company that made her such a monster. With that, she said a silent prayer for her soul to find Adam.

"Hey, Millie," Tyler said, breaking the silence. "Can you use your witch skills to zap me a passing grade? 'Cause with all this crap I missed a few papers and a test."

Amelia groaned. The last thing she wanted to think about was school. Never in her life had she missed so many classes. "I don't even want to think about how behind I am."

The frying bacon smelled wonderful. Usually Amelia hated the greasy smell, but today it made her mouth water in anticipation. The conversation spiraled on, chatting easily as if nothing had happened and Amelia was ecstatic at how easily Erin and Tyler blended with her family. Mabel served breakfast and, to Amelia's surprise, she joined them.

Mabel was just about to work on the mess when she stopped, plates balancing in her hands. She looked Amelia over, head to toe, and raised a questioning eyebrow. "You seem different. What happened to you?"

Different, Amelia thought. *Wow, that's an understatement.* She busied herself, sweeping crumbs off the table and dusting them onto her plate while she tried to think of how to answer that. Of course, she seemed different. Who wouldn't after all this? A bunch of excuses popped to her mind, but in the end, she settled on telling the truth. "I saw my Mom and my past."

Amelia locked eyes with Mitchell and she was sure she heard a few gasps from around the table, but she ignored them. A replay of her burning flashed through both their minds. Tears prickled her eyes and she felt his shame. Again, she wished she could fix the link, reassure him somehow, but for the life of her, she just didn't know how.

"What past?" Tyler asked and Amelia forced her eyes away from Mitchell.

She was about to explain when Angelle came to her rescue. "I'll fill you in some other time," she said, and Amelia assumed Mitchell must have confided in her.

Amelia mouthed a *thank you* and then she got up from the table. She didn't want them all to see her cry again and she knew the tears weren't far off. "I need a shower," she said and pushed in her chair. Everyone, even Lola, looked taken aback at her abrupt departure, but she didn't really care. She smiled—what she hoped was a convincing happy smile—at Mitchell. "I won't be long." He smiled back, sad and distant, but nodded so she turned and headed for her room.

"Amelia," Lola said, just before she left the kitchen, and she glanced back over her shoulder. "It doesn't completely suck that you're not dead."

Unsure of what to say, Amelia just nodded, and left the room.

****

Amelia let the steamy water cascade over her as she cried. She cried for her parents, she cried for Erin, she cried over her mistakes with Mitchell, she even cried for Kandi's death. She cried for what felt like hours before the tears stopped falling.

Had she made the right choice? She really wasn't sure and she wished—truly wished—that she could have had both, her parents and Mitchell.

Amelia pushed that idea out of her head, swallowed hard, and turned off the shower. She dried off, wrapped the fluffy bath towel around her, and wiped down the steam-covered mirror. She took a good hard look at herself, noticing for the first time the shimmering glow that surrounded her. For a second she didn't know what it was, but then it hit her: it was her—her magic—and she smiled.

She splashed some cold water on her face, brushed her hair and tied it up, and brushed her teeth. After spending way too much time on her make-up, she ventured out into her room to get dressed.

As she was digging through her closet to find the perfect outfit, she couldn't help but wonder why she still felt so miserable. Everything had worked out. Her friends were fine, she was alive. So why did she still want to curl up in a little ball and hide from the world? Amelia gave up on finding something to wear, threw on a housecoat, and padded her way out onto the terrace for fresh air, hoping it would help clear her mind.

The night was crisp and refreshing, and she inhaled two deep, invigorating breaths. Looking up at the velvety night sky, the stars sparkling like jewels, she searched for Cassiopeia, her favorite constellation. If only she could be like the great queen of the past, Amelia was sure Cassiopeia would have known what to do.

That's when she heard the soft splash of water. She glanced over at the pool and saw Mitchell leaping out and then gracefully diving back into the water.

Amelia laughed hollowly, suddenly understanding why she still felt so empty. Mitchell. Everything seemed to be boiling down to Mitchell and the broken bond. Last week she would never have believed it, but now she missed him. Missed the bond that she'd fought so hard against.

She racked her brain, wondering why the bond was still broken. She had accepted him. She loved him. Then it dawned on her and just as Madame Crystal and her mother had said, "Look inside yourself and you will know how to bring him back."

Amelia rushed back into her room. She picked out a pink and blue striped bikini and squirmed her way into it. Then she rushed outside. The cold night air prickled her skin into goose pimples and she snuck into the pear-shaped dome that covered the pool.

As Mitchell swam lazy laps, Amelia took a moment to admire him. His muscular form took on a silver tone in the glistening moonlight and her breath caught in her throat. Her heart started pumping, erratic little beats. It fluttered around wildly, jumping into her throat.

Mitchell must have heard the beating. He stopped swimming and his gaze met hers. "Hey," he said nervously. "I didn't realize you were there." He brushed water from his face. "I'll go."

Mitchell misunderstood her hesitation and instantly, Amelia felt his doubt and insecurities. She sat on the edge, letting her feet dangle into the water. "You don't have to go," she said just as nervously, and let her eyes drift to the clear, blue water. "I wanted to talk to you."

Mitchell hesitated for a second and then he swam over to her, placing his hands on either side of her, splashing lukewarm droplets of water onto her bare thighs. He waited until she met his glorious blue eyes before he spoke. "I need to tell you something first. I'm sorry for pushing all this on you. I should have talked to you first. I should have let you choose this life. I know it's not an excuse, but I was just so scared you wouldn't choose me."

"I get it. I saw everything. I get it." He reached over and caressed her cheek. "Mitch," she breathed. "I want this to work. But..."

"I know, love," he said, cutting her off. "I know it can't work between us. You don't have to say it."

Amelia bristled. "Oh, just shut up and listen," she snapped. "What I was going to say before you decided again that you already know everything was..." She paused for a second to give him a long glare. "It can't work if you don't stop trying to know everything. We're both gonna have to change. It's gonna be hard, but hey," Amelia smirked and raised a flirty eyebrow, "what fun would it be if it wasn't a challenge?" Then she got serious and whispered, "I don't want to live without you. I love you."

Mitchell looked totally blown away. He opened his mouth, closed it, then opened it again, and Amelia giggled. She'd never seen him speechless before, and it was just a little bit cute. He finally got his thoughts under control and said, "Sorry, but can you say that again. I don't think I heard you right." Amelia shoved him away playfully and he grinned. "I love you, too."

Without warning, Mitchell grabbed her around the waist and pulled her into the pool. Amelia squealed as the water splashed around them and then he leaned in and kissed her. The kiss started out soft and quickly turned urgent. He tasted wonderful, with just a hint of chlorine, and she felt herself deepening the kiss, trying to get closer. His tongue brushed against hers and her body ignited in fiery passion.

Amelia broke the kiss, lips tingling, and she licked them, savoring the taste. Then she leaned back just enough to meet his eyes and he groaned. When she was sure she had his attention, she tilted her head to expose her neck.

He hesitated, and she could see the concern flashing through his mind, and for a long moment, he didn't truly understand what she was asking him to do. When he realized, a soft smile touched his lips. "It's okay. You don't have to let me bite you."

"I know I don't have to. I want to." Mitchell stared at her, examining her face, and she could feel him pushing on the link, trying to get in. He wanted to be sure, really sure, that she meant it. "Mitch, please, I want you to do it," she said, desperation tinting her voice.

Mitchell kissed her, long and hard and then he let his lips travel down her neck. Amelia had expected the bite to hurt, but it didn't. It was nothing like the first time. There was no burning, no pain, but a massive explosion of feelings. Love... passion... and then, just as she had thought it would, the bond opened up and she was flooded with his feelings and she knew, suddenly, without a doubt, how much he loved her. His love seemed to envelope her in a cocoon of ecstasy.

It ended too soon and when he pulled away, they were both panting. "It worked," Amelia gasped in between ragged breaths. "It fixed the bond."

They gazed at each other, speechless for a moment, and Amelia could feel the soft hum of Mitchell searching through her thoughts, catching up on all he'd missed since the link had been broken. When Amelia finally caught her breath, she smiled teasingly and asked, "So what kind of a stupid name is "Dreams Come True Scholarship Fund" anyways?"

Mitchell laughed, the first genuine laugh she'd heard from him since they'd met. "I know, it's tacky, but I kind of thought…" He grinned. "Well, we met in a dream and when I found you it was as if my dreams came true." Then he chuckled, and his brilliant blue eyes twinkled. "The name just seemed to fit."

Amelia leaned into him and kissed him. "It's perfect," she whispered against his lips and then she kissed him again. For the first time in years, she felt as if she was finally exactly where she was meant to be.

ABOUT THE AUTHOR

Ashley Stoyanoff is an author of paranormal romance books for young adults, including The Soul's Mark series and the Deadly Trilogy. She lives in Southern Ontario with her husband, Jordan, and two cats: Tanzy and Trinity.

In July 2012, Ashley published her first novel, The Soul's Mark: FOUND, and shortly thereafter, she was honored with The Royal Dragonfly Book Award for both young adult and newbie fiction categories.

An avid reader, Ashley enjoys anything with a bit of romance and a paranormal twist. When she's not writing or devouring her latest read, she can be found spending time with her family, watching cheesy chick flicks or buying far too many clothes.

Ashley loves hearing from her readers, so feel free to connect with her online.

www.ashleystoyanoff.com
www.facebook.com/AshleyStoyanoffTheSoulsMark
www.goodreads.com/ashley_stoyanoff